Tears Shall Drown the Wind.

In all the world there was only the rock and the sea. The howling wind was drowned by the sea's thunder; the driving rain was lost in the sea's fury.

For the next eternity of moments only a few rational thoughts pierced Tory's mind. She took a fresh hold on the rock projection. She pretended the rock was Luc's chest, the chest that had offered her comfort and strength and security hardly more than a dozen hours before, at the beginning of this day that had lasted such a lifetime. A gigantic wash of water crashed over her, trying to suck her into the sea. But Luc would come, he would have to come . . .

ABRA TAYLOR

was born in India, where her father, a doctor of tropical medicine, treated both maharajahs and British viceroys. Exposed to exotic places and unusual people from an early age, she developed an active imagination and soon turned to writing. The author of numerous romances, she is today a beloved storyteller whose books are sought after by fans worldwide.

Dear Reader,

Silhouette Special Editions are an exciting new line of contemporary romances from Silhouette Books. Special Editions are written specifically for our readers who want a story with heightened romantic tension.

Special Editions have all the elements you've enjoyed in Silhouette Romances and *more*. These stories concentrate on romance in a longer, more realistic and sophisticated way, and they feature greater sensual detail.

I hope you enjoy this book and all the wonderful romances from Silhouette. We welcome any suggestions or comments and invite you to write to us at the address below.

Karen Solem
Editor-in-Chief
Silhouette Books
P.O. Box 769
New York, N. Y. 10019

ABRA TAYLOR

Wild Is the Heart

Silhouette Special Edition
Published by Silhouette Books New York
America's Publisher of Contemporary Romance

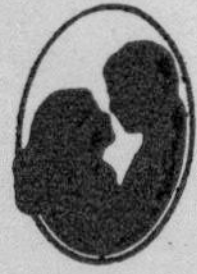

SILHOUETTE BOOKS, a division of Simon & Schuster, Inc.
1230 Avenue of the Americas, New York, N.Y. 10020

Distributed by Pocket Books

ISBN: 0-671-53603-6

First Silhouette Books printing July, 1983

10 9 8 7 6 5 4 3 2 1

Map by Ray Lundgren

America's Publisher of Contemporary Romance

Printed in the U.S.A.

Other Books by Abra Taylor

Season of Seduction

Published by SILHOUETTE BOOKS

Hold Back the Night

Published by POCKET BOOKS

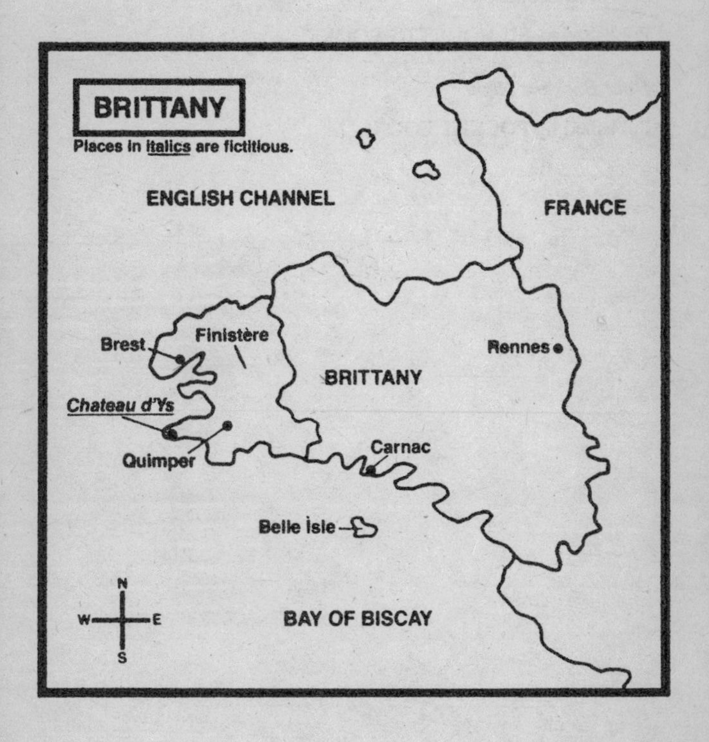
BRITTANY
Places in italics are fictitious.
ENGLISH CHANNEL
FRANCE
Brest
Finistère
Rennes
BRITTANY
Chateau d'Ys
Quimper
Carnac
Belle Isle
N
W
E
S
BAY OF BISCAY

Chapter One

"Monsieur Devereux is not in, mademoiselle. I believe I told you that on the telephone, only an hour ago?"

The secretary was formidable, as thoroughly bilingual as if she had been working for a big Paris corporation, and not in a boatworks in a quiet Brittany backwater. Her smile was polite and impenetrable. The smile said she could recognize a voice perfectly well, even when the voice was disguised. A real dragon of a secretary, in other words. Tory had already discovered as much, to her sorrow.

"You've been telling me that for three days," Tory replied with considerable exasperation. "And please don't bother repeating it, for I don't believe you! I know he's in, for I saw his car." After the taxi ride from Quimper, and before entering the office, Tory had walked behind the long, low, rambling stone building that housed the boatworks. In the landscaped parking lot there had been a designated space with a dark brown Mercedes parked in front of the nameplate.

"That, mademoiselle, is a company car. Monsieur Devereux is not in."

Tory cast a frustrated glance at the closed door to the inner office. The door had a milky glass window, and through it she could see a shadowed silhouette. Someone was definitely in there, and one didn't need a great deal of intelligence to know who it must be. She checked her watch. "Is he engaged for lunch?"

"I'm afraid, mademoiselle, that he is not in at all." The secretary's face was bland. "This is a personal matter?"

The question tended to confirm Tory's opinion that something might get her through that door if she hit on the right approach. "It's rather confidential . . . er, business. Important business."

"You are known to Monsieur Devereux?"

Tory hesitated. "It's been some years," she said evasively, hoping that the hint of a prior acquaintance might get her past the dragon. "It's a private legal matter, and it's not trivial. I came all the way from the States to see him."

The secretary trailed a cool glance over the clothes Tory had chosen with such care, hoping they would give her the advantage of appearing quietly self-confident. The oatmeal-colored blazer blended with her pale, toffee-colored hair, while the pleated tweed skirt and creamy silk shirt were businesslike but not aggressively so. Tory hadn't wanted to look like a hard-core career woman—but she hadn't wanted to appear too feminine, either. She hoped she looked and sounded like a lawyer.

The secretary, for one, was not overawed by Tory's appearance. "I assure you, mademoiselle, that the most confidential matters are often left in my hands. Perhaps you represent the American consortium? If so, mademoiselle, Monsieur Devereux's answer is still no, even if the offer has been increased. He cannot possibly undertake another yacht of that size at this time. However, if your business concerns something else . . ."

"It's not about a yacht," Tory said quickly, thinking she might have discovered the secret of gaining admission to the inner sanctum.

The little pursing of the secretary's lips made it clear that if it wasn't about a yacht, it could hardly have anything to do with Saint-Cloud et Fils, yacht builders extraordinary. "*Eh bien,* once again I must ask you to state your business," she said pleasantly. For three days Tory had been refusing to do so.

"I don't care to state anything, except to Monsieur Devereux himself." Because if I did, Tory added in her head, your evasive boss might never see me at all. After all, he had ignored that urgent letter two years before—or largely ignored it. The tardy answer had come from a law firm in Brest, not from Luc Devereux himself. And she didn't intend to be put off, not when she had come all the way to Brittany for the sole purpose of finding him.

"If you would at least give me your name," the secretary suggested tactfully.

Tory wanted to choose a name she wouldn't forget, and she didn't think a lack of inventiveness would make much difference in France. "Smith . . . Jane Smith." But she had hesitated a little too long.

The secretary's expression remained impenetrable as she wrote the name on a small memo pad. "I shall tell him you called," she said.

"Perhaps you'd also be good enough to give me the name of Monsieur Devereux's legal firm?" Tory asked pleasantly.

With no hesitation the secretary supplied her with a name and address in Brest. To Tory's satisfaction, it matched the name she already knew. She must have the right Luc Devereux. At that point the intercom buzzed, and the secretary depressed the button. *"Oui, monsieur?"*

So there very definitely was someone in that inner office, and the secretary's failure to use the person's last name didn't fool Tory for one minute. It was probably a deliberate omission.

The fluid, rapid-fire French that erupted over the intercom was far beyond Tory's comprehension, but she listened to the conversation with every instinct vibrating, hoping it might at least help her to recognize Luc Devereux's voice if she ever heard it again. There had been no snapshots amongst Laura's possessions, nor could Tory remember being given much of a description beyond the vague eulogies of dark, handsome, marvelous. After all these years it had been very hard to track the man to ground, and Tory still knew little more about him than the make of his car and the nature of his occupation, owner of a company that manufactured racing yachts. Two years ago she hadn't even known that. She had had to send the letter to an apartment he had once rented for Laura in Brest, in the hope that it would be properly forwarded. It had been, but with disappointing results.

Before the brief interoffice communication came to

a close, Tory noted with satisfaction that the secretary had at least passed the Jane Smith pseudonym along. So much for the fiction that Luc Devereux wasn't in.

The secretary reached for a large appointment calendar opened to the correct date in late spring and leafed through several pages. Tory, standing on the other side of the blonde oak reception desk, could see that all the pages were very nearly blank, including today's. Perhaps it was the woman's pointed way of telling her to state her business, or else. "Monsieur Devereux will not be available for several days. If you wish, I could make an appointment for next week."

"I'll wait today," Tory said firmly, earning only a lift of the other woman's brows.

"As you wish," she said pleasantly, flipping the appointment pad back to the correct date. She returned to her typewriter.

By the window of the glass-fronted reception area, there was a grouping of leather couches and chairs. Tory walked over to it and sat down, determinedly positioning herself so that she could not miss any comings or goings at the door of Luc Devereux's office.

Her back was turned to the view, but she had seen it all anyway on arrival. A quiet, sheltered cove. The Bay of Biscay sparkled by sun under a clean-swept blue sky. A long, picturesque stone quay. A large, sleek, spanking-new yacht had been anchored in deeper water a short distance out. On it a number of wiry, well-muscled workmen had been working at snail's pace, attending to assorted tasks, mostly checking canvas and fiddling with gleaming fittings. They had seemed about to put out to sea. Other workmen had been on the dock. Earlier Tory had heard them joking with each other in a very un-

French language that she had presumed to be the Breton tongue. She couldn't believe that the man who owned this idle, sleepy endeavor was too busy to see her. Nor could she believe he wasn't in the office.

Although it gave its address as Quimper, the boatworks was some miles beyond that walled old Breton town. It shared its well-sheltered, slumbrous bay with local fisherfolk—that, too, Tory had remarked on arrival. At the far end of the bay there had been a colorful variety of fishing craft resting on stilts in the low tide. From the lanterns on the boats and clues gathered during her few days in Quimper, she gathered that they must be sardine fishermen, who often plied their trade by night.

Tory had a long, long wait. The lunch hour came, with the secretary stopping to eat a packed lunch of sandwiches, but no one emerged from the inner office. Tory eyed the crusty French bread hungrily, her stomach telling her to go in search of food, and her mind overruling her stomach. He had to leave that office sometime!

But what if she didn't manage to corner him? What if his office had an exit leading directly out to the parking lot, which it adjoined? She didn't think it did, for she could remember seeing no doors at the rear of the building. As far as she knew, the only exits were at the front, giving onto the quay. If he wanted to leave that inner office, he would surely have to pass this way. All the same, the thought troubled her, but she could think of no way to find out, short of leaving her post. And she didn't intend to do that.

But at least he hadn't left yet. Through the milky glass window there were still occasional movements to be seen.

She set her mind to wondering how she might

discover where Luc Devereux lived, should she fail to connect with him here. He had no telephone listing in the Quimper directory nor, as far as she could determine, in any directory in this province of Brittany known as Finistère. Finistère: surely that meant land's end, world's end, or some such thing? How ironic, for she certainly felt as if she had followed him to the ends of the earth! Two weeks in Brittany and God knew how many phone calls; and nothing to guide her but that old apartment address in Brest, the name of a close-mouthed law firm, a belief that he was well-to-do, and the knowledge that his occupation had something to do with the sea. Even that hadn't been much help at first. A third of Brittany's population, Tory had discovered, made its living from the sea.

The secretary disposed of her lunch wrappings in a wastebasket and trained a cool look on Tory. "There is no point waiting, mademoiselle. Truly, Monsieur Devereux will not be seeing you today. He is not in his office, and if he were, I would not be able to disturb him."

Tory looked at the smoked-glass pane in the door and detected a definite movement. She returned the dragon's imperturbable smile and stayed firmly in place.

She didn't believe the woman. But if he did leave by some other exit, what would she do? Perhaps it would be possible to engage one of the workmen in conversation, provided any could be found who spoke English. In larger cities many Frenchmen could, but in rural Brittany it was less likely. All the same, this company did seem to have some dealings with American customers. If nothing else worked, it was worth a try. No one, but no one, could be less obliging than the dragon lady!

Tory had been pursuing that train of thought for several minutes when someone entered from outside. A man. With her eyes fixed on Luc Devereux's door, she didn't actually see him enter, and by the time she glanced sideways, he was crossing the office purposefully, his goal very clearly the same as her own—Luc Devereux's office. He halted at the secretary's desk and propped his hands on its edge, leaning forward with an air of proprietary familiarity while he exchanged a few low words. Tory listened intently, but she heard only the secretary's first name—Annette. Annette seemed to know him, too. A fellow employee, perhaps?

Asking to see the boss, probably. Tory still couldn't see the man's face, but he didn't look like a customer. He was wearing paint-stained white ducks, a well-worn blue T-shirt, and scuffed boat shoes. Dark hair curved over his collar, the cut a little too long to be described as anything but careless. He was a tall man, his build lean and hard. The powerful, wiry musculature of his shoulders and thighs suggested that he was quite capable of manual exertion; in fact, the line of sweat darkening the T-shirt between his shoulder blades suggested that he had recently been exerting himself quite strenuously.

"*Mais certainement, si vous voulez.*" With those words, the first Tory had been able to overhear and understand, the secretary slid out of her chair and vanished into the inner office, clicking the door closed behind her. So Luc Devereux was not quite as unapproachable as all that, when he wanted to be approached!

The man turned and looked at Tory incuriously, an idle glance that drifted away at once. He extracted a pack of Gitanes from his pocket and shook one out.

Then, with a frown, he started to rummage for a match. He found a wooden one and ignited it on a thumbnail, then cupped his hands to light the cigarette, still facing Tory. The match's flare flickered over a scowl and a deep scar.

Tory watched, wondering. . . .

With that grim expression and the scar on his face, he looked anything but easy to handle. The old wound had left a pale, jagged mark that sliced down from a broad temple, past the eye, and over a well-defined cheekbone. It was the most striking feature in a hard, handsome face. Tory wasn't blind to the fact that he was an enormously attractive man, in the prime of his attractiveness. The scar didn't detract from his dark good looks—in fact, it kept him from being too handsome. At the same time it added a dimension of intense excitement, of danger, of mystery. The very type of man she always avoided tangling with.

"Do you speak English?" she burst out.

His eyes came up to meet hers. His were granite-gray and had a hard, weathered look, as though they had seen quite a lot. They were the eyes of an experienced man. From the expression in them, Tory knew he was sizing her up just as she had been sizing him up, making all those man-woman assessments that were made whenever opposite sexes met. But she had made the first approach, so when he took some time to study her coolly, she couldn't in all fairness describe it as insolent. Tory wasn't used to that kind of appraisal, and it unsettled her deeply.

He ascertained the color of her eyes, hazel, and even slid a glance at her bare ring finger. His last long gaze trailed down to her toes, as if measuring her height and weight and a few other vital statistics as well. He didn't appear to be overly impressed. Tory hadn't expected him to be, because she had too little faith in her attractions. All the same, his brooding inspection started a little quiver deep in the pit of her stomach. Sexual awareness was a sensation she had managed to tamp down for some years, and it was disturbing to realize she could still feel it so strongly.

"Yes, as a matter of fact, I do," he said after a moment.

"Are you American?" she asked, astonished at his accent.

"Are you surprised?" he countered. "Some people do work abroad."

For another moment they looked at each other, making mental assessments. It occurred to her that he might think she was trying to pick him up. In this liberated age there were a lot of women who didn't hesitate to approach men, that type of man especially. Even living in old-fashioned Brittany, he must be subjected to it time and again. Tory smiled in what she hoped was merely a friendly fashion. "It's wonderful to find a fellow American," she said.

"I gather you're from the Midwest, Miss, er . . ."

He was asking for her name. Tory hesitated awkwardly before saying, "Smith. Ah . . . Jane Smith." She had had to think in order to remember the name she'd given before. She wasn't very good at lying and she changed the subject hurriedly, sorry to have flubbed the name again. She didn't want to tell him she was from Colorado, which wasn't to her way of thinking the Midwest, so she went on quickly, "I'm afraid I don't quite recognize your accent." It was very definitely American, but it had just a touch of British in it, too.

One of his dark brows had lifted sardonically at the name Jane Smith, but he didn't remark on it. All the same, the eyebrow was comment enough. "I've moved around a bit," he replied smoothly.

"A rolling stone? I think you've spent some time in the British Isles, too."

"Yes." He didn't tell her how long he had stayed there.

He sounded and looked like an adventurer, the sort who might very well have worked his way around the world, which would explain his presence in this place. She still couldn't quite decide what part of the States he was from. "Is that East Coast I hear in your voice?" she asked lightly. "New England?"

"Probably. Mostly, that's where I lived."

"Where?"

"Too many places to list. One of them was Cambridge, Massachusetts. I spent some years there, studying physics."

She uttered a little sound of surprise. "I thought you worked in this place! I expected you to be a boat builder, or—or perhaps a sailor of some sort." Had she wasted all this effort on someone who didn't know a thing about Luc Devereux?

"I am a sailor, and I am a boat builder, and I do work in this place. I'm a yacht designer, to be precise. At M.I.T., I learned hydraulics among other things—the laws governing water and wave movements. There is some science to the art."

Tory relaxed a little. So he did work for Saint-Cloud et Fils. It was worth pursuing the conversation. Still striving for small talk because she couldn't plunge directly into the questions she really wanted to ask, she remarked, "At first I thought you were one of the unskilled laborers."

"There are no unskilled laborers around here. I'm not the only one with a background in the sciences."

"No, I suppose not." So far, the conversation didn't seem to be going too well. He was still watching her with that cool, hooded look, his veiled eyes enigmatic behind concealing dark lashes, as though he were deciding whether it would be worth his while to pursue the acquaintance. And yet he hadn't been too chary with information about himself. She decided it was time to engineer the conversational switch, in case the secretary reappeared.

"Er . . . are you hoping to see Luc, too?" There. That first name should do the trick.

"Not really. There are some blueprints I need. Annette knows where they are."

"The boatworks doesn't seem too frantic today. I wonder why Luc's so busy?"

"On the contrary, things have been hectic all this month. There's a Greek client taking delivery in a few days."

She noticed that *he* didn't pretend his boss was out. "Hectic all month, for that one boat out there?"

"That one five-million-dollar boat out there," he corrected dryly. "You don't know much about yachting, do you?"

"Not a thing," she said quickly, wanting to get the subject back on track. She glanced at the door. Through the milky glass she could see a woman's shadow, hovering as if exchanging a few last words with someone. The secretary might emerge at any moment. Tory sighed rather dramatically. "I've been waiting for Luc for simply ages."

"I noticed." He gestured at the plate glass behind her. "Off and on, I've seen your head through the window."

Tory smiled again, more encouragingly this time. "The dragon lady tells me he's not in, but I don't believe her. Maybe I'd better give up and call Luc at home . . . oh, damn. He has an unlisted number, doesn't he?"

"If he does, and as you know him so well, wouldn't he have given it to you?" the man fenced, his granite eyes darkening scornfully. She knew he had seen through her ruse.

Oh, blast. Was he going to be a stone wall, too? Tory tilted her head to one side with the best imitation of flirtatiousness she could manage. "He did, but you know how it is. He wrote the number on a cigarette pack."

"Really?"

He looked so disbelieving that she could only conclude Luc Devereux didn't smoke. "Er . . . I made the mistake of throwing the pack away, when I finished it. You wouldn't happen to know the number, would you?"

The man studied her with cool insolence, a little mocking twist playing at the edge of his hard mouth. He was not deceived by her tactics, Tory knew, but she still hoped. She gave him her most engaging smile, the one she had kept in cold storage ever since the short, disastrous marriage that had taught her in the most painful possible way that her attractions and men's intentions were not to be trusted.

His lids drooped, dropping to the curve of Tory's throat and below. "I might be able to help you," he drawled, "if—"

The secretary chose that crucial moment to emerge from the inner office, a neat roll of blueprints in her hand. She passed them over with a pleasant smile and slipped back into her swivel chair. Tory could have wept with vexation.

"Merci mille fois, Annette."

"Ça va?" asked Annette.

"Comme ci comme ça," said the man with a shrug.

Tory had understood all that. Thanks a million. How's it going? Oh, so so. Not very illuminating conversation.

Then the man spoke in English. "Look, Annette, this young lady is very anxious to see Luc without delay. Is he in there or not?"

"Does the mademoiselle think I lied?"

"Indeed she does. Why don't you let her through the door so she can see for herself?"

Annette hesitated, then shrugged. "As you wish," she said.

The man strode toward the outer door, purposeful once more. Tory was already rising to her feet, with the ghastly suspicion that she had waited all this time in vain, when he came to a halt beside her.

"I'll pick you up for dinner," he said abruptly. It was a statement, not a question, and the arrogance of it took Tory aback.

Although fairly tall, she had to look upward to meet his gaze, a fact that contributed to the sensation of vulnerability that suddenly pierced her, as if a thousand butterflies were trembling in her stomach. She began to regret her earlier flirtatiousness. "I don't . . ." She bit her lip, pausing. He wouldn't be asking, she supposed, if he hadn't already done some calculations about her availability. No doubt he was another of those arrogant males who thought he could rush any woman into bed on short acquaintance. That strong, intensely virile type was always confident of success. Until this moment he hadn't seemed to be dazzled by her, but perhaps he was becoming bored with the local women. . . .

"I can't wait all day," he reminded her impatiently

and somewhat sarcastically. "We're taking the new job for another test run."

He was waiting for her answer, and she wanted to say no. Unwillingly, she was aware of his iron-hard thighs, his flat stomach, his strong muscled length. There was a little dusting of dark hair on his forearms, and she could almost feel the texture of it prickling at her fingertips. She looked away quickly, not wanting to feel such disturbing sensations.

But she could handle him, couldn't she? It was more than seven years since she had been bested by any man, and then only out of youth, vulnerability, and a painful lack of the defenses she had since acquired. And if Luc Devereux really wasn't at the boatworks, she had to find some way to reach him. At the moment this man seemed the only way. "All right," she said, trying to quell the peculiar quiverings she could only put down to apprehension. Information was her goal, not a date with a man as dangerously masculine as this.

"You're staying in Quimper?"

She nodded and told him the name of the hotel.

"Nine o'clock, then. I'll ask for . . . Jane Smith, shall I?" That little pause held a hint of derision. He must be well aware that she wasn't registered under that name.

"No, I . . . I'll meet you in the lobby." Not that she cared if this man knew who she was, except that he might pass the name Victoria Allworth on to Annette. Tory preferred to keep her identity to herself until she came face-to-face with Luc Devereux, who might or might not recall the first name but would most certainly remember the Allworth.

He saluted mockingly and started through the door.

"Wait! I don't know *your* name."

He paused on the threshold and turned his head long enough for Tory to see the mocking droop of his lids and the lazy, arrogant smile that had taken possession of those hard, handsome lips. "Doe," he said dryly. "John Doe."

Luc Devereux's brief smile faded as soon as he passed through the door, his quick stride taking him across the quay to where his men were waiting for him anxiously. He had not told the woman many lies, but he hadn't told her very many truths, either. He simply didn't have time.

An hour later, as the spray hit his face and the huge yacht pointed breathtakingly close into a stiff wind, he ought to have been feeling an intense thrill, the thrill of reward at the end of a long labor of love. Luc's painstaking craft was more important to him, he had always thought, than any woman would ever be. Mastery of a woman could never supplant mastery of the sea, for the sea—the great, beautiful, terrible sea—was the one mistress to whom a man could never be unfaithful. It was the Saint-Cloud blood in him, of course. What was it about the Saint-Clouds and the sea?

As always during a test run of this nature, a large part of his mind was occupied with the elements and the yacht's performance and the niggling adjustments that would have to be made after they returned to shore. To the man who sat beside him taking notes, he occasionally clipped out orders about tightening stays, adjusting winches, trimming rigging. But the orders were almost automatic, the observations the result of long experience and instinct rather than wholehearted concentration. For once, a part of him was still back on shore, with the woman.

He knew what she must have found when she passed through the door Annette always guarded so zealously. There was no plush office, but a clean, well-lit room with several drafting boards and a couple of draftsmen hard at work. His own desk and drafting board would be empty.

And if Annette showed her the rest of the place, she would be equally disappointed. The working space of Saint-Cloud et Fils took up most of the building, and it opened directly onto the quay. A stranger would see only a big, clean two-hundred-foot working area with the raw hull of the next commission filling half the space, and storage shelves and work-benches filling the rest. A very few, very skilled men would be working meticulously and conscientiously at a careful, unhurried pace. One didn't hurry when one centimeter's change in a curve might win a race or when one ill-designed stay or shroud might cost a man his life.

His secretary's intercom reached not only the inner office but the working area as well. He had been there when Annette told him that Jane Smith, the mysterious caller of the past few days, had finally put in a personal appearance. All day, as the yacht was being readied to go through its paces, Luc had been coming and going . . . and seeing that smooth, shiny shoulder-length hair in the window of the waiting room. And wondering what part of his past she might have come from. Damn her for turning up today!

Under the circumstances he might have relished the prospect of the evening ahead. Now that a few years had passed, his vital faculties were no longer impaired by the tragedy that had rent the fabric of his life, and of all Saint-Cloud lives. Normally he enjoyed women, and for the most part, nowadays, he enjoyed life. But at the moment he felt only the fierce need to concentrate and a dull, throbbing headache—the kind of headache that always accompanied attempts to remember.

Jane Smith. A lie, of course. And she had been lying when she told Annette that she knew him, for she very patently didn't. At first he had thought it possible that he might have met her very briefly at some point, and that the scar might have misled her. God knows, he had lived in the States long enough while learning his craft. But he had mentioned most of the highlights of his life and she hadn't jumped at any of them. Massachusetts, M.I.T., and yachting meant nothing to her. And she didn't know enough about him to be aware of his extreme fluency, his exacting and uncommon specialty, or his permanent address on the Saint-Cloud estates.

So where was the connection?

Besides, something told him he had never seen the woman before. Her looks weren't flashy enough to turn heads, but there was something hauntingly lovely about those level, wide-spaced eyes and that quiet, mobile mouth. And when she smiled, her whole face lit in an extraordinary way, giving an illusion of beauty that made her quite unforgettable. Surely, if he had ever seen those eyes and that smile before, he would have experienced some little flashback—one of those fleeting, ephemeral wisps of memory that taunted and teased, then vanished like dispersing mists, only to reappear in more substantial, graspable form.

There was very little, now, that he didn't recall. There had been no miraculous cure for the amnesia, but over the years most of his dim and unremembered past had been gradually and sometimes painfully recollected, reassembled, and reconstructed. The publicity attendant on the Saint-Cloud tragedy had added a good deal of confusion. There had been the usual chicanery resulting from the deaths of prominent men—crank letters, false claims against the estate, lawsuits, even marriage proposals from total strangers when it became known how much he stood to inherit, the boatworks being only the hundredth part of it. Sifting through to the truth of a blurred past had not been easy, but most of the claims had been disposed of and most of the memories had in time returned. With only occasional specters to haunt him now, the headaches had become fewer and farther between. But there were still some elusive ghosts troubling his mind. Was that slim, tall American woman one of them?

He'd find out, he supposed, once he told her that he was the Luc Devereux she wanted to see. He might have done that at once, but he'd been far too occupied today to spare the time for what might turn out to be a difficult interview. When she wouldn't state her business to Annette or reveal her true name, he'd become suspicious. And of course there was the matter of her come-on to a perfect stranger, when it was easy to see she was the sort who usually held herself in reserve. Manlike, he spent a moment speculating how far she intended to go to get the information she wanted. And oddly savoring the speculation.

Oh, hell. Luc gritted his teeth as a sudden thought occurred to him. Might she be a writer for some American magazine? Or a syndicated columnist? Perhaps one of those radio commentators who did interesting little sob-story pieces? With an international flavor, of course. She wouldn't have to know much about yachting to do a follow-up on the aftermath of Fastnet. The human interest angle. The tragedy of so many international yachtsmen lost at sea. It could very well be something like that. To an American journalist, Luc Devereux would be no more than a name on a list of survivors.

Fastnet . . . oh, God. That was one cruel memory he wished amnesia *had* obliterated. With remembrance of those wild storm-lashed seas, of falling masts and bloodied decks and screams drowning in the gale, the throb in Luc's scarred temple changed from dull to acute. Fastnet had been a race with death, a race in a yacht *he* had designed. That the Saint-Cloud men had lost their lives aboard that yacht was an affront to the family, who had reared him, a distant, bastard cousin, almost as one of its own. If he had to forget something, why couldn't he forget Fastnet?

And yet that part of the past still held him in its chains. Perhaps it always would, just as it chained the two women in his life, the two who were all that remained of the proud line of Saint-Cloud. Would he ever discharge the duty he owed to his aunt and his young cousin?

For his aunt, Tante Marie, he felt scant sympathy, despite the great debt he owed her for his upbringing. If the past imprisoned her, perhaps the prison was partly of her own making. His aunt was a woman of extraordinarily strong will; she would survive. But Aimée, lovely, innocent young Aimée, trembling on the brink of the future and held by the bonds of the past . . . why must *she* be shackled by the family tragedy? It was enough to lose father and brother without losing freedom, too. Aimée was the real victim of Fastnet, and it was for her that Luc felt the greatest responsibility. For now, there was little he could do to change the abnormality of his young cousin's life, but it disturbed him deeply. Another burden for his chained conscience.

Determinedly, Luc pushed away thoughts of the women to whom he owed such debts and shouted a command to come about. So far, with the small adjustments that had been made during the day, the test was a triumph. For the next short time, as the yacht moved like a great graceful bird into a new pattern of flight, the headache was almost forgotten. And then it returned, along with the haunting face of the mysterious Jane Smith. Journalism wouldn't account for the false identity unless the woman had a recognizable name. He doubted that she would at her age. She couldn't be much more than halfway through her twenties. Besides, she was staying at what must be the smallest, seediest hotel in all of Quimper—hardly the stuff of expense accounts.

Another false claimant against the Saint-Clouds, then? Or against himself? She must be. To Annette, she had hinted at legal complications. In other words, a veiled threat. Others had appeared and pretended a place in his past or cited promises that had never been made. The widely reported amnesia had encouraged imposters of all sorts, some of them with stories that sounded plausible enough but didn't mesh with the known facts of his life or the lives of the two dead Saint-Cloud men.

Another imposter, then. Her pretense of a previous acquaintance practically confirmed it. She was looking for money, of course, and hoping her threats would produce it without going to court. If she had any genuine claim, any story that could stand up to the harsh light of examination, her approach would have been more straightforward and presented through proper legal channels. She didn't look the type to try extortion, but Luc already knew to his sorrow that an innocent appearance didn't mean a thing. Through bitter experience he had learned that honest faces often concealed dishonest intentions.

A sudden anger washed through him. Damn the woman, anyway! She deserved a cruel lesson if her purpose was to take advantage of other people's cruel misfortunes. The pounding in Luc's scarred temple became acute, causing his mouth to harden into a dangerously thin line. Maybe Miss Jane Smith had met her match in Mr. John Doe.

Chapter Two

Tory had just emerged from the bathtub when the rap came at the hotel door. Her nerves didn't jump at the sound. After a long, luxurious soak they were a lot less frayed than they had been earlier in the day when she discovered that her wait at Saint-Cloud et Fils had all been for nothing.

In this hotel it was not likely to be a maid, so it must be that pesky female tourist who had a room across the hall, a retired English schoolmarm who was traveling alone and not relishing solitude at all. With a sigh of resignation, for she didn't wish to be unkind to a lonely maiden lady, Tory wrapped the well-worn hotel towel around her and went to the door. She had lots of time; it was no more than seven o'clock.

Clutching the towel to her breasts, she eased the door open a crack. She gasped. "Oh, Lord," she said, staring. "It's you."

"May I come in? Or must I stand in the hall, as thanks for getting you past the dragon lady?"

The question was rhetorical because he didn't wait for an answer. He was much more expert than she in the art of easing doors open. With no pushing and a good deal of smoothness, he engineered it.

With only one free hand, Tory couldn't make her objection very physical. One set of fingers had to stay in control of the towel, and the hand that did go up to stop him was immediately seized and kissed—a very un-American gesture. The imprint of his hard mouth seemed to burn some of the common sense out of her, and before she knew it he was in the room, with the door firmly closed behind him.

She jerked her fingers away from his mouth. "You're . . . early," she stuttered. Little bubbles seemed to be traveling along her arm, through her bloodstream, their source that mark that seemed branded on her hand. Hysteria perhaps? Why was he here two hours early? How had he found her?

"The wind started to die." There was a dark, watchful mockery in the man's eyes, a disturbing derision in his mouth. He knew he had unbalanced her. "We had to come to shore much earlier than expected. As I'd had no lunch, I saw no point in delaying dinner."

Her visitor's eyes scouted the surroundings. Whether from lack of interest or from tact, he made no comment. Tory's room was a small and dingy one, its only amenity the tiny attached bathroom without which she felt she couldn't exist.

"You'll have to go!"

"If I do go, I mightn't come back," he warned, sauntering farther into the room. He draped his lean length against one side of the bathroom door and faced her with a diabolical glint in his eye. "And please don't ask me to wait outside in the hall. I'm not a patient man, and I might decide to go on to dinner alone."

She couldn't let him vanish: he was her one link to the information she needed. "No, I . . . please wait. I'll change in the bathroom."

But between herself and that small haven was a wall of muscle—his shoulders and chest. At her words he didn't step aside, as she might have expected. She had left her underthings in the bathroom and wanted to get them on as soon as possible. But when he remained at his station she hesitated, every nerve jangling.

In the suggestive dimness of the room, the shadows that played on his face were unsettling, for they emphasized the amused quirk at the edge of his hard, sensual mouth. Because her window overlooked no scenic vista, only a view of other nearby windows, Tory had pulled down the blind before stepping into the bath. She had turned on only one small lamp. She quickly bent to flick another switch, hoping to change the room's atmosphere.

By artificial light the paleness of his scar stood out against the deep bronze weathering of his skin, the dark swath of his hair. He wore the civilized suit and tie as easily as he had worn casual clothes earlier, but there was still that elemental quality about him. She had known he would be dangerous, but not quite this dangerous. Those effervescent bubbles started to move into her lower limbs. Why did he have to be so damnably attractive?

She eyed the bathroom door nervously. Too much of him filled the space she had to pass through. "How did you . . . find me?"

"I bribed a chambermaid," he drawled, his eyes darkly sardonic. "I gathered the good lady had no memory for names. She couldn't remember which room Jane Smith was in, but she had no trouble at all when I asked for the cool, willowy American lady with honey-brown hair and the wonderful smile. That mouth of yours, Jane"—there was a little hesitation over the name—"is a lot less anonymous than your name."

The long, dark, smoldering look that accompanied the words unsteadied her more than she would have believed possible. For a moment, yearnings long dormant turned her legs to butter and sent small shivers of awareness sliding down her spine.

But then she reminded herself that men always used that sort of flattery, even when they didn't mean it. The compliment and the steamy look were only intended to soften her. She had heard compliments in the past and knew exactly where they were intended to lead. She stiffened, an instinctive reaction despite the fact that her graceful carriage didn't require any straightening. Her brief and painful experience with marriage had taught her a strong distrust of all attractive men, and in the years since, she had seen no reason to change her mind. That raking appreciation in his eyes wasn't a true compliment, only a statement of his intentions for later in the evening.

She wasn't ready to disabuse him yet. She tightened her hold on the towel. "You should have phoned up from downstairs," she said, keeping her hazel eyes level with some difficulty.

One dark brow tilted upward. "How could I? The desk clerk couldn't find a record of Jane Smith. And I didn't know your room number until the maid pointed me at it. Well, are you going to get dressed? Those long legs of yours would look very well on a beach, but not in one of the best restaurants in Quimper."

It was as if he were daring her to walk past him. She decided a towel was no way to be dressed when confronted by such a dangerous human barrier. It was simply too risky.

Never in her life had her legs felt so naked. Conscious that they were under close inspection, she crossed the bedroom and rustled in the tiny clothes closet until she found her bathrobe. She wished it wasn't light nylon, which, though eminently packable, had a way of clinging too suggestively. Turning her back to him, she put it on, allowing the towel to slide onto the floor only when she was safely covered. She tied the sash securely. She didn't want this whole thing to get physical, so she would simply have to play it by ear. Get dressed and out to dinner as quickly as possible, without antagonizing the man. When she found out what she wanted to know, she would drop him.

When she turned, her pulses leaped to realize that he had closed the gap between them.

"Before you do something about that beautifully scrubbed face," he murmured huskily, "I think we should introduce ourselves properly." Every nerve in her body quivered as his hands came up to her shoulders, closing over the silky fabric. His strong fingers caressed its surface, sliding lightly and slowly and oh, so suggestively. Tory felt as if her flesh had been totally sensitized. She wanted to scream.

"I told you, my name is—"

"Hush. I don't mean your name. I'm talking about another kind of introduction, the important one." As his face descended she was mesmerized by his eyes and the smoking message in them. If she had any doubts about what he expected from her before the night was through, those heavy-lidded eyes and the sensuousness playing over his firm lips set them to rest. She turned her head just in time. He made no move to force her mouth back to his, but the little line of kisses he laid along her jaw very nearly destroyed her sense of balance. His gently parted lips were not as hard as they appeared. They were soft, warm, seductive, and far too skilled, the lips of a vastly experienced man. She closed her eyes, breathed unsteadily, and then opened them again as he freed her without pressing his advantage.

"I hope you're not averse to kissing," he murmured with a velvet sensuality in his voice. "That would spoil my plans for later this evening."

"We . . . don't know each other," Tory objected, too breathlessly.

"I intend to correct that before the night is through." The arrogant little twist to his mouth declared that he was well aware of her reaction and quite prepared to wait. No doubt he thought the trembling of her flesh meant victory whenever he chose to claim it.

With one hand Tory anchored the gap at the vee of her neck, where the nylon had slipped to reveal a little too much of the curve of her breast. Escaping into the bathroom, she locked the door and leaned on it, breathing hard. Having sampled his intentions, she realized that she should have brought a dress in with her, a simple enough matter if she had only been thinking straight, which she hadn't. It was too late now to go out and fetch one. She reached for her underthings with trembling fingers and slid into the skimpy but vital apparel. Her heart was racing, her palms clammy, her throat on fire where his lips had laid those temptingly light kisses.

Another kind of armor went on with her makeup, which fortunately sat on a glass shelf in the bathroom. She was disturbed to find that her hand, the hand that had been pressed to his mouth, was shaking quite badly. Oh, damn. Hadn't she learned a thing since the age of nineteen? All the hard lessons taught by Griff Rammell should have given her some immunity to tall, magnetic men. The more sex appeal they exuded, the more they should be avoided. Attractive men were all the same—they took what they wanted and when they got it, they walked out. Griff had done it to her, and Luc Devereux had done it to her sister, Laura. And they had both made promises they hadn't kept.

She was still trying to straighten the line of her lipstick when he tapped on the bathroom door. His deep, sardonic drawl came through the door, muffled by the barrier it presented. "I've chosen a dress for you. Open the door and I'll hand it in."

After a moment's pause and a tug at the sash of her light robe, she acceded. Quickly she relocked the door. Then, dismayed, she looked at the garment he had chosen. To her way of thinking, it was only half a dress. "This has a jacket," she called out.

"I don't like the jacket. When I dine, I prefer to enjoy the view. A moment ago I saw enough of it to whet my appetite for more." His voice hardened. "Put it on."

She squeezed her fingers around the soft fabric of the dress, feeling trapped and badly unnerved. She hated displaying herself. Without the high-throated matching jacket, this flimsy little concoction of butterscotch silk concealed very little, at least on the upper half. The swinging, clinging skirt was perfectly decent, but the plunging halter neck was designed to afford tantalizing glimpses with every small bend and sway of the body. By no stretch of the imagination could a brassiere be worn underneath, for the back was bare above the waist.

"I'll be cold!"

His husky, suggestive laugh could be heard through the door. "I'll remedy that."

Tory took a good grip on her nerves, calming herself with the reminder that she could procure the jacket before setting off for the evening. Well, she thought militantly, thank God she had smallish breasts! In that area she was well-shaped, but not overendowed. When he saw the lack of amplitude, he'd probably be bored. She slid into the dress, brassiere discarded, and spent the next few seconds looking helplessly into the mirror with a contrariness that was purely feminine. Why couldn't she be just a *little* larger where it counted? She vented some of her mixed frustrations with a few furious strokes of the hairbrush.

She reminded herself that she didn't want to attract him anyway, no matter what he might think. What *did* he think? That she was the type for one-night stands? He must have decided something like that, for he couldn't have been more obvious about his intentions. He'd been undressing her mentally since he'd walked through the door. They might have been seafarer and streetwalker, for all the time he'd spent on the niceties—including the exchange of true names. Perhaps he simply didn't care. How badly this man had misjudged her motives for picking him up! *His* motives were transparent enough, as men's motives always were. One thing was certain—whether she managed to wheedle information from him or not, she wasn't going to let him back into her hotel room after dinner.

When she emerged he was leaning against a wall, arms crossed, brooding. For a fraction of time she thought she glimpsed something hostile in his expression, but then he straightened and approved the view.

"I'm ready to forget the dinner," he murmured as he swept her with a smoldering gaze that made no secret of his intentions, "you look quite edible enough for me."

She knew it was only the sort of flattery men used when they wanted something, but all the same it caused little flutters she ought not to feel. She felt half naked and fully vulnerable as his eyes probed her neckline. She tried to hold herself as tall as possible, a posture that made the inadequate fabric strain against her breasts rather than desert the vital areas altogether. She manufactured a bright smile and tried to get past him to the closet.

"Wait," he murmured. "I want to make sure I've chosen the right dress."

He seized her arms and forced her to turn to left and right. She knew he didn't miss much, for even though she stood very straight, the clinging silk delineated the exact shape of her breasts in clear detail.

"Very tantalizing," he decided in a smoky voice. Before releasing her, he lifted one hand to touch her ear lingeringly—a seductive gesture that revealed his intimate knowledge of ways to drive a woman to forgetfulness. Despite herself Tory shuddered and closed her eyes briefly. When they opened again, it was to see a knowing twist to his mouth. She recognized that kind of arrogance, the arrogance of a male predator who thinks the conquest is going to be easy.

But it won't! Tory declared to herself, twisting away. Even with her senses in a clamor, she knew she would soon be sorry if she did anything to encourage his advances. His hold was light and she escaped easily, thankful that he hadn't adopted more aggressive tactics.

Moving quickly but carefully, she went to the closet and extracted the other half of the dress. Before backing out of the closet to put it on, she bent to pick up a pair of dressy sandals. She had just straightened from slipping her feet into them when his arms came around her from behind. She gasped audibly, dropped the dress jacket, and straightened abruptly.

"Do you always react so wildly?" he murmured into her hair. And then he swept the hair aside, baring the throat beneath it. While his mouth dropped to explore the hollows below her ear, his hands smoothed her bare shoulders. Her senses reeled at the feel of him, the sandpaper texture of fingertips roughened by long days at sea, the warmth and hardness of his palms. And yet, like his lips, his fingers were not ungentle. While she stood frozen with a crazy explosion of sensation, one of his strong hands slid downward and insinuated itself intimately beneath the verges of fabric at her plunging neckline. The room seemed to spin. Momentarily dizzied by the outrageous liberty he was taking, she was too overpowered to move. She could feel his warm breath heating her throat, the moisture of his parted mouth laying delicate traceries on her sensitive skin. After the long years of self-denial, the wildly inappropriate intimacy of his touch caused her body to react like a geiger counter to uranium.

During that moment, while she stood frozen with shock, he curved his palm over the soft breast, testing its feel and fit beneath his hand. And then with his thumb he began to stroke her nipple softly and expertly, causing it to spring to life.

Belatedly she sprang to life too. Seizing his wrist, she dragged the hand from its intimate lodging, and in seconds she was halfway across the room. She turned to face him with color flaming hectically in her cheeks. The golden glint of anger released hidden fires in her warm eyes. This arrogant, overconfident male had presumed too much.

"I'm not the type you think I am," she said hotly. "Just because I agreed to dinner doesn't mean I intend to fall into bed before the night is through. You're behaving like a . . . an oversexed tomcat!"

His expression changed subtly, becoming more dangerous. A faint disdain touched his mouth. "I know precisely why you agreed to dinner."

"You're wrong!"

"Am I? You want information about Luc Devereux. You'll be glad to hear I'm prepared to give it. That's a promise . . . depending on what you're prepared to give in return."

"I'm not prepared to give *that,*" Tory said, tilting her head at a defiant angle.

He regarded her coolly for a moment, an odd glint hardening his granite eyes. When he spoke again, his voice was decidedly scornful. "How do you know what I want from you? It certainly isn't—as you so unromantically put it—*that.* I've been behaving like a tomcat only because you, Miss Jane Smith, have made a very amusing and very responsive mouse. I don't have sex on my mind. Even if you'd asked for it, I wouldn't have been willing."

Head held high, Tory tried to conceal her feelings, something for which she had no great talent because her expressive eyes usually gave her away. Perversely, although she didn't want him to act on desire, the innermost feminine core of her wanted very badly to be desired. She wetted her lips while she tried to think of something adequate to say. I'm glad you don't want me? I knew it all the time? I didn't respond to you; that was only your imagination? Did your boss set you on me to find out what I want? Now it was shame, not indignation, that colored her cheeks.

"You've been playing games with me," she said finally.

"Perhaps I have," he acknowledged grimly.

"You must have a purpose."

Reaching into the closet, he extracted a light spring coat and threw it at her. He snapped the closet closed before she could retrieve the rest of her dress. And before she could protest, he steered her to the exit, a veritable dynamo now that he had shed the pretext of being attracted to her in any way.

"Let's go," he directed. "Over dinner, we'll talk about what my purpose is. It might, Miss Jane Smith, have something to do with yours."

The restaurant was on one of Quimper's old streets, where timbered houses with overhanging gables shouldered each other as they had done for centuries. From walled gardens nearby, coral azaleas and hydrangeas honeyed the soft night air, but inside the restaurant there were other scents, the subtle aromas of excellent French cuisine. In a shadowed, intimate corner of the restaurant Tory was not too self-conscious about her decolletage. What did it matter whether he saw what he didn't want anyway?

As aperitifs were sipped, she remained unnaturally silent, her head still high but her eyes directed downward so that his hands, and not his face, were in view. Damn those hands for looking strong and competent. Damn them for being gentle. Damn them for being skilled in ways to stir a woman. Damn them for playing games with her.

Damn them and damn him for proving that underneath the scar tissue of the years, her old wounds were unhealed and as painful as ever. And she had thought she wasn't vulnerable anymore. What irony! Beneath the cool, collected adult surface of her, there was still a deep-down child, rejected and wanting to cry.

But grown women, especially self-sufficient grown women, didn't cry. "Exactly what game have you been playing with me?" she asked.

"A very small one—probably much smaller than you've been playing with me. We'll talk about it after dinner, shall we? I refuse to discuss it before then, for I prefer not to spoil my appetite."

Schooling her face to blankness, Tory studied the menu with pretended interest. If he didn't want sex, what was it he did want? He had to be acting on Luc Devereux's behalf. And yet he had promised information, and for that reason alone it was worth suffering through dinner.

"Shall I order for you?"

"Please do."

He chose lobster à l'Armoricain, a local specialty. "Not à l'Américaine, you'll notice," he pointed out after giving the order to the waiter. Tory studied the tablecloth fixedly while he told her that Armorica was the ancient name of Brittany; that the country had been renamed after successive waves of Britons, mostly Celts, had peopled the land; that one of the largest waves of immigration had come with the Anglo-Saxon invasion of England, and more with the Norman invasion.

"But it probably started before that, for the very earliest inhabitants were also Celts. King Arthur's knights are said to have come here in search of the Holy Grail, which supposedly lies in the Forest of Paimpont near Rennes—the last remaining stand of a larger forest where Merlin made his home. If there's any truth to the tale, those medieval knights may have left the legacy of curious names like Saint-Cloud."

"Saint-Cloud? Oh, yes—the name of the boatworks. It is an odd name." Tory lacked real interest, but hoped to lead him around to the topic that was on her mind. "I suppose Luc Devereux bought it from the original owners. How long ago was that?"

"We're not talking about Luc Devereux until later, remember?" His reminder was sardonic. "If the topic of the Saint-Clouds bores you, I'll pick another. What brought you to France?"

"You just told me to leave that topic until later," Tory said sharply.

He smiled grimly, acknowledging her point. "It seems we'll both have to wait," he murmured before returning to less touchy subjects.

The food arrived. As Tory didn't try to introduce any topics, he continued to talk about Brittany, where it seemed he had lived for some years. He seemed fond of the almost mystic Breton people, whose old, old language was closer to Welsh than to French.

With surface civility Tory asked some questions, most of which had to do with the local *pardons*.

Although the most important of those colorful religious ceremonies occurred during the summer months, she had chanced to see one since coming to Brittany, a solemn candlelight procession involving a whole village. There had been traditional costumes, banners, religious icons, and a good deal of pageantry, followed by an outburst of hilarity and high spirits. For an American, her dinner companion knew a lot about the local customs and costumes, the festivals, the legends and superstitions.

"Many of the local saints aren't recognized by Rome," he explained, "but that doesn't stop the Bretons from honoring them. They're a very individualistic, independent people. Almost mystic in religious matters—the Celtic heritage, of course."

The innocuous topics made the meal bearable, if still uncomfortable. He spoke of parts of Brittany she had seen, and some she hadn't—the heather-covered moors and rolling, rocky farmlands of the interior; the gleaming tourist beaches that stretched along the Côte d'Émeraude, the emerald coast to the north; the frequently seen wayside calvaries whose time-eaten stone spoke of great antiquity. He spoke of the pine-covered ridges and the jutting mauve granite cliffs that defined the harsher Atlantic shoreline, sometimes with a profusion of subtropical flowers growing in their protected lee. He spoke of yachting and the Breton love of the sea. Tory listened half-heartedly, hoping he might drop some clues about Luc Devereux, but the only thing he didn't talk about was his employer. Toward the end of the meal he broached a topic that touched closer to home.

"You've heard of Carnac, I suppose? It's similar to Stonehenge, which was also built by Celts. Thousands of huge megalithic stones set on end, perhaps for a sun cult of some sort. Menhirs, they're called. It's east of here, near—"

Tory put down her knife and fork. For some time she had only been toying with the lobster, anyway. She lifted her eyes for one of the few times since their arrival in the restaurant and found him looking at her narrowly. Having eaten with more gusto than she, he had already finished his meal.

"I know all about Carnac," she said in a decidedly discouraging way. Silence fell between them while the hovering waiter removed the plates and brought coffee. No desserts had been ordered, but Tory accepted a strawberry liqueur, a local specialty. "Look, do you mind if we stop this small talk? I'd really like to know how to get in touch with your employer. Are you going to tell me or not?"

"Yes, I am. But first, as your part of the bargain, I want you to tell me a few things about yourself. The ones I couldn't find out, Victoria Allworth, by looking at your passport."

Tory paled. So he had made himself very free with her things while she was in the bathroom! "You went into my purse," she accused.

He shrugged, indifferent to her reaction. "I had to do something to fill the time. Jane Smith couldn't possibly have a past, and I have a feeling you do."

She looked at him steadily and antagonistically. Her hands resting on the edges of the tablecloth formed tight fists, the knuckles whitening. "I think we've already established that Jane Smith isn't of any real interest to John Doe."

"I'm not satisfying your curiosity until you've satisfied some of mine."

She kept a tight rein on her voice. "I will if I must,

but I prefer to leave my past out of it. If you want to ask about my present life, go ahead."

"Consider yourself asked. Start anywhere, and tell everything."

She steadied herself to do that, in part at least. It wasn't so much to ask, if the reward was a small piece of information that seemed remarkably hard to come by. And as he already knew her name, anything else he passed on to Luc Devereux was of no particular importance. "I have the usual number of parents. That's present tense, because they're both still alive." She paused and narrowed her eyes. "Don't you think it's time we dumped the John Doe, too? Then I mightn't feel as if I'm talking to a total stranger."

"First things first. Finish your story, then I'll tell mine. Your parents, you were saying?"

"Poor but reasonably honest. My father owns a struggling small-town newspaper. My mother also works for the paper, because he can't afford to pay staff at the going rates. They sent my sister to Europe and me to college, and as a result the parlor is papered in mortgages and the front porch is papered with bailiff's notices . . . oh, God! You don't want to know all that sort of thing, do you? Everyone has a story like that."

"I'm not sure. Go on."

"No brothers. One sister. We're twins, but not identical. In fact, we're opposites. She's very pretty and fragile and . . . well, let's just say we're not alike, although we were always very close. You know how it is with twins. She has a child, my nephew, Nicholas. What else is there to tell? You saw nearly all the vital statistics on my passport. Except my occupation, I guess."

"Which is?"

"At the moment, nothing. I'm unemployed."

"Unemployed?"

"I'm a geologist. The unemployment is temporary, I hope. I sent off a number of applications just before I came to France, but it takes time to get responses. I quit the last job."

"Why?"

Her gaze was very level because she wanted him to hear this. It was an exercise in pride to let him know she wouldn't have been available, even if he had wanted her. "Because of the boss. He was big, blond, handsome, and thought he was God's gift to women. I can't tell you whether any women shared the opinion, as there were no other women in that wretched, godforsaken little corner of Alaska to ask. I know what my opinion was. I got tired of fighting him off, and after three years of bruises I couldn't take it anymore. Does that answer all your questions?"

"No. Why on earth would you work somewhere you describe as wretched and godforsaken in the first place? And stick it out for three years?"

"Money," she said, looking him straight in the eye. "Lots and lots of money. There were big bonuses."

"I take it you like money," he observed dryly. "Divorced, or just determinedly single?"

"Now you're getting into the past," she said coldly. "Any more questions, or shall we go on to the subject of you?"

"Smoke?" He offered a cigarette.

"No thanks. I don't." That pretense needn't be sustained, either.

Lighting his own, he frowned. Then he looked up, blue smoke curling around his hard, handsome features, the scar contributing to a forbidding tautness in his face. "What do you want from Luc Devereux?"

She stared at him stonily, trying to keep her expression noncommittal. She wasn't going to answer that one. "It's time to go on to the subject of you," she said after a minute of loaded silence.

Their eyes were locked in a war that was only now being declared. The surface civility covered hostility, resentment, caution, and, in Tory's case at least, a great deal of unresolved sexual tension. The atmosphere in the little restaurant was pregnant.

"I just did," he said softly. "I repeat, mademoiselle, what do you want from me?"

A long, long silence stretched between them. Tory had become very pale. At last she put her napkin on the table, a gesture that had a touch of quiet finality about it. "I think we'd better leave this restaurant," she said very carefully, "before I punch you in the nose."

Chapter Three

They had arrived by taxi, but no taxi was pulled up at the restaurant's canopied exit when they emerged. Tory started to walk very quickly, not waiting to see if one could be flagged. Her actions weren't conscious—they were prompted by a need to clear the blind rage from her head. If he hadn't kept pace, she would have stopped. Now that she had him, she couldn't afford to lose him. But it seemed he didn't intend to let her lose him, anyway. His long stride matched hers.

They passed through a large square, through narrow streets, through alleys poorly lit. She hardly saw the great cathedral of Saint-Corentin, whose great Norman spires and rambling, curiously skewed construction had filled her with awe only a few days before. She hardly saw the closed bookstores and music stores, the shop windows with their pottery and Quimper ware, the stone park benches emptied for the night. She hardly knew what twisting path they traveled, or how many minutes went by. At last, underneath a street lamp, in a solitary place by the great shadowed ramparts of the ancient town, her heel caught on a broken paving stone. She came to a halt and started to drink great gulps of the night air.

He seized her upper arms and turned her to face him. "Hadn't you better explain yourself?"

Tory answered him in the only way possible for her at the moment. Her rage was wordless. She balled her hands into tight little fists and expressed the pent-up anger of the years, battering at his chest until her hands were sore and her arms hurt from the effort. Her teeth were gritted and her chest was heaving with sobs and there were tears streaming down her face, gleaming in the light of the golden street lamp, but she wasn't conscious of those things. She just kept battering.

And battering.

And battering.

For some minutes he held her and allowed it, although his grip on her upper arms tightened to prevent the angry drumming from becoming any more damaging than it was. At last he said tensely, "I'm a man, not that granite wall. There are limits to the punishment I can take without responding in kind. Do I have to stop you forcibly?"

Suddenly it all drained out of her. All of it. The fury, the strength, even some of the despair.

She stopped, simply because she was incapable of going on. The power had gone from her fingers. They opened, trembling, and spread for one instant against his suit jacket. Then her hands dropped to her sides. She was exhausted, so exhausted she could hardly stand, so exhausted her lungs were too torn for the wrenching sobs to continue. A terrible weakness invaded her legs. Swaying, she desperately needed to lean on a shoulder, but remembering whose shoulder it was, she backed away. The wall was right there, and she used it for support.

"Feeling better now?" he asked after a few moments of watching her. He hadn't tried to touch her.

"No," she said. Even her mouth felt weak, and she had trouble forming the word. Her lips quivered. The slow slide of tears no longer afforded relief. She hated having him see her like this, but she didn't quite have the strength to stop those tears, that sign of feminine weakness.

But at least some of her anguish had been spent and some of her rational faculties had been restored. In the dim light of the shadowed street she could see his scarred face well enough to determine the dark, grim expression on it. She recognized how easy it would have been for him to strike her in return, but the thought caused no cautionary prickle of alarm. She didn't care. Hadn't he done all the hurting he could do?

He waited until her tears stopped of their own accord, watching closely as if he didn't quite trust that she was in possession of her faculties. "Now will you please tell me what that was all about?"

She couldn't answer for a moment because she couldn't believe he would say such a thing. He must have known from the moment of seeing her passport, from the moment of discovering her last name. All through dinner he had been aware; even in the hotel room he had been aware. She realized why he had taken a taxi to the restaurant—the secretary, Annette, must have told him she would recognize his car. She stared at him dully, wetting her lips while she tried to think what advantage he might be hoping to gain. He was going to deny the whole thing, she supposed.

"Please don't pretend," she said.

"I'm not pretending. I really don't know. Or if I ever did know, I've forgotten."

She uttered a little mirthless laugh, some of her strength returning with cynicism. She managed to straighten against the wall, using only one arm as a prop. "Forgotten? I don't believe that."

"Believe it or not, as you please. Nevertheless it's true. If you look at my face, you can see the reason."

The scar? She did look at it, at the cruel way it cut downward from his hairline, the skin pale and long since healed. Even in this poor light it was the most remarkable aspect about him, a distinctive feature one could hardly miss. "I suppose you didn't have that scar eight years ago."

"No. It's newer than that, by several years."

"And you're going to plead amnesia," she said bitterly.

"I'm not pleading anything. I'm simply telling you there are some things I don't recall."

"And I suppose you're going to tell me my sister is one of them. That you don't owe her a damn thing!"

He hesitated for a moment, dark suspicion evident in the lowering of his brow and the tight set of his mouth. "Yes," he said harshly. "I am going to tell you that. Do you think this is the first time a woman has tried to throw some past relationship in my face? If I ever knew your sister—which has yet to be established to my satisfaction—I've forgotten her. Your last name meant nothing to me."

Oh, God, what a pretender! "Even if you had forgotten," she said in a tense, trembling voice that shook with hatred, "there was my letter to remind you. You could have looked into it then, two years ago. I despise you, Luc Devereux, for what you did to Laura."

That brooding darkness was still in his eyes, the faint hostility. "Laura . . ." The repetition was no more than a thoughtful rolling of the name on his tongue, as if testing its syllables for sound and size. Tory knew it had to be another pretense.

She relinquished her hold on the wall, finding that she could do without it. She thrust her balled fists deeply into her coat pockets, for she didn't want to be tempted to reach again for support. Pride demanded that she stand on her own two feet. Her legs were still shaky but capable of supporting her; returning anger gave her some focus.

"Even if you have had amnesia—which has yet to be established to *my* satisfaction—how can you be so cavalier about the women in your past?" she bit out tightly. "Especially when the woman is your *wife!*"

Instantly his mouth became utterly expressionless. His eyes moved away from Tory's face to a point somewhere behind her shoulder, and although there were only the close, shadowy stone ramparts to see, he appeared to be staring into a very far distance indeed. He was so still that Tory began to think he might actually be trying to search his mind for clues to some lost memory. She could see moisture filming his temple, causing it to gleam beneath the street lamp. A muscle near the scar seemed to be throbbing, its cadence matched to the pulsing of her own heart.

She saw other things, too, now that she knew who he was, and having seen them, marveled at her slowness. The dark gray, deep-set eyes. The black hair and brows. There wasn't a great resemblance, but the coloring was the same. And there was just a suggestion of a cleft in his chin where Nicholas's deep baby dimple was now disappearing and beginning to change into a more manly mold.

At last he shook himself back to the present. He looked back to Tory, his face now hardened and watchful despite the little lines of worry around his eyes. "I think you'd better tell me more," he said slowly. He took her elbow in a firm grip. "Shall we go back to your hotel? It's not far from here."

The tiny hotel room was not a very comfortable place to talk, for its drab furnishings included only one chair. Tory, who was shivering now, kept her coat huddled around her as she sat down on it. Luc remained on his feet. She would have done that, too, but her legs no longer felt capable of the effort.

He stood near the bed, tall and tense, his face schooled in unrevealing lines. "I don't concede that what you say is true, but I'm willing to listen. Now tell me about your sister."

"About your wife," she corrected bitterly.

"That's not an established fact."

"All the same, you married her."

"When?"

"Nearly eight years ago."

"Has she any proof of that? A marriage certificate?"

"Not that I know of. I imagine you kept it."

"Anything else? Wedding pictures?"

"I know some things about you. You're from Brest."

He looked a little pale. "I don't deny I was born in Brest. But anyone could discover that, and I wasn't raised there. You'll need to produce more concrete evidence than that, something to corroborate your claim. Perhaps a record of—"

"There's Nicholas," Tory interrupted. "Isn't a child proof enough? Oh, he doesn't go by your name. As far as Nicky knows, his name is Nicholas Allworth. At the time, Laura was so cut up about the whole thing that she couldn't bear to hear the name Devereux. Her maiden name was used on the birth certificate. As he was born in the States, she wasn't—"

"Exactly when was this child born?" Luc interrupted curtly.

"Seven years ago." With angry eyes Tory defied him to deny his paternity. "He was born four months after you wrecked Laura's life," she added bitterly.

"Wrecked her life . . . !" The words exploded from him. He ran his hand around the back of his neck, a gesture that was part annoyance and part frustration, but it also gave him a somewhat trapped air. "Look, Miss Allworth, can you manage to sound a little less accusatory? I'm trying to be cooperative, by listening to what you have to say. I can't believe I wrecked anyone's life."

"Do you deny it's possible you married her?"

"I don't deny it flatly, because there are outside possibilities. But I don't admit it, either! I don't mean to sound callous, but if your sister wants to make some sort of claim, she'll have to have proof."

Tory sprang to her feet. She was very near tears again. Her eyes were luminous, large and sparkling with anger. "Perhaps I do have some pictures after all! When you were looking through my purse, you should have looked at the snapshots. I have something I'd like to show you."

The snapshots were in a plastic fold in her wallet. She found them and took them out. First she handed him one of Laura—soft lovely Laura, with wind blowing her light brown hair and a gentle, ethereal smile on her glowing face. Luc paused over it, frowning.

"Is this recent?"

She was watching him closely to see his reaction. "Yes, very. I took it just before leaving the States. She looks almost exactly the same as she used to."

"She's very beautiful."

"Yes."

Dismissing the picture, he handed it back to Tory. "That doesn't prove anything to me, I'm afraid. I simply don't remember the face." Sardonically he added, "Where and how am I supposed to have met her?"

Tory's eyes hardened. "Near Carnac—where I know you've been."

His face became closed, disbelieving. "Go on. Remember, my memory's less than perfect."

"After high school Laura came to France to study language. That was nearly eight years ago, when she was eighteen. She was to start at the Sorbonne in the fall of that year. Before university began, she spent the summer bicycling around the country with a group of American students in order to improve her fluency. At the beginning of August they all went to see the menhirs at Carnac."

"You'd better remind me of the details," Luc put in sarcastically. "What was I supposed to be doing there?"

"You had been sailing, I remember her telling me that, and something needed repair. You must have put in somewhere nearby. As you had to hang around for a few days, you checked in at the inn where the students were staying. You struck up a conversation with Laura. It wouldn't have been hard—she would practice her French on anyone who would talk back. There was a whirlwind courtship. By the time Laura wrote home about it, you'd been married for a couple of months and had just finished a long honeymoon. The marriage didn't last long. Most of the time, Laura was at your apartment in Brest while you were off at sea. I can't tell you all the details. Eight years is a long time."

"It certainly is." Something biting had entered Luc's voice, an edge of testiness. "I dislike people taking advantage of my faulty memory. Shall we call a halt to this charade?"

"Charade? If you can't use your memory, try using your eyes!" Enraged, she thrust the picture of Nicholas into his hand. It was a good, clear color shot, a close-up. Nicky's grave little face had not put on a smile for the camera. He was not an unhappy child, but he was grown-up beyond his years.

She was watching Luc's face again. Was it imagination, or was there a whitening of the skin around his mouth? A certain tautness to his lips? An unsteadiness of breath? He certainly looked at the picture long enough.

"Well?" Tory asked.

He placed the picture carefully on the bed, where he could still see it if he chose. Then he turned back to Tory, his face unfathomable. "I don't deny there's a certain similarity in coloring." His words were cautiously chosen. "I would have to know more, of course. Much more. Dates, places, facts. As you say, eight years is a long time. Why isn't your sister here in person? It might simplify getting to the heart of this matter."

Tory could feel the old choke of anguish in her

throat, the pain that twisted in her heart so deeply that she sometimes thought she and Laura must have been born joined, and separated at birth. "Laura . . . couldn't come. She hasn't been well for a long time."

"Oh? But the picture of her . . ." Luc brought himself up abruptly. "In any case, even if she can't appear in person, she can certainly provide a few hard facts. Place of marriage, for one. That would be a starting point."

Tory's voice became very controlled. "That's not possible. She can't even be asked. You see, Laura's is an illness of the mind. Some years ago she . . . retreated from reality altogether. She's happy most of the time now, because she lives in a dream world of her own. But she has setbacks, and certain things cause them. Your name is one of those things."

"I see." Luc sat down on the edge of the bed, heavily. Tory could no longer see his face. His head was lowered and his elbows rested on his knees, the hands hanging loosely between them. It was a posture of dejection. If Tory hadn't lived for so many years with the knowledge of what he had done to Laura, she might have felt some pity for him. Instead she felt a cold, hard ball of hatred.

"Tell me more. Where does your sister live?"

"She's in a home now," Tory said. "She has been for three years. She's well cared for."

"And the boy?"

"My parents look after him. He . . . doesn't see Laura anymore. A couple of years ago when I was attempting to trace you, I tried asking her some questions, with very bad results. Now she can't even bear to have Nicky go near her, because he brings back the past. The doctors decided it was best to keep them apart."

Luc's voice was gruff. "And what terrible thing am I supposed to have done to her?"

"She would never talk about it, because she was too cut up. It must have been sudden, for she was in very bad shape when she flew back from France. She was shaken and on the verge of collapse. She hadn't even thought to pack her things or tell us she was coming. She just . . . arrived. She's never been the same since."

The deep depressions, the suicide attempts, the times when Laura had just curled into a ball for days on end, her sad eyes staring into nowhere. Tory wasn't going to tell everything. On a few occasions she had tried to talk Laura into divorcing Luc Devereux. Laura had become hysterical and physically violent. Three years ago, because it was hard for a young child to grow up under such a shadow, arrangements had been made for the home, a private psychiatric clinic. Tory had taken the unpleasant job in Alaska to pay for it. It had been a blessing when Laura, aided by tranquilizers and good psychiatric care, had finally slid into that dreaming world in which she now lived most of the time. In it she was happy.

"I take it you've come to me for financial help."

It was a terrible hardship to say it, but she had to. "Yes. Laura's care costs quite a lot, and I may not be able to land another field job. I'll take anything I can find when I get back to the States, but it may not pay as much as I was making in Alaska."

"So that's why you worked there."

"Yes."

"You said something about a letter you sent to me."

At that reminder, the anger Tory had banked for the past few moments began to burn once again. "I wrote you two years ago. Amnesia or not, I don't know how you could have ignored it."

"I didn't even see your letter," he said. "My lawyers always handle the more ludicrous claims, without showing them to me."

"Ludicrous! You must be—"

"Over the past few years I've received a lot of letters," he cut in, his voice heavy. "Not just yours. At the time of my . . . accident, there were a couple of deaths in my family. There was a lot of publicity, too. My amnesia was widely reported in the press. Many people tried to take advantage, and a few still do. I have to make sure you're not one of them."

Tory sucked in her breath. "After what I've told you, how can you—"

He glanced up, his eyes hard. "Because I have to!" he said harshly. "How do I know what's truth and what isn't? How many children in the world have gray eyes and black hair? How many newspapers have printed the story of the Saint-Clouds? Of the money I inherited when they died?"

"No newspapers I've read!" she cried. "I'd never even heard of the Saint-Clouds until a short time ago, and I certainly didn't know they were dead—whoever they may be! I thought it was just the name of the boatworks!"

His flare of hostility faded, to be replaced by a more resigned air. "The Saint-Clouds are well known in Brittany. I'm distantly related to them, and as my own parents were dead, they brought me up as a member of the family. I suppose you really didn't know of the connection, or you'd have known where to find me." There was a weary note in his voice as he passed a hand over his brow, pressing his fingers briefly to the temples. "All the same, I have to have proof. I have to know whose child that is."

"Then you still deny you're Nicky's father!"

When he answered, his voice was careful again. "I'm absolutely sure I'm not, but I intend to investigate the possibility, at least. Does that satisfy you?"

"In other words, either I come up with proof, or you don't intend to help!"

"I didn't say I wouldn't help. If I have any responsibilities, I'll discharge them. But first I have to know what my responsibilities are! Doesn't it occur to you that there might be some mistake? Luc is a common enough name, and Devereux isn't exactly unique."

From her long search, Tory knew that was true enough. She had tried every Devereux in Brest, in Quimper, and in a dozen other places as well—all without luck.

"It's possible your sister married someone, and he may have even gone by that name. But it seems she told you very little, and nothing you've said so far leads me to believe it was me. You knew nothing about my home, my family, my relationship to the Saint-Clouds . . ." He glanced at the photograph lying on the bed, a casual glance that seemed to dismiss its importance. "What if your sister married some other man?"

Tory was not going to admit that possibility. There were too many coincidences. The lawyers in Brest; the occupation to do with the sea; the color of his hair and his eyes; even such scanty physical description as Laura had given in her letters. They all matched. How many men in Brittany by the name of Luc Devereux would fit the profile of Laura's husband? Surely only one.

Luc went on. "If your sister can't provide information, then you'll have to. You must know a little about this supposed marriage. Old letters, addresses. As it seems to have happened in Brittany, there must be a record of it somewhere. With such clues as you have, we'll start a search next week. I don't have time until then."

"And I don't have time *then,"* Tory said desperately. "I'm leaving on Sunday."

"You can't." It was a curt, clipped decision. "Do you really expect me to confess to something I didn't do, on a stranger's say-so? You'll have to stay while this is sorted out. I imagine it won't take more than a couple of weeks."

Tory slumped back down on the chair, feeling thoroughly defeated and dispirited. To have come this far, only to find success still tantalizingly out of reach. At some point during the conversation, she had accepted that the amnesia was not a pretext—Luc's willingness to investigate seemed to confirm that much. Under the circumstances she could even grudgingly concede his need to see some kind of proof, and a photograph of a child with similarities of coloring wasn't proof enough.

What a wretched trick of fate, that her lack of proof should be matched by Luc Devereux's lack of memory! In one month, unless some bills were paid, Laura would have to be taken out of the home. That would be hard on her and even harder on Nicholas. Tory couldn't risk spending extra time in Brittany only to have Luc Devereux reach a conclusion she had long since reached on her own: There was no proof readily available. Besides, she didn't have money to stay. She had used her severance pay to come to France, and there simply wasn't enough left to continue paying for the dreary hotel. She could hardly ask Luc Devereux for a loan.

"I would stay," she said, "but I have to get home and continue hunting for a job."

"If you won't help me look for evidence, then you can't have much faith that I'm the man," he noted dispassionately.

Tory's eyes returned to him, hostility kindling in them again. "Oh, I have faith in that, but I don't have hope of finding proof of any kind. I'll admit, I've already done a good deal of searching. Letters to authorities, that sort of thing. I think the marriage may not have taken place in France. You were yachting at the time, you and Laura."

"As this . . . marriage broke up so very long ago, there may have been a divorce. What man would want to remain tied to a woman for that length of time without doing something about it? Perhaps that's why your sister became hysterical whenever divorce was mentioned."

"Or perhaps you simply deserted her for another woman and didn't worry about the legalities! That would have made her even more hysterical. If you walked out when she was five months pregnant, it might have triggered her flight from France."

Luc mulled that over for a moment. "Whoever the man was," he said with deliberate inflection, "he might have proceeded with a divorce on his own."

"Impossible! If you had, the courts would have sent Laura some kind of notification. She had never made a secret of *her* background. You most certainly knew our home address, because at the time you shipped over all the things she had left in France—without so much as a note to go with them, I might add. Besides, if you'd been divorced, wouldn't your lawyers know about it? Yet two years ago they simply said there had been no marriage and denied financial responsibility out of hand. They told me that if I wished to pursue the matter, claims would have to be pressed through proper legal channels, with proper documentation. I didn't proceed because I knew I could prove nothing."

"And that's why you came to see me in person."

"Yes," Tory said, resenting his sarcasm but feeling suddenly too deflated to react. "I had thought you would know the answers to the past. I had hoped that even if you couldn't be taken to court, you might be willing to help."

"Out of the goodness of my heart."

"Look, I don't think there's any point in going on with this," she said tiredly. "I might have known you wouldn't have the conscience to help. I see I was pinning too many hopes on this trip to France."

Luc was studying her with a brooding darkness on his face. "I'm afraid I can't let you leave now."

"You can't stop me, either. I have to get back to the States and find a job."

"Don't you see I have to know the answers just as much as you do?" His voice was harsh. "I'm sure I didn't marry your sister, but I'd like to know who did. If there's a marriage certificate somewhere with my name on it . . ."

Abruptly he cut his words short and became brisk and businesslike. "I gather your reason for refusing to stay has something to do with the cost of this hotel. I won't offer to cover the bill, for I don't wish to be turned down. Nevertheless, I must insist that you stay in France. This week is a busy one for me, but on Sunday I'll be free—the day you intend to check out anyway. I'll pick you up at noon that day. You're moving into my home, and there you'll stay until the truth is determined."

Tory's mind made a lateral leap into remembrance of some of the things that had transpired before dinner. For the past three hours the dark magnetic attraction exerted by Luc Devereux had been the last thing on her mind. Now it flooded back in full force. Apprehensive about her emotional future, she bent her head and stared at her knees with a returning consciousness of her response to the one man in all the world she ought to feel no attraction for. She was glad she was sitting, because just thinking about it made her insides turn to jelly.

She looked up again and found his dark, enigmatic eyes trained on her. She was aghast to find that she still felt that electric attraction, against all dictates of mind and reason. Nervously she clutched the throat of her coat and felt the color draining from her face. Perhaps the attraction he exerted was even stronger now, because there had been some bonding in that wild, angry physical assault of hers, when she had lashed at him and released such floods of long-dammed emotion. At this moment Laura's problems, and the desperate need to solve a financial crisis, were not the things on Tory's mind.

"I . . . can't," she said, shaking her head.

"You must," he returned flatly and autocratically. "Are you concerned about the propriety? There's no need to worry. The Château d'Ys is a household of women."

"The Château . . . Deece?" She thought she must have misheard the name. *Dix,* perhaps, the French word for ten?

He told her how to spell it. "Two women of my

family live at the Château d'Ys. Tante Marie—that's my aunt, Madame Saint-Cloud—and also her young daughter, Aimée. There are servants as well. I have my own quarters in the château, quite separate from the others." It still sounded too close for Tory's liking. "I prefer not to tell my aunt the true reason for your arrival, but I'll work up some plausible story. I'll phone and let you know what it is before Sunday."

Appalled by the thought of a continued close contact she wasn't sure she could handle, Tory still demurred. Shakily she said, "Look, I see no need to stay. At this point I have to trust to your integrity, whether I like it or not. I'll write down everything I know and put it all in your hands. Perhaps you can put investigators on it. Either you'll decide to help or you won't, and—"

"There is some urgency, mademoiselle," he interrupted curtly, the Gallic form of address giving his voice a foreign ring. "Do you think you're the only person who needs to solve the riddle of the past? I must know, just as you must know. Marriage isn't the only matter in question. If this child Nicholas has some claim . . ."

"It isn't a claim against an estate we've been talking about," Tory said, leaning forward tensely. "It's help for Laura. That's all I want."

"And if you want it, you'll have to help me," he returned grimly. He studied Tory for a moment more, as if reaching some critical decision in his mind. At length he offered curtly, "Stay for a couple of weeks and help me get to the truth of this. In exchange I'll cover all your sister's expenses for . . . let's say, three months. That's a payment for your services, not an admission of liability."

A vast relief coursed through Tory. Three months

of paid bills made the risk of close encounters worth her while. "In that case I will stay. But you can't be so certain you're not married to Laura if you—"

He sliced through her words. "Don't you see my position? Legal or not, this child may be—" He cut himself short, evidently unwilling to add the "mine," which would admit to a possibility of paternity. "There's another point, an important one that should have occurred to you. What if I should want to marry?"

"Marry?" Tory paled and repeated the word faintly. "But if you never got a divorce, you couldn't possibly get married again! That's bigamy!"

His face was a mask. "Please don't load your comments. Your words suggest I've been married before, and I don't choose to concede that I have. But as to the rest of your remark, exactly. I'm a bachelor" —he paused to add the right amount of emphasis— "but not a confirmed one. I hadn't planned to stay that way forever. If my name's on a marriage certificate somewhere, I need to know about it—whether I got married or not."

"You did," Tory said stubbornly, earning only a deep scowl.

Luc stood, impatient to be off. "I'll tell my aunt to expect you Sunday," he said tersely.

She nodded her acquiescence and rose to her feet while he went to the door, sick with herself because she was so very conscious of all things about him. Even after he had left the room, she had only to close her eyelids to bring back disturbing recollections of his lean hard length, his supple strength, his sexual impact. She remembered how his hand had felt on her breast and how his parted lips had felt on her jaw. She hated herself for remembering. Why had she let those things happen before finding out who he was?

The ferment of unwelcome sexual feelings conflicted with long-harbored hatreds, and Tory was restless and wretched for a long time after Luc left. Belligerence such as she had displayed tonight wasn't a normal part of her nature, but for years her inner tensions had all been channeled in one direction, and one direction only. To her the name Luc Devereux had come to be anathema. Hating him as she did, how could she experience such intense shuddering reactions at the mere memory of his touch?

It wasn't until twenty minutes later, when she was turning down the cover of the bed, that she realized he had taken the snapshot of Nicholas.

So he must be the right Luc Devereux, no matter how much he denied it. Anger welled back to the forefront of her feelings, and attraction was forgotten in the intense and instant surge of antagonism. Damn the worm!

Not that she had doubted his identity for one minute! There simply couldn't be another man named Luc Devereux . . . a man with dark gray eyes and black hair . . . a man who could turn a woman's world upside down with one touch, one smile, one smoldering look. . . .

Chapter Four

Tory didn't intend to waste the days until Sunday. Now that she had located Luc Devereux and had a few more clues to his past, there was a good deal of groundwork to do. The few letters Laura had written from Brittany had long since been thrown away and many of their facts had been forgotten, but there was always hope that some of those misty details might be recalled with help. Knowing more about Luc Devereux and his family might provide the needed boost to her memory.

He had mentioned past publicity, so some local newspaper seemed a logical place to start. Quimper not being an overly large town, Tory located one without trouble. The difficulty didn't begin until she tried to communicate. Her French simply wasn't up to the task, and the receptionist didn't speak much

English. Nor did one or two other employees standing by, looking curious.

The name Luc Devereux brought only a blank stare, but the receptionist recognized the name Saint-Cloud readily enough. However, she seemed reluctant to part with any information. Tory tried to convey that she wanted to see someone, a reporter perhaps, who was familiar with the family's story.

"They die," the woman said, finding a couple of English words she knew. *"Ils sont morts, tous morts.* You know, die?" She added some more sentences, all in French, that Tory didn't understand.

Matters seemed to be at an impasse. After a few more attempts Tory turned to go, realizing she should have brought a French dictionary along. She was about to leave the office when a man's voice stopped her.

"You ask for the Saint-Clouds, mademoiselle? Perhaps I am of help."

He was a few years younger than Tory, not much past twenty. He had a thin, pleasant, polite face. His pale blue business suit was not quite the garb of a reporter, but because of his youth she thought he must be one.

"Thank goodness," she said, sagging with relief. "Yes, I do need help, and quite badly."

"I fear, mademoiselle, that the help I give is perhaps not the help for which you have desire. This *journal,* this . . . newspaper, it will dispense no information about the Saint-Clouds without permission of the owner, the publisher." His English was rapid but not perfect, rather quaint in the old-fashioned choice of words. "That is what one tells you at the desk. She cannot help you, mademoiselle. However, if you wish to know more, and will state your reason . . ."

She could hardly tell him the real one. "I've been invited to stay with the family for a couple of weeks. I know so little about them that I thought—"

His attention seemed riveted. "Stay with them? You stay to visit, at the Château d'Ys?"

"Why, yes." If he knew where they lived, he must know a good deal about the family. And he had warmed to her, too, his thin young face kindling with interest. Tory's hopes rose.

"For two weeks?" he asked. What caused that instant curiosity, that intensity, that element of disbelief and surprise in his voice?

"Yes."

He seized her arm as though he had no intention of letting her out of his sight. It might have been he, not she, who was in dire need of information. He called a few words to the receptionist and said to Tory, "Come, we will leave this place, for we wish not to be interrupted, *n'est-ce pas?* There is a little café, it is not grand but it is quiet. Then we talk, yes?"

The café was really an inexpensive crêperie, not yet open for lunch. Only the sidewalk part was in operation. As it was a warm day, the outside chairs were peopled by a few customers in working clothes, dawdling over carafes of local Muscadet and eyeing the unhurried passersby. It was a typically French scene in the sleepy morning sun, but Tory had not quite grown used to the sight of people drinking at this hour of the morning. She refused the offer of wine, preferring coffee. For himself, the young man ordered Chouchenn, a honeyed mead made from an old Celtic recipe.

From somewhere in the far distance, a schoolyard probably, came the distinctive sound of the *biniou,* the unusual bagpipes of Brittany. Schoolchildren practicing for a concert, no doubt. Although Tory had been told the name of the musical instrument that emitted the plaintive, poignant wail, she was not quite used to the idea of hearing that particular sound in France. Yet why should Scotland have a monopoly on bagpipes?

Tory's companion had chosen the most private of tables, in the shadow of an awning; no one else was seated nearby. As soon as the order for Chouchenn and café au lait had been placed, he introduced himself. "I, mademoiselle, am Jacques Benoit. It is my father who is owner and publisher of the newspaper where you have come this morning. The Benoits and the Saint-Clouds, they have always been close, for many, many years. We have known the family . . . oh, a long time. The friendship is one of many generations. So you see, I know of matters you would learn from no other person. I am able to help you . . . perhaps."

There was just the smallest hesitation over the last word. Tory gave her own name, hoping he wouldn't ask the reason she had been invited to stay at the Château d'Ys. Unfortunately he did.

"Luc Devereux invited me," she said.

To Tory's relief, that seemed to satisfy the young man. In fact, it seemed to please him a good deal. His thin face glowed. "You are a friend with Luc?"

"Yes," Tory answered cautiously. She couldn't very well say she was his sister-in-law without arousing curiosity about things she couldn't discuss.

Jacques Benoit eyed her with satisfaction, drawing his own conclusions. Luckily he didn't question why Luc had told her so little about the Saint-Clouds. "You must be his very good friend, then, I think. Luc, he would not invite you to meet his family if you were not his very, very good friend indeed. *C'est bon!* It is as I hoped, exactly."

Fortunately the waiter arrived with the orders at that moment. Tory made no effort to correct the young man's mistake. Having reached what appeared to be a fount of knowledge, she wasn't about to shut off the source.

"I will tell you of the Saint-Clouds, mademoiselle, but there is a small thing I wish in return. I wish that you deliver for me a message—and the answer also, it goes without saying. Perhaps, if it is as I hope, there will be more messages to follow." He paused and added, "It will not be hard for you. The message is for Aimée Saint-Cloud. The daughter of Madame Saint-Cloud, yes?"

Tory could only imagine a youthful romance not encouraged by the family. "I'm not sure," she said cautiously. Meddling in what might be a tricky situation could jeopardize her own position with the Saint-Clouds, and she wasn't ready to do that.

Jacques leaned forward persuasively. "I have hope, mademoiselle, to tell Aimée Saint-Cloud of my regard. I am not allowed to see her; yes, this I confess to you most freely. But the reason for it, I do not understand. In the time of the Saint-Cloud sadness our little newspaper was most careful to show respect. There were things we could have printed and did not. Believe me, I have given no offense. In the time of most grief it is only the Benoit family that is allowed at the Château d'Ys. *D'ailleurs,* before that, for all the time when Aimée was a little girl, I saw her often. My father used to joke that someday the house of Saint-Cloud would be joined to the house of Benoit. Me, I used to make the noises of scorn at such a thought, for the little Aimée, she was so young. A child, no more.

But then two months ago I looked again, and saw with new eyes. . . ."

He paused, sighed heavily, and went on. "For some years I was away to study at the Sorbonne and did not see the little Aimée. Then, two months ago, in the time of her birthday, my parents, they drove to the Château d'Ys with a present. I myself was not expected, but I went. With my family I am allowed through the gate. Since that day I have not been permitted to see Aimée, and my family is no longer welcome at the Château d'Ys. Why? Because I smile at her, and she smiles at me? My letters go unanswered. There is no reason given. Is it Aimée who will not answer, or is it her mother who does this thing? This I must know. If it is Aimée who refuses to see me, this I accept, because I must. And if not . . . *eh bien,* the message you return to me will tell. *Je vous en prie, mademoiselle.* Is it so much to ask? Aimée is nearly a grown woman now, and I wish to hear her mind, not the mind of her mother."

"How old is she?"

"In years, just seventeen. In life . . . perhaps a little less. This I confess to you, because you will see it with your eyes. It is the way she has been kept from the world. The Château d'Ys, it is between the Crozon Peninsula and the Pointe du Raz, the place where the tip of Brittany reaches far into the Atlantic. There the coast is wild, and the cliffs high, and the sea strong. The estate is well walled. Aimée goes to no school, she meets no person of her own age. And always there is *la gouvernante* . . . the governess at her side. It is for this reason that it is hard to learn of Aimée's feelings. Do you not see that I must know, when no hands have touched, and only the message of the eyes has been exchanged? Believe me, there is no bad in my intention. In my family all things are done slowly, in the very old way. If Aimée has no regard for me, then I assure you I will not trouble her again, and I will try to . . . mend my affections. I beg of you, mademoiselle."

His earnestness was moving, and it certainly didn't sound as though Jacques Benoit had been carrying on with Aimée Saint-Cloud in any manner that should upset even the most vigilant of mothers, as Madame Saint-Cloud appeared to be. Was one message so much to ask? Touched by his plight, Tory agreed to the request. "But maybe I'll have trouble speaking to her privately, too," she said.

"Ah, you will find a way." Jacques Benoit sank back in his chair, looking deeply relieved. "Now, what is it you wish to know? I am of sympathy, mademoiselle, for I understand. I know that Luc will tell you little, for there are many things of which he will not speak . . . including, to my sorrow, the matter that is close to my heart. *Eh bien,* where shall I begin?"

"You might start with Luc's exact relationship to the family," Tory suggested.

Jacques began to fulfill his part of the bargain with a will. "The Saint-Clouds, they raised Luc as if he is their own son. Luc's father, he had been a Saint-Cloud, a far cousin, the captain of a ship. He died at sea, in the time before Luc was born. He did not marry the woman Devereux, Luc's mother. Of the mother . . . it is best to talk little of the mother. She was a woman of the town of Brest, where the French sailors make a port, and sometimes a . . . a sport." He laughed somewhat embarrassedly at his own small joke. "Need I say more? When the Saint-Clouds offered to take the boy, she gave him up with gladness. Perhaps even with relief, for she had no great means, and it would have been difficult for a woman such as she to keep a child. Luc grew to a man at the Château d'Ys. In all things but name, he is a Saint-Cloud."

"A few years ago there was some Saint-Cloud tragedy," Tory prompted quietly. "What was it?"

"Ah, yes, mademoiselle, a great tragedy. A tragedy not only for the Saint-Clouds, but for many yachtsmen of the world. It was the Admiral's Cup Race of England. For that cup there are five races, and one of them is known as Fastnet, from the name of the rock in the Irish Sea where boats must turn. Most certainly you have heard of Fastnet?"

"I'm not sure . . ." For Tory, it stirred only the dimmest of recollections, something to do with disaster. "Wasn't that on the front pages a few years ago?"

"Yes, mademoiselle. It is from Fastnet that Luc has his scar. And it is at Fastnet that the last of the Saint-Cloud men died, along with many yachtsmen from all countries of the world . . . Americans, British, French. There was a storm in the Irish Sea, most sudden and most terrible, with waves as high as"—he gestured at a building of five stories—"as high as that. Men were injured, boats were sunk, masts were snapped. And for this, although it was an act of nature and of . . . of providence, I think Luc feels some blame."

"How many Saint-Clouds died in the race?"

"Two. There was the old man, the admiral, and his son."

"Admiral?"

"*Oui, mademoiselle.* That was the uncle of Luc, and husband of the Madame Saint-Cloud you will meet. The admiral, he had little love for business, but he had a great love for the sea. He was in a high post of the French navy. When he was not at sea for duty, he was at sea for sport."

"And the son? Was he also in the navy?"

"Armand Saint-Cloud? Armand, no, he was not a man of the sea. He had the smart head for business." Jacques took a moment to clarify the relationship. "Armand was the brother of Aimée, although he was older by many, many years. Between the two children of the Saint-Clouds, there was a great space, a space of twenty years. It is not so strange. Madame Saint-Cloud, she married very young. And also, mademoiselle, the admiral, he was always much away at sea. With such absences, there were no children born between."

Tory's interest in the Saint-Clouds was limited, except in matters where their lives pertained to Luc's. "Why would Luc feel blame for the deaths?"

"Perhaps, because it was he who designed the yacht in which they sailed, and it was he who took benefit from their deaths."

"Oh?"

"The will of the admiral, it left most things, all but the boatworks of Quimper, to his son, Armand. But if Armand did not survive him, then all things would go to the male relative most close in blood. Armand left no sons, for although he and his wife had been married for many many years, they were, how do you say it . . . blessed with no children. For this reason the man of closest blood was Luc. I think, mademoiselle, Luc would have preferred to inherit only the boatworks and leave all else to the Saint-Cloud women. But the admiral, he had been most careful about telling his wishes. There was income for the women, but the big things, the important things, they were to go to a man, and only to a man."

"I see," Tory said guardedly. Jacques Benoit was describing Luc Devereux as a man of considerable conscience. Could that be the same Luc Devereux who had so casually destroyed Laura's life? Cynically Tory doubted that Luc's motives were quite as pure as described. With a fortune in hand a man could easily pretend not to want it.

"There were no other Saint-Clouds? No cousins?"

"No, mademoiselle. Over the centuries too many Saint-Cloud men have died at sea. Perhaps I should explain more, so you will understand. The Saint-Clouds are a very old family of Brittany, a family of the sea. Although there is land in Brittany, it is not rich land, and so it is from the sea that most of men's riches come. The Saint-Clouds have always been very rich. They own fleets of fishing boats and they own places where the fish is put into cans. In Brest they build ships, and these are used for the exports and the imports, which they also control. It is for all these businesses that Armand Saint-Cloud had the clever head. But for most men of the family, it is the sea that calls. In the French navy, in time of war, there are always Saint-Clouds. Captains, admirals of the fleet, even . . . ah, leaders of the French navy, I do not know the English term. The list is long and of great honor, and it goes back for many centuries. For the navy of France, Brittany is always the"—he searched for a phrase—"the spine, that is the word, I think?"

"Backbone?" suggested Tory.

"Yes, backbone. And of that Breton backbone, the Saint-Clouds have been a very strong part. Saint-Clouds have fought in every great sea battle in the history of France. In World War Two many escaped to fight with the Free French, and many, many died. The admiral—the uncle of Luc—he survived that bad war. So did the father of Luc, but only for some years."

Jacques paused for a reflective moment over his coffee. "Most Saint-Cloud men have died in times of war. But even when there are no wars to fight, the Saint-Cloud men go to sea. They have amused themselves with the sailing and racing of yachts, not little ones but the great yachts of the ocean. There are many big races in the waters around Brittany—races where other nations come to enter—and for many years Saint-Cloud yachts won them all. But the admiral, he wished for his yachts to win all the great races of the world. To do that, mademoiselle, one must have more than great skill. One must have the right boat. It is for this reason that he sent Luc to learn of the art of building great racing yachts. He sent him to America, where the greatest of all racing yachts are built."

"I knew he'd been to college there," Tory said. "I'd have known by his accent, if nothing else. It's quite amazing."

"Ah, yes. But of course Luc spoke English from the cradle, like all Saint-Clouds. At the Château d'Ys the governesses have always been English. There is reason that Brittany means little Britain, yes? For some the old ties have not been forgotten. For the Benoits, too—although in England our family is known as Bennett."

Tory studied the passing pedestrian traffic while she tried to think of more questions to ask. A pair of wrinkled old women clip-clopped past wearing the wooden clogs, the old-fashioned bunched skirts, and the elaborate starched headdresses of the Breton national costume. Usually such outfits were reserved for feast days and *pardons,* but a few of the older women still clung to the revered old ways, scorning more modern costume. Tory had been told that more than a thousand different styles of *coiffe* existed, and that those versed in the differences could tell a woman's village by her headdress.

"The old ladies, they come from Plougastel, near Brest," said Jacques Benoit, seeing the direction of her eyes.

Brest—that reminded Tory of another subject she ought to pursue. "Can you tell me more about Luc's mother?"

"I do not know more, mademoiselle. I know little except that she was not a woman of—" Jacques halted, but Tory was sure he had been about to say "virtue." "Not a woman of breeding. The woman is dead now; she died a few years after Luc's birth. *Eh bien,* mademoiselle, have I satisfied your curiosity for the moment? For me the business of the day awaits."

"Oh. Of course."

Tory would have liked to continue the questioning, but Jacques had cast an anxious glance at his watch. He rose to his feet and pulled out her chair in the most polite way. He had the manners of an Old World gentleman, continental and rather endearing in a young man of his generation. Before they parted he said, "It has been most pleasant, mademoiselle. If you will be good enough to take lunch with me later in the week, I will give you the letter for Aimée Saint-Cloud. And then, if there are other matters you wish to ask, you may ask them."

Tory's arrangement to stay at the Château d'Ys was confirmed in a phone call later that same morning. When she returned to the hotel, there was a message from Luc Devereux, along with a handsome check—more than enough to cover three months of Laura's expenses.

This time, when she called the boatworks, Annette put her directly through. Impatiently Luc brushed aside her acknowledgment of the check. "I've been thinking about the rationale for your stay at the Château d'Ys," he started. "I have to invent something that explains why we must spend a good deal of time together. Journalist? You wouldn't be welcome at the Château d'Ys. Something to do with yachting? No, for you might give yourself away. Personal friend? I'm afraid that wouldn't answer, either. It has to be business, for I want no questions asked about our exact relationship."

"Then you do admit we have one," Tory said tersely.

"I certainly don't. Do you have some very efficient looking clothes?"

Tory conceded that she did. "I even have horn-rimmed glasses. I wear them for reading."

"Good. I want you to look intelligent."

"I thought I did," Tory replied sharply.

Luc chuckled, a low amused sound that caused her fingers to tighten over the telephone. "Not when you're angry," he murmured. "However, perhaps I used the wrong word. Scholarly might be a better choice."

"Exactly what occupation are you going to pin on me?" Tory asked suspiciously.

"I haven't decided yet, except that it won't call for lipstick, mascara, or dresses with nonexistent necklines. For the time being you'll have to hide your attractions. Look, I have to go. See you Sunday?"

When Tory hung up, she was disturbed to realize that her fingers were shaking. And why? She had already decided, quite on her own, that it wasn't a bad idea to spend the time at Château d'Ys looking as plain as possible. But her reasons, she had to admit, were not quite the same as Luc's.

Tory's next meeting with Jacques Benoit provided a little more information, none of it of great consequence. He confirmed a number of things she already knew. The wide reporting of the Saint-Cloud story at the time of the Fastnet tragedy; the continuing morbid fascination of the French press, particularly in Brittany; the fake claims against the estate—Luc Devereux had lied about none of those things. Nor had he lied about the amnesia.

It appeared that, like most amnesiacs, he had never had trouble remembering the everyday things ingrained from birth and learned in school—language, customs, skills. Only his memory of people and places and events had been affected.

"But there is little, now, that he does not remember," Jacques added. "At first, mademoiselle, there was much. But faces, places—when he sees these things, slowly they bring back the past. It is the putting together of a puzzle, a . . . a jigsaw, I think you say? It takes time, and it takes much searching of the mind. It has been most painful for Luc, yes? In the beginning it brought him headaches, for it was hard to think of those things he did not know. But always, in time, he remembers."

"Always?"

"Always, I think. Although, one time, I heard him say there are some things a man would rather forget."

And very conveniently, too, Tory reflected bitterly,

when one of those things was an unwanted wife. If what Jacques Benoit said was true, then Luc Devereux ought to have had some vague stirrings of memory on seeing the photograph of Laura. And yet he had pretended no recollection at all. If he was going to keep denying everything flatly, why had he bothered to take the photograph of Nicholas? Oh, damn. She had forgotten to confront him about that. Yet perhaps it was as well she hadn't. Having a photograph of his son might give him time to get used to the idea, and even stir what small conscience he might still possess. . . .

Let him keep the snapshot. But after taking it, how did he dare deny he was the man?

"I've given the matter a great deal of thought," Luc told Tory during the drive to the Château d'Ys. "From this moment on you're an expert in the science of hydraulics. Water and wave motion. A recent graduate, with knowledge of the latest data in the field. I've retained you to help me with some problems of design."

"You're joking! If anyone asked me a question, I couldn't even wing it."

Tory turned to stare at Luc, although she had been avoiding doing that since their departure from Quimper. She had been facing the view from the passenger window, preferring to devote her attention to the landscape on that side—an uneven patchwork of rocky fields where wildflowers grew and small black and white Breton milch cows grazed on sparse grasses, shaded by a few treed windbreaks.

Luc's attention remained on the road, the unscarred side of his profile strongly delineated against quite a different scene. While Tory had been watching out her own window, they had been passing the twisting coastline and the blue Atlantic. Little islands dotted the quiet inlet they were passing. Along this sheltered part of the shoreline, stone cottages with slate roofs nestled close against the water, with bursts of color to show that spring had long since come to their granite-walled gardens, in air made balmy by warm Atlantic currents.

"Of course you can," he disagreed coolly. "If questions are asked, you can answer in almost any way you wish, and no one will be the wiser. As you've had some background in the sciences, it shouldn't be hard. In any case there's no choice now. I've already informed my aunt of your occupation."

"Oh, God," groaned Tory.

"I've told her my problem is an urgent one requiring some evening work, and that's why you must stay at the Château d'Ys. Otherwise she would expect you to book into a hotel. As I often do preliminary design work at home—I have a studio set up for it—it's an explanation that makes sense. But it's a fiction we'll have to keep up, I'm afraid."

Tory was afraid of the fiction, too. How many evenings would she have to spend alone with Luc Devereux? His competent hands on the steering wheel of the car were enough reminder of thoughts she ought not to think. She watched those hands, skin pricking, and couldn't quite find strength to tear her eyes away. The lean suede trousers taut across his muscled athlete's legs didn't help, either.

"You're putting me in a hell of a position, Luc," she said tightly, working out some of her inner tensions. "What if I make some sort of slip?"

"You're making one right now." Luc's reminder was level. "I've retained you, remember? You'll have to make some attempt to bury all that antagonism of yours, for it doesn't suggest the right relationship. Nor can you continue to call me Luc while I call you Miss Allworth."

Tory was seriously thrown. If she had called him by his first name, it hadn't been consciously done. "Have I been doing that?"

"Yes."

"I wasn't . . . aware. It must be subconscious. I suppose it's all those years of thinking of you as Laura's—"

"The reason isn't important, but the result is. I don't want any subconscious slips, so there's only one solution, easily explained by American casualness. I'll call you Victoria."

"Actually most people call me Tory."

"Tory?" He mused for a moment and then laughed, a warm, husky sound that sent shivers sliding over her skin. "In some odd way that suits you better. A woman with fists like yours doesn't deserve the lady-like name of Victoria. My chest took two days to get over the punishment."

"Please, I'm not proud of that outburst," she said stiffly. But she wasn't ready to apologize for it, either.

After some minutes of driving in silence, he returned to the subject of her coming charade. "Naturally most of our searching will be done by day. That should be no problem, as Tante Marie will imagine you're going to the boatworks. However, we won't be there."

"What if she phones you during the day?"

"She won't," Luc said, "for the simple reason that there's only one telephone at the Château d'Ys, and that's locked into my quarters. In the rest of the château there's no telephone at all."

"No telephone . . . !"

"Tante Marie had all of them taken out, over my protests," Luc admitted, his voice studiedly casual. "My aunt, I might add, is quite a strong-willed woman."

"All the same, no telephone . . ."

"It may seem a little odd, but Tante Marie has her reasons."

No telephone! No wonder Jacques Benoit had not been able to get in touch with Aimée Saint-Cloud. Could it be that the girl's mother was trying to prevent all outside contact with all young men? Tory had the strong notion that it was so. An admirer who wanted very much to get in touch with a young girl would most certainly try to do so by telephone. Suddenly Tory was very, very glad she had agreed to Jacques's request. Placing confines like that on a teenager, in this day and age, was positively medieval.

"Why do you have an unlisted number?"

"I used to get a lot of crank calls, and I prefer to have Annette field that sort of thing. Anyone who knows me well enough knows my home number."

With curiosity piqued, Tory might have asked more about the Saint-Clouds, but Luc was already onto other matters. "As my workload will be less hectic during this coming month, we'll spend time going over some of the ground covered by your sister during her . . . marriage." That small hesitation told her that he was not yet prepared to admit to any past relationship, legal or otherwise, with Laura. "Carnac, for one, as that's where your sister supposedly met me. Brest, of course. And any other locations you can think of."

"I've been trying. Perhaps if we spent some time with a map, something would ring a bell."

"It's a way to start, at least." He drove in silence for a few minutes, and then asked casually, "Does Belle-Île mean anything to you?"

"Not really. It's an island, is it?"

He frowned as if he hadn't liked her answer and quickly returned to other matters. "I may have to drop you off in Quimper once in a while, on the days when I have genuine business to attend to at the boatworks. Fortunately, like all the Saint-Cloud enterprises, the company has an excellent business staff, so once my Greek clients have taken delivery, I should have a good deal of free time. Mostly I confine my activities to the design side. You'll have a few other days entirely to yourself, the days when I must chair meetings for other Saint-Cloud concerns."

"I hear there are quite a lot of them."

"Yes, but each has its own managerial staff. For years the Saint-Clouds have been—as they say in America—kicked upstairs."

She wondered if Luc regretted his dry words the moment they had been spoken, because they might be interpreted as a reference to the Saint-Cloud deaths. His brief scowl was followed by a stone mask of an expression she already recognized. By now she guessed that Luc must don that expression whenever he wished not to reveal his true feelings. If he had any!

Temporarily Tory shelved her antagonism in the hope of extracting more information. "I hear you studied boat design to please your uncle," she observed.

Immediately the scowl returned. "Who told you that?"

"Er . . . I can't remember. I have to admit I asked around about the Saint-Clouds. You told me so little."

"What else did you hear?"

Tory held her breath, but she couldn't pretend she had learned nothing. "The story of Fastnet, of course. Other than that, only bits and pieces."

"If someone gave you the impression I studied yacht design only to please my uncle, then someone is sadly mistaken. The field is one I would have chosen for myself. As a boy, I liked nothing better than visiting the family shipyards in Brest and the boat-works in Quimper."

After a moment he added, "There is a saying, mademoiselle, that every Breton is born with the sea flowing around his heart. And in these parts there is another saying—that a Saint-Cloud is born with the sea flowing *in* his heart. Despite my name I'm a Saint-Cloud. The sea is my first love, my great love . . . my *only* love."

She knew he was telling her in this new way that he could never have been seriously involved with Laura. "Are you telling me the sea is the only woman in your life?" she asked, deliberately sarcastic.

"No," he said, his face unrevealing. "There have always been women in my life—and you're about to meet two of them."

The coast is wild, the cliffs high, the sea strong. That description should have prepared Tory for the bleak physical aspect of the promontory that confronted her, but it hadn't, perhaps because she had grown accustomed to a sleepier, softer Brittany. As the Mercedes emerged from a deep rock cut that had hidden the Château d'Ys until this moment, she sucked in her breath at the raw grandeur of the sea-battered promontory and the building that dominated it. It looked more like a small medieval fort than a château. With stories of Saint-Cloud wealth and picture-book visions of Loire Valley châteaux in her head, she had expected something mellowed and infinitely more gracious, even though she knew that the poor proud soil of Brittany had given rise to few luxurious structures.

The château had been built with typical Breton disregard for symmetry. It was not overly large. It stood guard over the craggy coast like a solitary feudal outpost, with a few randomly placed round turrets relieving the severity of slate roof, hewn granite stone walls, and narrow slitted windows. Battlements overlooked the sea, suggesting a walkway of some kind—a cruel place to walk on a stormy day, Tory reflected wryly.

And yet it was not a totally unfriendly scene. The view dominated by the château had two aspects—one the majestic Atlantic cliffs, where breakers crashed far below and threadbare grasses bent to the prevailing wind; the other a more promising view. In the low lee of the château, protected by its bulk, there was a walled orchard of twisted apple trees, pink with the blossoms of late spring. Below the sheltered orchard, pine trees grew and the land became craggier again, but the pink-laced boughs rising above the old stone wall were lovely. Perhaps the place was not going to be quite as forbidding as it had promised at first sighting.

"I'll park first, if you don't object to walking a few feet. There's no point leaving you to stand alone at the door. As I still consider the château my aunt's home, I can't suggest you walk right in without me."

The garage was housed in a stone outbuilding a short distance from the château entrance. Luc maneuvered into one of its spaces, parked, and collected Tory's suitcase while she stepped out of the car. He took her arm in a firm grip. As Tory emerged into the open she had to tuck her hair behind her ears in an effort to prevent it from blowing across her eyes and nose. At once the elements made a mockery of the effort.

There was some relief from the prevailing wind when they crossed the cobblestone forecourt and approached the front entrance. In the shelter of the building the salt air was balmy, the sunshine syrupy under the swept blue sky. The great Gothic front door was a massive one, heavily carved in weathered oak. Above its arch there was a heraldic stone shield, its design almost effaced by time and salt air. Tory tried to pick out the symbols it bore and belatedly remembered the horn-rimmed glasses. In seconds they were in place, looking properly scholarly with the quiet tweed suit she wore.

Luc put down the suitcase to open the door, a two-handed task because of its great weight and age. The knocker was a curious cast-iron fish. Over the rim of her unneeded glasses Tory glanced at the escutcheon above the door. It bore a tree and an odd looking fish similar to the knocker, the fish not surprising after what she had heard about the Saint-Clouds. There were also some words in old, old script. She tried to decipher them, letter by letter, without success.

"I take it that's the family motto," she observed. "Is it in Old French?"

Luc paused in the act of opening the door. "No, in the Breton tongue. The derivation is Celtic."

"What does it mean?"

"'From the sea we come, to the sea we return.'" His face was almost without expression.

"It sounds almost like Charles Darwin's theory of evolution."

"The Saint-Clouds anticipated him by a few centuries, then," Luc observed dryly. "Those words have been there since the Middle Ages. The first Saint-Clouds arrived in Brittany by the sea, and I believe they chose that motto and those symbols because they hoped to return someday, by sea, to the land of their roots. They abandoned that thought in time, but over the years the motto's grown to have other meanings."

An ancient male servant, desiccated by age, greeted them in the hall. He looked to be long past his years of usefulness, and Tory had the feeling that one puff of a stiff Atlantic gale might have blown him away altogether. His watery eyes were lit by a smile when he saw Luc. While they exchanged a few words in French, Tory's eyes swept a large, gloomy entrance hall chilled by old stone walls that must have been many feet thick. The stone floor added no warmth. Tapestries and ancient weapons hung between old, heavy wall sconces encrusted with candle drippings of more recent vintage. To one side of the hall a wide opening, more than a doorway, revealed a great room, almost a hall. Tory guessed it to be the main salon of the château. Its formal furnishings included a good deal of dark oak, more old tapestries, and an impressive number of branched iron candelabra.

Other servants arrived on the scene and Luc introduced them. None spoke English, except—with severe limitations—the elderly Émile, who had answered the door. "And Aimée's governess, of course," Luc added, "but as this is Sunday, she's off. The schoolroom is closed for the day."

The schoolroom? It made Aimée sound very young, hardly more than a child. Tory had visions of tunics and white blouses, the sort of uniform worn by French schoolchildren and often seen on the streets.

"Émile says you're to have the Green Room. He'll show you there now, before I take you to my aunt. Evidently she's in the orchard, with Aimée." It was the sort of day that might well bring the occupants of a chill stone building out of doors to sit in a sheltered spot. "I'll meet you back here in the hall," Luc added.

Tory followed the manservant up a great baronial staircase that divided halfway up. Along a dim hallway hung with yet more tapestries, Émile opened a door. The room Tory had been assigned had a beamed ceiling, plaster walls, and a huge old bed. It took its name from the color of the curtains and bedhangings, not from the walls. It was as medieval in feeling as the lower hall, but to Tory's relief, less chilled. Warmth crackled from a great fireplace, giving the room a friendly glow.

And blessing of blessings, it had an attached bathroom. In broken English Émile managed to communicate that the convenience had been added some years before, during a renovation of the château. After a look at the fixtures Tory decided wryly that it must have been about fifty years before. A glance in the bathroom mirror gave back a suitably bookish reflection. She squared her shoulders and followed Émile back down the stairs to meet Luc.

As they walked together into the sunshine, he thrust a clipboard into her hands. "Window dressing," he explained. Tory riffled through the attached papers and saw some very incomprehensible jargon, all English although it might as well have been Greek.

"Is all this really necessary?"

"Can you think of a better reason for us to spend the rest of the day together? One look at that and no one will dare ask questions."

The orchard nestled close against the protected side of the château, using its bulk as an effective windbreak. The other three sides were fenced by the high wall of rough stone Tory had seen on arrival. Once Luc had led her through a tall wrought-iron gate leading into the enclosure, she saw that it was far more than an orchard. True, most of the raked space was filled with old, well-tended trees. But in one cleared place, hiding close in the protection of the château's walls, sheltered flowerbeds offered a mixed bouquet of colors against the weathered gray granite. Larkspur, phlox, azaleas. It all smelled hauntingly of the sea, for the pervasive tang of seaweed fertilizer competed with the perfume of the blossoms that filled the flowerbeds and laced the branches of the trees.

Beneath the bent boughs of a purple lilac, several stone benches rested on flagstones dappled by sun and shade. Two women were seated there, the older in gray, the younger in white.

"Oh, how lovely," Tory breathed.

She was talking about the garden, but the words would have applied just as well to the young woman in white. Aimée Saint-Cloud was beautiful.

The two Saint-Cloud women rose to their feet as Luc and Tory approached. Luc performed introductions, first to the woman he called Tante Marie. Thirty-five or forty years before, Madame Saint-Cloud might have been as lovely as her daughter, but time had taken its toll. Age had made her bones more prominent and grayed her hair, and the stern lines of old griefs had left indelible marks on her face. All the same she was a handsome woman, gracious if somewhat tense. Tory wondered if she detected a small reserve between Luc and his aunt, not exactly coldness but a certain lack of warmth.

"And this is young Aimée," Luc said, his manner gentling as if he were speaking of a half-grown child.

"I am so glad you are here, mademoiselle," Aimée said in a soft young voice. She looked as though she had lived all her life in a walled garden. Eyes like anemones. A dark cloud of long hair. A young mouth fresh with innocence and unawakened womanhood. A delicate heart-shaped chin with the character not yet as strongly formed as in her mother's face. No wonder Jacques Benoit was smitten!

"Young woman" was the wrong description for Aimée, Tory decided. The word "girl" wasn't quite correct, either, for there was something very grave and very adult about Aimée Saint-Cloud, even though she was not long past her seventeenth birthday. She was half a child and half a grown woman, and she trembled on some delicate brink between, as if she had never lived through adolescence at all.

Madame Saint-Cloud gestured graciously at a bench. "Please, mademoiselle, forgive us for waiting outside, but it is not every day the wind allows us to enjoy the sun in such a way. Sit for a moment and tell me of yourself. I know Luc is in a hurry to put you to work, but that can wait a moment, yes? How nice for Aimée and myself, that he had reason to bring you here. It is not often that we enjoy the pleasure of a visitor."

Having made guesses about Aimée's overprotected upbringing, Tory had half expected to have reservations about Madame Saint-Cloud, but it was harder to judge now that she had met the woman. Hers was a proud, sad, strong face, and one had to remember that life had robbed this woman not only of her husband, but of the grown man who had been her only son. Perhaps she simply wished not to be robbed of her daughter, too, at least until Aimée reached a somewhat riper age.

Tory answered a few questions, finding the talk tough going because her supposed occupation was as mysterious to her as it was to everyone else. Luc fielded the question about Tory's supposed accreditations.

"She's going to be modest about her degrees, so I'll list them for you." He did. Tory was as impressed as anyone at her credentials. "Now she's doing research on the dynamics of wave interreaction. Very advanced theories, far beyond anything I studied."

"I think, mademoiselle, that you must be devoted to your career," Madame Saint-Cloud observed. "You must explain more about these . . . dynamics."

Tory glanced at the clipboard. "Er . . ."

"It's far too technical to describe," Luc cut in. He described some of it all the same, causing everyone's eyes but Tory's to glaze. That put an end to career descriptions, for the time being at least. When talk turned to more general matters, Aimée Saint-Cloud leaned forward and listened eagerly, as if she thirsted for news of the outside world. She burst into a question about clothes.

"Is it true that in America, girls of my age wear blue jeans all the time? Even on the streets?"

"Even in Quimper," laughed Tory, astonished. Had Aimée lived *that* protected a life?

Madame Saint-Cloud looked as if the subject displeased her greatly.

Luc asked, "Have you been longing for a pair of blue jeans, Aimée? Perhaps, ah, Tory could buy you a pair in Quimper."

"Tory?" Madame Saint-Cloud stiffened. On her tongue, although she spoke English fluently, the name had a decidedly foreign ring. It suggested displeasure.

"It's hard to be too formal during the working day, Tante Marie," Luc said casually. "As everyone else at the boatworks calls me Luc, I can hardly expect Mademoiselle Allworth to call me Monsieur." He turned to Tory, mild mockery in his granite eyes. "Sorry, I've done it again. Never mind, I'll get used to the Tory in time."

Madame Saint-Cloud seemed satisfied by that, but still on watch. She looked at Tory quite carefully, as if trying to reach some decision. "As long as Mademoiselle understands," she said.

"Oh, Mama—"

Understands? Tory certainly didn't. There were undercurrents between the other three that didn't quite make sense. Madame Saint-Cloud's displeasure at Luc's use of a first name. Luc's overlong explanation, when no particular explanation should be needed. And Aimée's wretched expression, as if her mother's last remark had caused dismay. To Tory it caused only puzzlement. What was she supposed to understand?

"Hush, Aimée." Madame Saint-Cloud's expression had turned stern. She spoke some sharp words to her daughter in French.

Aimée subsided, her dark lashes fanning downward over her young cheeks. She looked a little pale. Oddly she said, "I am sorry, Luc, truly sorry. I did not mean to offend."

Luc rose to his feet impatiently, as if the whole exchange had left a bad taste on his tongue. "That's not necessary, Aimée. Tory, come with me. We have a long afternoon's work ahead of us. Will you excuse us, Tante Marie?"

As Tory followed him back to the château a few tiny questions were teasing at her mind. Why would Aimée think she had offended Luc? And was it her imagination, or did Madame Saint-Cloud not like her nephew very much? Reserve and a faint antagonism emanated from her when she spoke to Luc, the distance in her voice curious, considering that she had raised him as her own son.

Well, if she didn't like Luc, she probably had good reason. The sort of man who had wrecked Laura's life might very well have wrecked other lives, too. The bastard!

Chapter Five

"I can't think of another thing," Tory was saying a few hours later, with far more antagonism than was called for. She must have said it a dozen times already, and still Luc persisted. He had gone over the ground time and again. Exactly what year had Laura been married? She told him. What month? August, within a week of meeting and falling in love. What exact date? Unknown. What things had she said about her new husband? Vague things. How well had he spoken English? Laura had been learning French and hadn't mentioned that. Why had he spent so much of his time at sea?

"Laura never made that quite clear," Tory had told Luc more than once. "We knew you had money, though, because of the yacht you rented."

"Rented?" He homed in on that.

"Why, I . . ." Tory was unbalanced for a moment, wondering why she had used that word. It could have been subconscious, a hint given in some forgotten letter, or it could simply have been that she didn't know people who owned yachts, as Luc undoubtedly did. And if he hadn't owned a yacht himself eight years before, he would probably have had access to some yacht owned by the Saint-Clouds.

"I don't know why I said that. It could just as well have been owned. Certainly Laura never lacked. Whatever other wretched things you did to her, you were generous, I'll grant you that."

"He," Luc had corrected, so frequently that even Tory had begun to think of Laura's husband as "he." In self-defense, however, she didn't allow herself to make that slip out loud. It would have been admitting a doubt that didn't exist.

During the course of the afternoon Tory had dredged up a few unimportant details, some of which were part speculation. She remembered that news of the marriage hadn't been received until about two months after it had taken place, when the long honeymoon cruise was over. She remembered something about a beard being shaved off at the end of the cruise. She remembered that the crew on the yacht had numbered only two, both Bretons. Although Laura had been in France to learn the language, she had not been able to understand their conversations, which had been held in the Breton tongue. Tory also thought it likely that Laura, who hadn't been keen on cooking, might have eaten out quite frequently during the few short months she lived in Brest.

And still the barrage of questions continued. The entire afternoon had been spent in the studio of Luc's apartment, which, with its crackling fire, was much homier than the rest of the château. It was living and working space both, with one end of the large room devoted to framed charts of coastal waters, models of yachts, and a handsome old oak drafting board with a high antique stool.

Tory and Luc were seated more comfortably in the living end of the room. The low timbered ceiling, thick pile rugs, and deep furniture created a feeling of intimacy that Tory found unnerving—a sensation perhaps due in part to the large bedroom she could see through an open door. For much of the afternoon she had felt uncomfortably warm, a heat that seemed to generate itself from some internal source whenever Luc Devereux leaned too close, or whenever she caught the male musk of him, the faint scent of tobacco, the salty tang of his skin. A part of Tory's unwarranted antagonism, although she didn't care to admit it, was because she wanted not to notice those things.

Luc was straddling a straight-back chair and facing her like an inquisitor, too close for comfort. "And why do you think his occupation had something to do with the sea?" he pressed. "He could have been idle rich. A weekend yachtsman, in it for the pleasure."

"Because Laura said your work was always taking you off to sea, even after the winter set in. That can't be the best time for pleasure yachting. Anyway, she was absolutely right. Your occupation does have something to do with the sea."

"It's not *my* occupation that's in question. It's *his.*"

"And you're him!"

"Am I?" Luc frowned. He rubbed a hand around the back of his neck, a gesture of growing irritability. "I beg to differ. You haven't produced one shred of evidence to prove that I'm the man you're looking for.

Only a name your sister gave you . . . and that could be coincidence."

"The letter I sent to Brest reached your lawyers!"

He shrugged indifferently. "Another coincidence. Possibly the landlord in Brest didn't know where to reach the man who had rented the apartment, and asked around until he located a Luc Devereux. Not necessarily the same Luc Devereux."

"You mean there's more than one? I feel sorry for the women of France."

The tight flare of Luc's nostrils matched the increasing grimness of his mouth. "Do I have to remind you this is supposed to be a joint search, not an opportunity for a lot of one-sided accusations? Ever since we met you've been attacking me in one way or another. If not with your fists, then with your tongue. I'm trying to cooperate, but you put a considerable strain on my patience." He paused and formulated a question he had not asked before. "Exactly how old was this man your sister married?"

Tory had no very close idea, but didn't want to admit it. "Now? He would be your age—exactly."

"And exactly how old is that?" Luc asked dryly.

Tory didn't know, but she plunged. "Thirty-eight."

Luc cocked a dark brow in surprise. "How clever of you," he murmured mildly. "People don't usually get my age correct. How did you guess?"

"I didn't guess," she retorted. "I used mathematics. Thirty plus eight."

"Really," Luc bit back, his voice now edged with heavy sarcasm. "It happens I'm thirty-six. Scars do tend to age a man by several years."

Tory glared at him, conceding nothing. "All right, it was a guess. But how can I be precise after all these years? I'm not certain Laura ever told me your age. As I've told you, she had a tendency to be vague."

"Then he could have been younger or older than me?"

"Younger than you . . . unlikely. Laura preferred older men. Older than you, I doubt that too. I imagine you and Laura's husband were born on the very same day."

Luc's jaw twitched, but he controlled the annoyance. "And you say he had a beard when she met him. A new beard."

"I don't remember saying it was new. How would I know?"

"Short and swashbuckling, you said." It was one phrase of Laura's that Tory hadn't forgotten. "You also mentioned that the beard was removed at some point, when his holiday was over and the honeymoon came to an end. I got the impression that the man was normally clean-shaven."

Tory cast a meaning look at Luc's well-razored jaw. "What a coincidence," she murmured.

"It's a coincidence I share with several million other Frenchmen. What color was his hair?"

"Dark. I told you how she described you. Tall, dark, and handsome, those were Laura's very words. Don't you agree they fit perfectly?"

"Somehow," Luc said, "you manage to make that sound like an insult of the first order. Did he speak the Breton tongue?"

"Obviously. You talked with your crew, didn't you? Just as you talk with your employees at the boatworks."

"Did it ever occur to you that your sister mightn't have been married at all? That she might have concocted a husband because she didn't dare tell your parents she was living in sin?"

Tory's eyes fell. "Laura wasn't an angel," she said, her voice briefly muted. "But my parents already knew that, and she'd have no reason to lie. Look, doesn't anyone ever eat in this place?"

"Soon. We eat around sundown," Luc said, with a glance at his wrist. Tory's unwilling eyes were dragged in that direction, too, to a view of his muscular forearm. Uneasily she stirred in the deep wing chair where she sat. Perhaps Luc was feeling warm, too, for he had removed his jacket and rolled up his sleeves. He spent a moment pushing buttons on his digital stopwatch and explained, "Setting the alarm for half an hour from now. That should give you enough time to dress for dinner."

"*Do* you dress?"

"Yes."

"Nice of you to warn me," she said in less than friendly fashion, although she had guessed that the Saint-Clouds wouldn't dine in day clothes and had prepared herself.

Luc gestured impatiently. "If you'd forget about how much you hate me for a few minutes, we might actually start to get somewhere. Is another half hour of cooperation too much to ask? All this is supposed to be in your interests, too. By the way, why *do* you hate me so much?"

Tory leaned forward tensely. "I've told you about my sister's condition. Am I supposed to love the man who did that to her?"

Luc's eyes were speculative. "I think there's more to it than that," he remarked. "You really don't trust men, do you?"

"I don't trust you."

He scowled, muttered a few vehement words to himself in French, and reminded her grimly, "I could pack you out of here and offer to see you—or your sister—in court. Is that what you'd prefer?"

Tory subsided. "No," she admitted reluctantly.

Luc waited until he was sure she was suitably chastened, and then he asked a new question. "Exactly when did your sister return to the States?"

For reasons best known to herself, that was an easy one for Tory. She gave him the precise date. "It was a Tuesday," she added.

"Odd you should recall the exact day so easily," Luc remarked, giving her a curious look.

"Something happened to fix that day in my mind."

"What?"

"Look, does it matter? It had nothing to do with Laura."

"I'll decide that when I hear what it was," Luc said, that watchful expression still on his face.

"Really, it wasn't important! And it had to do with my life, not my sister's."

"Tell me."

"It wouldn't help you one bit! It was just one of those crazy coincidences that happens to twins. You know, like getting a cavity in the same tooth at the same time. Now can we drop it, please?"

"No," Luc stated in a hard voice, looking at her steadily and incisively. "You're going to tell me about it. We have nearly half an hour, and I have a feeling your experiences aren't quite as unrelated as you say. Perhaps I'm through with the questions about your sister after all. I intend to learn more about you."

Anxiety was like a gigantic rubber band, tightening around Tory's chest. She wanted not to breathe. She had to escape those probing eyes, that commanding voice, that intent and unsatisfied curiosity in his face. "If you're through, then I'm leaving," she declared, jumping to her feet.

Instantly Luc was on his feet, too, and Tory's wrist was seized in a grip of steel. She tried to twist away, only to find herself pulled hard against the wall of his chest. With her arm wrenched behind her and manacled to her back, she couldn't struggle free. For one long moment they stood like that, the length of their bodies locked close against each other, both breathing hard, both battling some war of wills. Their eyes were locked, too, dueling now without words. And then Tory began to lose the battle. Something that was not antagonism began to liquefy her limbs, the quivering warmth licking its way along curves too closely fused to Luc's superior strength.

His grip on her arm softened, but she wasn't aware of that. She reacted without reason to the simple, overwhelming physical power of his maleness. Now his hold was not on her wrist but on her senses. He was so close she could see the fine details of his eyes, the darkening granite gray and the black pupils, the definition of each individual lash, the little lines around the edges that revealed the depth of his experience. She could almost taste the hard curve of his lips. She could almost feel the abrasiveness of his shaven jaw, the heat of his mouth, the texture of his scar. She thought about touching those things, about exploring them with her lips and with her fingertips. For a moment she forgot who he was and who she was and remembered only that he was a man and she was a woman. She didn't think of the dangers in the moment; she didn't think at all.

Her body melted against his, issuing an invitation more meaningful than words would ever be. Her eyes glistened feverishly; her mouth parted and quivered. With her tonguetip she moistened her lips, a thoughtless provocation to the kiss that seemed to tremble in the air between them. Half expectant, half scared, she lifted her face.

With a slowness that mesmerized her, Luc's head descended. He toyed with her lips, testing their outer textures, brushing his mouth against the soft surfaces that were helpless to resist him. It was not a kiss but the preliminary to a kiss, a teasing experiment with her lips. She ached with unnamed needs, the primitive woman in her receiving too readily what her mind would have rejected.

Tory could not have said how her hands became free to entwine in his hair, but they did. The vital texture was an aphrodisiac to her fingertips. It was too long since her hands had been in a man's hair. It robbed her of reason, chased away all thoughts of old hungers and old hurts, scattered the deep-seated fears and the remembrance of social taboos. She dizzied to feel the breadth of shoulder, the might of muscle, the warmth of man. With her sense of right and wrong disjointed for the moment, it seemed wrong only that there was fabric between them. Desperate to be held and mindless of the consequences, she allowed herself to cling to his powerful physique. For one moment of shaking weakness she longed for his domination, she quivered for his mastery. Trembling with forbidden feelings, she laced her fingers in that dark hair, shamelessly seeking the deepening of a kiss she should never have invited at all. Her rational mind would not have permitted it, but her rational mind was not in control.

Her invitation was a torch to dry tinder. Luc had the needs of a man, the strengths of a man, the weaknesses of a man. His passion flared wildly and recklessly, fanned to instant flame.

With a low groan he twisted one hand into her hair, winding a silken swath around his hard fingers, against the nape of her neck. His other hand slid to her buttock, capturing her close against him and bending her backward at one and the same time. His kiss deepened instantaneously and commandingly, a driven response to her complete offering of herself.

Instantly Tory froze. It was a conditioned reflex, caused by his swift transformation to predator. When she felt the strong surge of his desire, the leashed power burgeoning readily against her thighs, a sudden fear assailed her. Remembrance was like a wash of cold water, although for one excruciating instant she remained as she was, submitting to the hot fusion of mouths and the burning command of his hands, feeling him hardened and imperative against her, tempting fate for one more wild moment. And then she tore her mouth away. "No, Luc, no. Stop!"

His mouth fell to her throat, but he didn't release her right away. He held her hard and close, his breathing ragged. His clenching fingers became painful in her hair. For a moment the hand clasping her buttock tightened its claim, too, imprisoning her against his body to the point of hurtfulness. She could not escape the intimate awareness of the strong need that suffused him, nor could she escape the knowledge of his desire's forbidden goal.

And then she was free. Immediately Luc turned his back, his shoulders hunched and tense in every muscle. With clamoring heart Tory sank back into the wing chair. Her legs felt too wobbly to support her. She was disordered and shaking very badly, conscious that she had been doing the unpardonable, making love to her own sister's husband. If she hadn't come to her senses, what might have been done? And she couldn't entirely blame Luc. It would have been her own fault, her own guilt. Given the witless invitation she had issued, nature and a man's body could hardly fail to react. Luc had responded as almost any man would have responded to any woman who offered herself—and he didn't even have the constraint of believing himself to be her brother-in-law. Tory felt almost physically ill to think that she had been so sinfully weak, a traitor to herself, a breaker of strong taboos, and with a man she had every reason to hate. She couldn't understand herself at all.

For the first time the room felt very chill. She wrapped her arms around herself, shivering uncontrollably. She felt she couldn't talk about what had happened, because to talk about it was to admit the existence of an attraction she shouldn't feel. When he turned back to face her again, controlled once more, she was still huddling in the safety of the wing chair, feeling almost as drained and enervated as she had felt after releasing emotions of another kind with her fists.

Luc remained on his feet, his manner as dispassionate as if nothing untoward had taken place. Either through power of will or through lack of real involvement, he had managed to tamp down all traces of desire. His expression was distant, a deliberate attempt to ignore the intimacies that had just taken place.

"Now tell me what happened to you that day," he directed in a calm voice.

Tory shook her head, still wordless.

"It can't have been good, as you likened it to a toothache," he noted dryly. "Who was the man?"

"I don't know why you think . . ."

His sardonic, perceptive eyes made Tory's protest trail to a halt. Of course, he knew there had to be a man somewhere in her past. At age twenty-six, she would be an anomaly if there weren't.

"Because it was one of those twin things. You said so earlier. Your sister was having man trouble, so it follows." After some moments of silence on Tory's part, he added evenly, "If you refuse to tell, then I'll have to do some guessing on my own, with the clues already at my disposal. You're some years past the age of consent, and I can't believe that all that locked-in passion of yours has always gone to waste. I imagine you consented at some point in your life. What was it, the end of a lovely affair?"

Tory steadied herself by gripping the arms of the wing chair. If he guessed, his guesses were going to be all wrong, and she didn't want him to think she was the type who went around having affairs. She armed herself with a defiant expression.

"No," she said. "It was the end of a rotten marriage. Maybe not as bad as Laura's marriage to you, but bad enough. And that's all I intend to say, for I don't care to talk about me."

Luc, however, did care to do so. "You must have been very young."

"I was. Now will you drop the subject? It's not a nice one, and I don't want to talk about it."

"A bad marriage . . ." Luc looked at her thoughtfully. "Is that why you mistrust men so much? And I don't mean just me. On very small evidence you're absolutely convinced your sister's husband was the lowest of the low."

"Make that a little more personal, and I'll agree

with you," Tory said, trying for a surface restoration of spirit to cover her inner churning.

"I refuse to say *me*, when I don't choose to believe it was me."

"And I don't choose to believe it wasn't!"

"Let's keep this talk on a rational plane. You have no idea what happened to send your sister scurrying back to the States. Why assume it had to be the man's fault—whoever the man may have been? From things you've said, he doesn't sound like a complete rotter. He was generous, attentive when he was around, and presumably likeable enough, because your sister liked him enough to marry him. Who knows what may have happened? Perhaps he simply died. Did you never think of that possibility? Or perhaps your sister became involved with another man, had an extramarital affair."

"Laura was in love. She wouldn't have done that."

"No? If she had one tenth of your instant response—"

Tory rose slowly to her feet. "How dare you say that," she said, trembling. "After taking advantage of me . . ."

"If you recall, I didn't take advantage," he responded in a steely voice, with only the smallest hint of scorn in the proud set of his mouth. "Although I believe I could have, if I'd cared to pursue the matter."

Tory's hand cracked across his face, proving that some of her responses were very instant indeed. Regret followed instantly, but there was no pause in which to apologize. Luc's eyes turned black with fury. Before Tory could twist away, his face closed over hers. His lips this time were hard, hurtful, and demanding. They pried hers apart in a savage, intrusive kiss that proved he was not always as patient with a woman's aggression as he had been that night in Quimper.

It was intended as punishment, a payment for the ready, spitfire attack of her flattened palm. His mouth seared hers brutally. At the same time he inserted his hand beneath the sweater she wore. Without any attempt to remove her brassiere, his hard fingers clamped mercilessly over one breast, a declaration of conquest.

In the first impact of the kiss there was a wild leap of exhilaration in Tory's blood, and she reacted with passionate, primitive intensity. Instead of resisting, she arched briefly against him. Beneath his palm her nipple turned taut, and beneath his lips her mouth declared instant surrender. And then the fear began to flutter somewhere deep inside. . . .

Which of the two conflicting instincts she would have followed, she was never to know. The low, intrusive sound of Luc's wrist alarm broke the spell of the savage kiss.

Tory jerked herself away from him, becoming conscious only then that Luc's arms had not been around her at all. She pressed her fingers to her burning cheeks, sick with mortification. Oh, God. Had she no resistance at all, no shred of conscience or common sense to protect her from her unnatural and mixed-up responses to this man?

Luc scowled downward at his wrist as he shut off the alarm. Where her hand had connected against his cheek, a faint suffusion of color surrounded the paler scar tissue. Then his eyes came up, darkly scornful as they took in her flushed face, her stung lips, her disordered clothes.

"Let that be a lesson to you," he said in a harsh voice. "I want your attacks no more than I want your advances. Need I remind you again that I'm made of flesh and blood? I have reflexes and I have responses. When I'm hit, I want to hit back. When I'm invited to kiss, I want to kiss back. Provoke me again and I may do more!"

"You, you . . . bastard!"

Luc's mouth twisted sardonically. "I don't believe you can think I'm your sister's husband at all," he said with deep irony, "or you wouldn't respond to me so strongly. Do you have any idea how transparent you are?"

Tory jerked her eyes away from his and started to straighten her clothing. "This sort of thing can't keep happening," she said unsteadily. "It's not natural."

"It seems natural enough to me," Luc remarked wryly. "But then, I'm not burdened by thoughts of mortal sin, as you are."

Desperate to hide her inner tumult, Tory smoothed her hair. Preparatory to leaving for her own room, she gathered her purse and also the glasses she had put aside on coming to Luc's rooms. She walked to the exit and turned to face him, once more girded in the armor of antagonism.

"As you're so sure it's all a mistake on my part, why did you walk away with that snapshot?"

Luc's expression didn't flicker by a muscle. He inserted his thumbs between beltline and shirt, against the flat of a stomach taut and lean with frequent exercise. The posture managed to be casual and aggressive at one and the same time, and it also drew attention to something Tory hadn't noticed until now. At the start of the last blazing kiss she had actually pulled the back of his shirt free of his trousers. Oh, lord, what things was she capable of when her unreasoning body took over?

"What snapshot?" Luc asked blandly.

Tory merely answered with a nasty look and left with all the dignity she could muster. But once through the door, she fled along the dark ringing halls of the Château d'Ys as if all the forces of hell were in hot pursuit.

As Tory dressed for the evening she was still writhing with wretchedness, sick about her internal frame of mind. She tormented herself with anguishing thoughts about her instant and explosive reactions to Luc Devereux. Her feelings confused her beyond belief. What was wrong with her, that she could be so wracked with longing for the very man she had spent so many years despising? The one man of all men for whom she should feel nothing but contempt? The one man of all men she shouldn't desire?

And even if there had been no Laura to consider, how could she feel that way when she knew full well how men like Luc Devereux used women?

Once changed, she looked in the mirror with despair. She had brought no long dinner dress to France and hadn't cared to spend the money on acquiring something for which she would later have little use. As a compromise, in Quimper she had purchased a long knife-pleated skirt of light wool, a fawn shade that would go with all the neutral beiges, browns, and earth colors that comprised her normal wardrobe. Later it could be shortened, and for now it could be worn with almost every silk shirt she owned. At the time it had seemed a good solution, but now it seemed too . . . tailored and ordinary. Her anguish increased. What internal demon made her want to look feminine and alluring for the one man of all men she shouldn't attract?

When the soft tap came on her door, she had just finished attacking her hair with fifty furious strokes of a hairbrush. As she was totally dressed, she went at once to answer, expecting that it was a call to come to dinner.

It was Aimée Saint-Cloud. One of the servants, an aging maid, hovered behind her in the hall. Aimée's eyes widened a little when she saw Tory. "Why, you are quite lovely, mademoiselle," she said, making the unguarded remark with an element of surprise. At once Aimée flushed. "I did not mean that, mademoiselle, in the way it may sound. With your glasses, you have a very nice look. But—ah, it is your eyes, *n'est-ce pas?* I could not see them so very well before."

Aimée herself was far lovelier, a fragile and exquisite creature in something young, floaty, and pink. She looked like a nineteenth-century portrait. In contrast, Tory felt overly plain, underdressed for the evening. But Aimée's compliment was a genuine one, and so was Tory's smile as she murmured an acknowledgment.

"Are you prepared, mademoiselle, to come for the dinner? Mama has asked Françoise to fetch you, but I have told her it is perhaps best if I come also on your first night here, as Françoise speaks no English."

"Er . . . first I have to find my glasses." As the spectacles weren't habit, Tory couldn't instantaneously remember where she had put them. She had wanted an excuse for a moment alone with Aimée Saint-Cloud anyway, and this seemed a perfect opportunity. She gestured at her eyes, for the benefit of the maid. "I can't see to find them. Won't you come in and help me?"

As soon as Aimée walked through the door, Tory closed it firmly to shut out prying ears and eyes. "I have a note for you, Aimée, from Jacques Benoit," she said hurriedly. "Wait a minute and I'll get it."

Aimée became instantly still, her attention riveted. "Jacques . . . ?" she whispered.

Tory knew exactly where to find the note, and in seconds it was in Aimée's hands. For a moment Aimée simply stared at it as if she could not believe such a message had actually found its way to the Château d'Ys. Then, with unsteady fingers, she tore open the seal and turned her back on Tory while she perused the contents, not once but many times. Several minutes passed before she tucked the note deep in her bodice and turned to face Tory again.

By the time the note was read, Tory had found her glasses and restored them to their unaccustomed perch on her nose. As she was slightly farsighted, they tended to blur her vision a little when not used for reading. She could not see Aimée's expression too well, although she thought there was a shimmer of excitement in the young girl's eyes.

"You saw Jacques?" Aimée was touchingly eager for news of the outside world. "Please, mademoiselle, tell me everything."

"There's nothing to tell, except that he thinks of you all the time." Tory smiled warmly. "He's a very nice young man, Aimée. If you have some answer for him, please let me have it soon. I'll get it to him the next time I'm in Quimper."

"Yes . . . yes, there will be an answer. I will push it under your door tonight. But tell me, mademoiselle. Jacques, is he . . . well now? Or is he still so very sick, as Mama has been telling me?"

Tory hesitated, for it was hard to tell a young girl

that her mother had been lying. "He didn't look at all sick to me, only anxious to hear how you are," she said gently. "Now shouldn't we go, Aimée, before your mother starts to wonder why we're taking so long?"

Gradually the pleading look left Aimée's face, and she turned to the door. "Mama will be wondering already," she said quietly, with a very grown-up calmness. By the time she turned the handle, her face was schooled into unrevealing smoothness. As they worked their way down the stairs, Tory reflected that the adultness she had sensed in Aimée Saint-Cloud was very real, the result of often having to hide her true feelings.

Dinner was served in a large, dim, darkly paneled place, a dining hall rather than a dining room. Heavy branched candelabra offered the only illumination, and a banked fire the only warmth. Tory found it gloomy, chilly, and too redolent of a time when discomfort and formality had been a way of life. At the Château d'Ys there seemed to be none of the armies of servants that might once have attended such a household in other eras. Old Émile served the meal while Françoise vanished into the kitchen, presumably to help the cook.

The table was far too long for four people, and they all sat at one end: Luc at the head, with Tory on his right and Madame Saint-Cloud on his left, flanked by Aimée. Below them stretched ranks of empty chairs, candlelight flickering over impressively carved oak. Ghosts of Saint-Clouds dead and gone seemed to hover in the air, and the weight of other centuries was oppressive.

Perhaps it was that heavy aura that caused Tory to sit through much of the meal with head bent to her gold-rimmed plate, listening to the others talk. She knew she was far too silent. She joined in the conversation, but awkwardly. She ate, but without knowing what was going into her mouth. She had trouble drawing her eyes away from Luc's hands, the strong fingers and their shadows infiltrating her thoughts, causing an acute ache somewhere in the region of her heart. Once, when she dropped a table napkin, he stooped to pick it up, and when he pressed it into her hands, she reacted too strongly, fingers jerking in the moment of contact. By the time the meal drew to a close, Tory was filled with despair about herself and total admiration for Aimée, who seemed to know a great deal more about concealing feelings than she herself ever would.

Luc, too, was in a silent, brooding mood. After dinner the four retired to the more comfortable but still imposing salon opening off the entrance hall. Émile provided a tray of after-dinner liqueurs. The women settled themselves, but Luc excused himself on the pretext of needing fresh air. Taking his liqueur, he strolled to the far end of the room, where wide French doors, presumably installed during the château's renovation, gave out onto the parapet Tory had seen on arrival. He opened them and walked out into the night, closing them behind him to keep the chill evening breeze outside. By the little light that escaped through to that shadowed place, Tory could still see his dark shape.

But at least he wasn't close at hand to affect her as he had done throughout the meal. Tory dragged her eyes away from the door and actually began to hear what was being said. Her answers became less automatic. She even began to think of a few questions, polite ones so that all the burden of conversation was not left to Madame Saint-Cloud and Aimée, who had kept up far more than their share. A query about the renovations led naturally to the topic of the Château d'Ys, and Tory remarked, "It's a curious name. Is it a family name, or does it mean something in the Breton tongue?"

"Ys? It is a Celtic name. Brittany was a land of the Celts for many centuries before it became joined to France. The tale of Ys is a legend, of which there are many in Finistère—so many, mademoiselle, that this part of the Breton coast is sometimes called the Coast of Legends. I take it you have not heard the story."

It was Madame Saint-Cloud who had answered. As she did so, her eyes turned to the French doors, soon followed by Tory's. Beyond them Luc could be seen leaning on the battlements, gazing out into the night, with the ceaseless pound of the Atlantic far below. The sight of him distracted Tory for a moment, and she forgot to respond to Madame Saint-Cloud's words, which could have been either statement or question.

"Of all the legends of Brittany, the legend of Ys is the one I most like to tell. I am happy, mademoiselle, to have a new audience."

"I'd love to hear it," Tory said belatedly, realizing she was supposed to have done the prompting sooner.

Madame Saint-Cloud's voice took on a faraway quality, almost hypnotic, the tone of voice sometimes used by a person repeating an oft-told tale. "If you were to follow the coast in the direction where Luc is now facing, you would come in time to the lost city of Ys. It is less well known than the vanished island of Atlantis, mademoiselle, but like Atlantis it is supposed to lie buried beneath the sea. The story is so old that only its memory remains, that and a very ancient granite cross, a Celtic cross which is covered with the lichen of many centuries. It is told that Ys lies in the waters of the Baie des Trépassés."

"Trépassés?" Naturally enough, Tory supposed the word meant "trespassers."

"To translate, it would be the cove of dead men, mademoiselle," came the unexpected answer. In the moment of silent rumination that followed, Tory wondered if Madame Saint-Cloud's mind had traveled back to the two lost members of the Saint-Cloud family. Of course, it must have. A woman who had lost both husband and son would naturally spend a quiet moment with her memories at such a time.

"If there is truth to the tale," Madame Saint-Cloud's faraway voice went on, "at one time the city of Ys was surrounded by a great wall, a . . . dyke such as they have in Holland, yes? It kept the sea out, and the city safe. In this dyke there was a gate, and the gate had a golden key. This key to the great city was kept at all times by the king of Ys himself. The king, mademoiselle, had a daughter. Her name was Dahut."

"Dahut?"

"Yes, a Celtic name. The princess Dahut was sick with love for a young man who lived beyond the city walls, and in her longing she thought only of herself. One night, when her father slept, she stole the golden key from his pocket and went out to meet her lover. While she lay with him, the tides and the winds rose, and the waves grew strong. As the gate was not locked, the sea came in and destroyed all the great city of Ys and drowned all of its inhabitants—yes, the family of Dahut, too. Now it is said that when the sea whispers and moans against the rocks, it is the beautiful siren Dahut, who to satisfy her selfish need for love, makes men die. And when the sea roars and rages in that sad cove of dead men, it is only the thunder of a thousand sorrowing church bells, ringing beneath the—"

The snap and tinkle of breaking crystal brought the monologue to a halt. Madame Saint-Cloud and Tory both turned to the sound. Aimée was staring at the broken stem of a liqueur glass, as if she could not believe what she had done. Her face was pale.

"You are not cut, Aimée?" Her mother's voice held sharp and instant concern.

"No. I . . . I am sorry, Mama. It was empty, but—"

Madame Saint-Cloud relaxed. "Then it is no matter. Come, sit over here by me, and Émile will sweep the glass a little later. Perhaps, my child, it is the talk of drowning, yes? But you know we must not avoid mention of such things."

She patted a space beside her, and obediently Aimée moved to it. Then Madame Saint-Cloud turned to Tory, her face controlled and proud. She was somewhat tense as usual, but if she had unhappy feelings, they were well under control. Her eyes wore the tracery of old sorrows, but they also wore acceptance. "I must tell you, mademoiselle, that some years ago Aimée's father and brother were both lost to the sea. Aimée loved them very much, her brother, Armand, especially. He was much older than she. As my husband was always away, and Armand always here, to Aimée he was like father and brother both."

Madame Saint-Cloud seemed to feel that more explanation was needed. "My husband, mademoiselle, was an officer of the navy, and he also had a great love for the racing of yachts. For these reasons he was almost never at home. Aimée knew her father very little. Armand, however, was always at hand, for unlike my husband, my son spent little time at sea. All the time Aimée was growing, he lived here with his wife. He managed the family concerns, a matter for which my husband had little love. The sea, mademoiselle, was my husband's whole life. He had no patience with the shore."

"Luc told me that . . . that Saint-Clouds are born with the sea flowing in their hearts."

"It is so of most of the men, certainly," Madame Saint-Cloud said, a ghost of regret passing over her face. "I was a widow of the sea, mademoiselle, for many years before I became a widow in truth. Me, I have learned to live with the past and to think of the future. So you see, you must not feel disquiet when such things are talked of. It is best to talk of them, yes? That is why I did not hesitate to tell you the story of Ys, although the bones of so many Saint-Cloud men lie buried beneath the water." Her eyes turned to the leaded glass doors again, and to Luc's dimly discerned outline against the bulwark of the shadowed granite battlements.

Tory felt she ought to say something but could think of nothing to say, except banal things that weren't appropriate. It was evident that Madame Saint-Cloud preferred to hold emotions in and wished to put the past to rest. Murmured condolences would only sound insincere.

"Unlike the city of Ys," Madame Saint-Cloud said a moment later, with her eyes still fixed on the parapet overlooking the sea, "the family of my husband is not quite destroyed. Not yet! I was not born a Saint-Cloud, mademoiselle, but I have been a Saint-Cloud for too many years to allow an end to a name that has been honored for so many centuries. Some day soon my nephew will take the name for his own. The Saint-Clouds will survive. There is still Luc."

Tory felt as if she had witnessed a declaration of some magnitude. Despite the hush of Madame Saint-Cloud's voice, it sounded absolute, as if a decree had been issued. Tory became conscious of Aimée's bent head, of the extreme paleness of her young cheeks. Perhaps she was upset by her mother's failure to mention her as a surviving Saint-Cloud.

"And Aimée," Tory said.

"And Aimée," echoed Madame Saint-Cloud.

Aimée's head did not lift, nor did the dark lashes that were fanned downward over her pale cheeks. But Tory had to wonder if the girl found it so easy to hide her feelings after all. Could Aimée still be thinking of the Celtic princess, Dahut?

Chapter Six

Although Tory found a slim letter under her door the next morning, some time passed before she had an opportunity to deliver it to Jacques Benoit. Luc, on shepherding her to his car after breakfast, informed her that the working hours of the next three days were to be spent in Brest. Unhappy at the prospect of spending so much time in his company, Tory suggested, not for the first time, that he hire a firm of detectives to do some of the investigation. She told him the days in Brest would be wasted. She had been through it all before—the questions that had no answers, the guesses that had no confirmations.

"As you're so certain the man is me," Luc said dryly, "hadn't I better see the scene of the crime? That's the way most of my other memories have come back."

"And if these particular memories did come back, would you even admit it?" Tory asked too sharply.

Luc gave her a strange look as he snapped the passenger door closed. Seconds later, easing into the driver's seat, he murmured, "You do have a low opinion of men."

"Not all men," Tory retorted pointedly, discarding her horn-rimmed glasses for the day.

Brest was something less than an hour's drive from the Château d'Ys. The town overlooked a magnificent view of a vast natural harbor large enough to accommodate a dozen navies, in a great blue bay defined by the Pointe de Penhir to one side, the Pointe de St. Mathieu to the other. Beyond the harbor's shelter lay a vast expanse of uninterrupted Atlantic, stretching all the way to America. From her former stay Tory already knew Brest fairly well. Rebuilt following the devastation of World War Two, it was less picturesque and considerably more impersonal than the ancient town of Quimper; nevertheless, it had its charm. As one of France's great seaports it was an exuberant place, alive and colorful and thriving. The harbor was busy with all manner of vessels, from great steamers to squat tugs. Alongside the giants of ocean commerce threaded the schools of small boats belonging to the Bretons who took their living from the dangerous coastal waters nearby.

Tory had read that Brest was the rainiest of French towns, and on this occasion the weather seemed to confirm that reputation. It drizzled off and on all that first day, a foretaste of what was to come for the next two. It was a soft, warm, benign rain that wouldn't have been unpleasant but for the way one's hair stayed lank and damp, and the way one's body seemed to steam up beneath the plastic raincoat that had to be worn so much of the time. In Tory's case the discomfort was not always due to plastic. Whenever Luc took her arm or brushed against her body or stood too close to her in an elevator, the clammy warmth that invaded her skin couldn't be blamed entirely on the weather. Her inner writhings still continued.

The apartment where Laura had lived was in one of the newer and more luxurious buildings, not far from the waterfront. First they tried the owner of the apartment building, whose offices were elsewhere. He claimed to have no personal knowledge of past tenants, beyond a list of names. If he had forwarding addresses, he refused to hand them out. He suggested the writing of a letter as the only way one might contact former occupants—unless, of course, the agency that handled all rentals chose to dispense additional information. The rental agency did not so choose. They claimed to have kept no old records and suggested asking at the building itself. The building was large and impersonal, and the doorman of eight years before had long since left. Laura's former apartment was occupied and couldn't be seen. With the passage of years the tenants of other apartments had changed over several times. Tory had known all those things, but Luc had wanted to confirm them for himself.

"Any twinges of memory?" Tory asked Luc after the hours of fruitless questioning.

"Of course not. If anything were familiar, I'd have let you know."

Tory merely gave him a look that said she didn't trust him to do any such thing.

That was only the first day of the search, and the second was even more trying. Tory and Luc trudged the pavements of Brest, going into every small shop within walking distance of the apartment. With the picture of Laura in hand, Luc put the questions. Tory could understand neither questions nor answers, but she could understand the general gist. Two or three of the older merchants did indeed vaguely recall the woman in the photograph, although they didn't seem to recognize Luc. In fact, when he gestured at himself for Tory's benefit, they shook their heads emphatically. To Tory that didn't mean he wasn't the man. Would Luc have been accompanying Laura to the butcher's or the baker's? That was hardly likely!

The third day they concentrated on restaurants. At first they traveled on foot, preferring the misty drizzle to frequent reparking. But when the closest places yielded no results, they took to the Mercedes to try restaurants farther afield. After several unrewarding tries their path took them off the beaten track to a discreetly elegant inn where, after the surreptitious exchange of an enormous banknote, the haughty maître d' condescended to consider Luc's query. As the lighting in the place was very dim and intimate, he had to carry Laura's likeness to a lamp. He spent a long time puzzling over it as though he might indeed recognize it. Luc spoke to that man for some time. As it wasn't the kind of place where voices were raised, Tory couldn't hear everything—not that she would have understood, in any case.

Tory eyed the surroundings askance as they finally sat down to have lunch in the same place. Their intimate table was in a secluded alcove, closed off from the eyes of other patrons by swagged curtains.

The plush banquette offered no choice of placement but one, side by side, with bodies practically touching. Tory, who had never been in a restaurant with such exotically private seating arrangements, reflected not too happily that it was exactly the sort of place where a man might bring his paramour. It whispered of illicit assignations.

She waited until two very dry martinis had been brought. "Well, did he recognize you?"

"Obviously not," Luc said dryly. "I had to tip the man generously to get him to even talk with me."

"I saw him squinting at your face." The squint hadn't seemed to result in obvious recognition, at least to a distant observer. But she wasn't about to say that to Luc.

"I asked him if I looked familiar. Besides, in this place you have to squint to see anything."

And that included the prices on the menu. There simply weren't any, usually the sign of a restaurant where the costs were too astronomical to mention. The place, Tory decided, was too discreet for words. If Laura had ever eaten here, she had certainly eaten well. A discreet waiter gathered the overly discreet menu after Tory discreetly chose a plain omelette, not wanting to be too indebted for the meal.

"But he *did* know Laura," she stated.

"He wasn't sure."

Tory thought Luc was lying. "He spent long enough looking at her picture! And why did you have so much to say to each other?"

"She reminded him of his daughter. I heard the story of his entire family, I fear, as price for this prime table. Worth it, don't you think? As soon as we walked in, I was told in a very haughty fashion that reservations were absolutely essential and that most tables were permanently reserved. Our soggy condition didn't help."

Tory stared at Luc, frustrated. "You must be telling me the truth, I suppose. If you'd made reservations here in the past, he might at least have remembered your name."

"Exactly," said Luc, with the coolness of a man who has proved his point.

"Of course, he may have remembered it and you haven't told me."

"Then why," asked Luc, "didn't he remember my face?"

Tory felt as if they had returned to square one—almost.

If the morning had added anything to her store of knowledge, it was that Laura's former apartment wasn't very far from the Saint-Cloud shipyards and canneries. She had seen a sign. It had meant nothing to her during her earlier investigations, but now it meant a great deal. She hadn't made a point of this on sighting it a short time before, but now she broached the subject to Luc.

He was unperturbed. "Of course I knew the two addresses were close to each other. But exactly what does that prove, except the very opposite of what you hope? If your sister's husband happened to be involved with the Saint-Cloud enterprises in any way, he'd have had no reason to be absent from his new bride so often. He'd have been home with her every single night."

"But *you've* been involved with those enterprises, and you don't actually work there," Tory said, feeling she had scored a point. "You work near Quimper."

Luc's face was absolutely unrevealing, although his eyelids grew heavy with mockery. "In that case," he drawled, "why wouldn't I have rented her an apartment in Quimper?"

Tory sighed and slumped a little, weary from the morning's long walk. "I don't know," she admitted wryly. A new thought occurred to her, and her eyes narrowed accusingly. "Unless . . . unless you'd ever had a mistress living in Quimper. Have you?"

He came back with a bland, "Haven't I told you, my memory's impaired?"

"That's not a direct answer! You've also mentioned that other women have turned up out of your past from time to time. I don't know why it never occurred to me before! Of course, you couldn't keep two women at the same time in a place the size of Quimper. It would get around. Did you ever have an apartment in Quimper?"

"Yes, for a time. I gave it up after my uncle died, when my aunt asked me to move back to the Château d'Ys."

"I'm surprised you agreed."

"I would have preferred not to, because it's a little far for commuting, and I prefer my independence. However, I thought my aunt needed at least one able-bodied man around the place, and she refused to hire any. Theoretically the place belongs to me, so I feel some responsibility for the safety of the occupants."

"Well, then," said Tory. "It's obvious what you were up to eight years ago. You were keeping another woman while you were married to Laura."

"Was I?" His words were heavily sarcastic. "Ask yourself another question, my friend. If I had married your sister, why wouldn't I have introduced her to my family? They live close enough to Brest, less than an hour's drive."

"We were talking about whether or not you had a mistress in Quimper! Did you?"

Luc began to look coolly amused. "I'm going to pretend I didn't hear that, on grounds that even listening to this nonsense of yours may tend to incriminate me. If you won't tell about your past love life, why should I tell about mine?"

"Because you're the one with something to incriminate yourself about! Anyway, I don't have a past—" She halted, stopping herself just in time as the red-coated waiter pushed a silver-laden trolley of hors d'oeuvres into the velvet enclosure. After serving with a flourish, he departed, leaving behind him delicious odors of pâté and escargots and other delicacies Tory hadn't ordered.

"Don't have a past what?" Luc prompted.

"Don't have a past worth talking about," Tory said stiffly.

"Odd," Luc murmured. "I have the distinct impression you stopped yourself on the verge of saying past love life. A strange remark for a woman who used to be married. Were you never in love with your husband?"

Tory paused in the process of spearing a snail, her slender fingers rigid with tension. She stared back at Luc, defying him to guess the truth of her marriage. "Of course I was in love with him once. I said yes to him, didn't I?"

"Is that as far as it went? Words and no more?"

"Of course not! I know what you're implying, but there was nothing . . . *wrong* with Griff. He was a perfectly normal male."

Luc's face was unreadable in the shadowed alcove,

but she could feel his eyes searching her, looking for clues to her past just as she had been looking for clues to his. "I wonder," he murmured.

Tory put down her fork. "If you ask one more question about my marriage, this whole meal is about to go to waste. I'll have to leave."

"That bad, was it?"

"That's a question!"

Luc gave her a long, narrow look and abandoned the subject. Through omelettes, buttery sugared dessert crêpes, and some very exotic accompaniments, the sparring continued, all of it centered on the subject of whether or not Luc had ever been married to Laura. Tory continued to insist he must have been, and he continued to insist it was the least likely of possibilities.

"Then who *was?*"

"That's exactly what I'm trying to find out," Luc said with exaggerated patience.

Between the jousting they also discussed plans for the rest of the week. Luc had a board meeting the following day, which would leave Tory some free time at the Château d'Ys. On Friday he would be going to the boatworks, and Tory's day would be spent in Quimper—opportunity, at last, to deliver the note about which Aimée had asked several times, either with anxious looks or with hurried whispers.

"We'll go to Carnac next week," Luc informed her.

"Perhaps you'll be convinced when you see the register of the little inn where you stayed eight years ago," Tory said. "They *keep* old records there."

Luc grew very still. "Oh?"

"The register's signed."

Luc answered carefully. "Anyone can sign another man's name."

"Yes, but there's another point. The Luc Devereux who signed in at an inn near Carnac was the same Luc Devereux that Laura married. If you and Laura sailed on to other countries—as I know you did—you must have had identification. Probably a passport. Don't you see, it *must* have been you?"

"There's another possibility. Perhaps in Carnac we'll discover that the signature isn't mine at all. In that case what will you do?"

Tory dipped her head, suddenly assailed by that confusion of reaction that seemed to have become part and parcel of her daily life. "Go home," she said in a low voice.

The meal drew to a close, its end marked by a bill discreetly presented in a handsomely flocked ruby-red folder with gold tassels. Luc scarcely glanced at it. He inserted a breathtaking number of francnotes, waved the waiter away, and remarked, "I think we've found out all we're going to find out by pounding pavements. Can you amuse yourself for a short time this afternoon? There's a small matter I must attend to. I'll drop you at a boutique near where I'm going to be, so you can while the time away."

"And where are you going to be?"

"If you must know, at the local newspaper. I thought I'd flip through the files for the period your sister lived in Brest. As you don't speak French, you'd only slow me down."

Tory had already gone through the eight-year-old files, a painstaking process that had produced no trace whatsoever of the name Devereux. She knew Luc would find nothing. Nevertheless, she said with deliberate sarcasm, "What is it you intend to do? Cover your traces?"

Tory's constant digging had clearly frayed Luc's

temper. He turned sideways, facing her more directly, and rested his left arm on the back of the banquette behind her shoulder. There was annoyance and scorn in the downward twist of his mouth. "You're not prepared to give me credit for one iota of human decency, are you? If I were to uncover any evidence that I was involved with your sister, you'd be the first to know."

Tory glared at him defiantly. "You must think it's possible, or you wouldn't be going to all this trouble, would you? And you made off with that photograph of Nicholas. Proof positive that you're the man!"

Luc glowered at her, his jaw working and his eyes darkening with some dangerous emotion. Where their bodies almost connected, heat seemed to emanate from him in waves. Inadvertently and against her will, she thought about the night she had assailed him with her fists. Aroused to anger, Luc Devereux was a thoroughly dangerous man. She had sensed it and ignored it that night, but she couldn't ignore it now. She knew that in some way she had pushed him too far.

And yet, as if driven, she taunted, "Well? Answer me that one!"

"I'll answer it," he said grimly, "in a way that should tell you exactly what I think of your logic. If I were married to your sister, I wouldn't dream of doing what I'm about to do. . . ."

With that, his left hand closed over her shoulder to prevent easy retreat. Beneath the tablecloth his right hand pinioned her knee, the fingers imperative in their seizure. His face descended toward hers, his mouth and his eyes filled with sensual demand.

At once Tory started to struggle, because his hand

fastened on her knee advertised his intentions clearly. But she had no opportunity to protest in words or screams, because in the next moment her lips were sealed in a breathtaking kiss. He dominated her easily with his mouth and one powerful arm, pressing her against the banquette.

His hand at her skirt insinuated itself intimately, finding the silken surface of nylon beneath the cloth. Slowly, heart-stoppingly, his fingers traveled higher, seeking a vulnerable goal protected only by the flimsiest of apparel. He clamped his hand possessively over that secret and wildly responsive part of her, claiming instant authority. And there, despite her struggles, his hand stayed lodged.

Tory tried to push at his head and tear his intrusive fingers away from her thighs, but in her heart she knew that the choked little animal sounds deep in her throat were not mere sounds of denial. She fought against the domination and at the same time she desperately wanted it. Some unruly part of her, a pagan part where desires ruled instead of fears and scruples, almost wished they were alone somewhere—completely alone so that he could follow through to some reckless completion, an act of subjugation she feared and would fight, but which she desired in her innermost self.

It seemed a wild eternity, but it was probably no more than fifteen seconds before Luc freed her, detaching himself so abruptly and so completely that for a moment Tory's hands were pushing at empty air. There was nothing left to fight.

"If that was a black sin," he said harshly, "then my soul is damned—but so is yours. If you really think I'm the man who married your sister, then the reactions you've been having for the past few days aren't exactly moral. Lusting half the time for your twin sister's husband doesn't leave you exactly—"

He halted mid-sentence and muttered, "Good God."

He was staring at her with deep disbelief, only half crediting what he saw in her face. Tory tried to hide the expression, but her internal disorder was such that she simply couldn't. Her eyes were wide and fearful, her mouth trembling with uncontrolled emotion, her chin quivering too.

"Good God," he repeated. "Half of you is starved for sex, but the other half is scared witless that you might respond to my touch. Do I really affect you so strongly?"

Tory tried to bring her facial muscles back to normal. Mortified to think herself so easy to read, she wanted to sink right through the banquette seat and emerge in some other part of the world. Were the emotions that wracked her really that plain to see?

"Surely you didn't think I was going to follow through, with no more than a curtain to hide us?"

"No," she whispered.

"Relax, Victoria," he said with a sudden gentleness. "I don't have any designs on you at all."

Severely shaken, she started to pull herself together. She had an unrealistic sense of having been discarded—as if she, not he, had started the whole humiliating thing. When they left the restaurant a few minutes later, she was unnaturally subdued and silent. She had been very thoroughly kissed, and although she had struggled and felt panicky she had wanted the kiss to continue. Was there no way to control this terrible longing that was growing inside her?

Chapter Seven

Luc could not have been more uncommunicative after his visit to the newspaper office, nor Tory more awkward and chastened. She had spent the hours of separation not in shopping, but in scuffing along the rain-washed streets of Brest, thinking. She had thought first of her mixed-up feelings, until she could bear to think of them no longer. And then she had forced herself to think about Laura and Luc.

When they met at the car at the agreed hour, Luc didn't bother telling her he had found nothing, and she didn't bother asking. She simply didn't have the heart.

Like dry rot in strong timbers, doubts had started to eat at the construction of things she had long believed. She would not have admitted it to Luc, but the three days in Brest had been responsible for her change of heart. His willingness to search for the past could not be faulted, and despite her sharp statements to the contrary, she was beginning to think that if he found the truth he would face it. The episode in the posh restaurant had also created nagging doubts. Despite Luc's evasiveness, she was fairly sure the maître d' had recognized Laura's picture, and she was also certain the man hadn't recognized Luc. Yet in a restaurant of that nature, wouldn't they have always been together? It wasn't the sort of place where Laura would have lunched with lady friends.

Luc's advances to her, much as it shamed Tory to think about them, had also contributed to her growing sense of uneasiness with old conclusions. Could Laura have been married to some other man, as Luc had suggested more than once? Someone with access to his identification? Not a Saint-Cloud, because the two dead Saint-Cloud men had been married. Besides, one had been too old, and the other had had an occupation that didn't take him to sea. Possibly there was another Devereux? Or perhaps a Saint-Cloud employee, who for reasons of his own had chosen to use someone else's identity? People did things like that when they wanted to live high on the hog but didn't want to pay the bills. Perhaps Laura's husband had been existing on credit and bad checks, and his house of cards had come tumbling down. If Laura had found out her husband was a cheat and a liar, that might have been enough to send her running home to the States in such a terrible frame of mind. It was wildly farfetched but it was just possible.

Perhaps the doubts had crept in only because Tory so desperately wanted to doubt, but once given a tiny toehold in her imagination, they were hard to dislodge. She began to think she must have made a mistake.

That night was a restless one, for she tossed and turned with her uncertainties and wretched recriminations. She could no longer delude herself about her feelings for Luc. He had called those feelings lust, but by now she knew they were far more than that. The confused feelings reached deep into her very core, causing terrible storms inside. The preoccupation with him filled all her dreaming moments, and most of her waking ones too. She had a sense of helplessness and inevitability, as if an ironic fate was ruling her destiny in the most cruel way possible. It altered nothing that the attraction wasn't mutual. She felt as if she were attached to Luc by some invisible and powerful force of nature she couldn't fight—like a comet plummeting to certain disaster, or a rudderless raft being sucked by strong currents into a fatal whirlpool.

Truth had the taste of bitterness, but the truth was that she was in love—unthinkably and unspeakably and shamefully in love. It might be that the sea flowed in Luc's heart, but it was Luc who flowed in hers, not peacefully, but with the tumult of a great tidal wave sweeping a destructive path.

During the long unhappy night that followed, Tory recognized that since meeting Luc her goals had undergone a sharp reversal. Once, she had wanted to prove that he was the man her sister had married; now she wanted to prove that he wasn't. Otherwise how could she live with herself?

Exhaustion had put circles under Tory's eyes the following morning, and she had reached no decisions. But she knew she could not rest until she discovered all the truth and swallowed it, however unpalatable it might be. Luc's memory of the past might be impaired, but the memories of other members of his family were not.

"About those blue jeans, Aimée," she said at breakfast, in the hearing of everyone but Luc, who had already departed for his board meeting. Present at the table were Madame Saint-Cloud and the English governess, a stiff-spined and strict woman of sixty-odd years, who joined the family for meals on all days but Sunday. They, as well as Aimée, were listening attentively as Tory continued, "I might be able to pick them up tomorrow, as I have another errand in Quimper. I believe Luc promised you a pair?"

That last was added for the benefit of the two older women, in case blue jeans were on some list of forbidden items. It wasn't merely a way to let Aimée know that her message to Jacques Benoit was about to be delivered. In truth, Tory was looking for an excuse to have some private moments with the young girl, a thing that seemed remarkably hard to arrange. This wasn't the best of excuses, but it was the only one she had been able to think of.

"If you would come to my room sometime today, Aimée," Tory went on, "you could try on the blue jeans I brought with me, so I can get an idea of your size. When can you spare a few minutes? Any time will do; I have the whole day free."

Aimée's slight hesitation over her glass of freshly squeezed orange juice wasn't matched by any hesitation in her voice. "Perhaps Mademoiselle Pritchard will decide, for it is she who must excuse me from the lesson."

Miss Pritchard, the English governess, nearly scotched all Tory's carefully laid plans. "There's no need for that," she said crisply. "I do all the shopping for Aimée, and I have all her sizes. I have quite a number of things to buy for her at this point, anyway.

New underwear and so forth. If jeans are to be permitted, I'll put them on my list."

Perhaps that accounted for Aimée's rather demure and quaintly youthful wardrobe. Frustrated but by no means defeated, Tory was casting about for some objection when Miss Pritchard added unexpectedly, "However, as you have the day free, I wonder if I could ask a great favor. Aimée's education has been devoted to literature and languages and Latin, but I'm afraid it's been somewhat lacking in the sciences. It would be helpful if you were to give her some instruction in your specialty—oh, nothing complex, of course, for Aimée hasn't the foundation. With your background it seems a shame to let the opportunity go to waste. Would you mind?"

"An excellent idea," said Madame Saint-Cloud.

Tory opened her mouth, let it hang that way for fully one second, and then closed it again. She nodded agreement, too overcome by inward mirth to risk saying anything out loud. After all her unhappy introspection, it was a relief to discover that her sense of humor was intact. If only Miss Pritchard knew!

"Come to the schoolroom, then," Miss Pritchard instructed, "at nine o'clock."

Tory managed to keep her face straight. She turned to Aimée. "Is there a way to climb down the cliffs to the sea?"

"Yes."

"Good, for I always like to start with a field lesson. There's no point drawing diagrams and expounding formulas unless you've already observed the waves closely and watched the way they interreact. So thank goodness it's a fine morning! Wear your very oldest clothes, Aimée, and be prepared to get wet. You do swim, I hope?"

"Oh, dear, that lets me out," Miss Pritchard sighed. She had back trouble and slept on a board, as Tory well knew from mealtime conversations. "I might be able to paddle my feet, but that long climb down the cliff is beyond me. I suppose I may as well drive into Quimper and attend to Aimée's shopping."

Tory concealed a smile by hiding it against the rim of her coffee cup. Praises be for Miss Pritchard! Tory couldn't have arranged it better if she had arranged it all herself.

During the wait for nine o'clock, while she located blue jeans, an old shirt, and a pair of sunglasses that might pass for prescription, Tory mentally enumerated some of the riddles she hoped to solve during the morning, none of which had anything to do with the mysteries of hydraulics. During the several days spent at the Château d'Ys, she had not been unobservant. Although the working hours had been spent in Luc's company, there had been plenty of opportunity to study the Saint-Clouds. Already she knew a fair amount about the household.

She was primarily interested in solving the riddle of Luc's past, but Tory had the notion that in solving that, she would also have to resolve some of the other mysteries that shrouded the Saint-Cloud family. It wasn't mere idle curiosity. She had the odd sense that all the Saint-Clouds were linked in some strange way, a web of destiny in which she herself was inextricably caught. She couldn't imagine why it might be so, but the feeling was very definitely there. On the surface she had to acknowledge that the Saint-Clouds, the dead men and the living women, could have had nothing very much to do with the mystery of Laura's and Luc's past. All the same, Tory had a strong sense of connection—in part, because although Luc had been brought up by such a prominent family, Laura hadn't mentioned it. Why had he not introduced her to the Saint-Clouds? She had been presentable enough. Why had he not even mentioned the marriage to his family at the time? If they had known about it, Luc would most certainly have found out while becoming reacquainted with his past, after the amnesia. And why would he have failed to tell Laura about his background? It wasn't one to be ashamed of. All those reflections tended to support Luc's contention that no marriage existed in his past.

But there was another view. Might there be some reason Luc shouldn't have married Laura at the time? He could very well have kept the union secret if he had known that the Saint-Clouds were going to disapprove. And Laura *might* have known about his background all along. She had always been inclined to vagueness anyway, and her few letters from Brittany had been exceptionally vague. Perhaps her failure to mention the Saint-Clouds had been deliberate, because she knew that secrecy was required. Or there might have been some casual reference at the time, something Tory had long since forgotten. Those possibilities argued in another direction and suggested that Luc could very well have been married to Laura.

Tory hoped a private conversation with Aimée might give direction to her thinking. Besides, she was curious about Aimée herself. All week Aimée's plight had kept pricking Tory's mind—at least, whenever her mind was not wrestling with other, more personal matters. There was something strange and poignant about that lovely, lonely child-woman, a combination of eagerness, sadness, and hesitancy, along with a subtle strength of character that made Tory wonder if Aimée was quite as compliant with her mother's wishes as she appeared to be on the surface.

By now Tory was in no doubt that Aimée was being deliberately protected from influences of the outside world. It was clear that since the death of her father and brother, and possibly even earlier, she had been given an overly sheltered upbringing. Tory's ears and eyes would have told her that Aimée was unnaturally removed from people of her own age, even if she had not heard it from Jacques Benoit. The servants were all aged; the governess was strict and nearly always at Aimée's side; the estate was remote from any town or village. Cliffs and sea protected it on three sides, while imposing rock formations and a tall, wickedly spiked iron fence with a barbed-wire top guarded it on the fourth. Trespassers, the signs warned, would be electrocuted. The gate was kept locked. The fence might have been erected to protect against people coming in, but Tory made mental note that the dangers it promised would just as effectively prevent someone from getting out. Every time she saw the fence, Tory could not help but think of the story of Dahut, a legend she had heard twice more since the first telling. It was, indeed, Madame Saint-Cloud's favorite tale.

There were other riddles, most of which could not be solved by outright questions to Aimée. Madame Saint-Cloud's overprotectiveness was puzzling, and so was the little tenseness in her manner. She had come to terms with the loss of husband and son, and she had done so with a strength and patient acceptance that were impressive. Why was she so very afraid of losing Aimée to a more joyful fate? Young Jacques Benoit didn't have marriage on his mind anyway, only the first tentative stages of romance. His intentions seemed honorable enough. As the son of old family friends, he ought to be acceptable to Madame Saint-Cloud. It wasn't the largest mystery in Tory's mind, but she thought that the solution to it might help her with the solution to matters close to her heart. If she could learn to understand the strange Saint-Clouds, might she not understand Luc?

"I wouldn't want to be doing this on a stormy day," Tory was saying half an hour later as she and Aimée clambered down a precarious path on the cliffside. There were only jagged rocks for handholds, and in places little more than narrow shelves of granite to support the feet. The top of the cliffs towered more than a hundred feet above the sea. The drop seemed alarming to Tory, although Aimée told her that the Pointe du Raz, Brittany's tip, was three times the height. A long fall was a distinct possibility and not a very pleasant one, for on this hard-toothed granite rockface one would be ripped to shreds long before hitting bottom. Madame Saint-Cloud's curious over-protectiveness certainly didn't seem to extend to the dangers of nature!

Aimée, in shorts and tank top, was like a young gazelle, much more skilled at the climb than Tory. With one arm she carried bathing suit and towels, along with the clipboard and notes that Tory had brought along for the sake of appearance. Even so, she seemed to have no trouble maintaining her footing.

There was a strip of clean beach at the base of the cliff. The sand was soft and Tory sank onto it gratefully, kicking off the light sneakers she had worn. Her bathing suit was under the jeans, although she didn't think she'd go in. The water looked too dangerous. The lap of waves at the beach was not too strong, but beyond the shore, breakers dashed against fanged rock formations, suggesting undertow and all manner of hazardous things Tory was supposed to know about but didn't.

Aimée sat down, too, more tensely. "You see Jacques tomorrow, then," she said.

"Yes."

"And you will give him the note?"

"Yes, Aimée, I will."

"You are sure?"

"Unless I can't reach him for some reason. I'll try my hardest."

"But even if you do not see him, you will deliver the letter? You promise?"

"I promise, Aimée."

Aimée seemed to relax. With a sigh, she turned to contemplation of the water. "I come to this place sometimes, when I wish to be alone. It is a good thing, yes, that the climb is not easy for older feet? Sometimes, when the water is more calm, I swim. When it moves swiftly around the rocks, it pulls hard at the body. Is this a part of what you will explain to me?"

"I don't intend to explain a single thing, Aimée. Use your eyes and your senses and you'll know as much as you'll ever need to know about waves. Including when to stay out of them! This isn't a working day for me, and I absolutely refuse to work. I just wanted company for the morning. I didn't think a holiday would hurt you, either."

With a light laugh that sounded like bubbles bursting, the first purely adolescent sound she had made,

Aimée threw herself full-length on the sand. She was released from the morning's studies and loved it.

Tory kept the talk simple and idle at first, not wanting to alarm Aimée into putting up her guard. Gradually, out of a pattern of seemingly innocent questions, she began to form a picture of the Saint-Cloud household in previous years, the years when Aimée had been growing up.

As a child Aimée had not known Luc very well, because he was nearly twenty years older than she. He had moved away from the Château d'Ys at college age, before Aimée was born. He had spent some years learning his craft in the States, but there had been frequent short visits to France and the Château d'Ys. After returning permanently, a taste for independence had kept him living on his own. Most of these things Tory had already known.

"I used to call him *mon oncle* until Mama told me I must call him Luc," Aimée said, sounding very wistful as she stared out to sea. "Really, he is only a very distant relative, but to me he was always like a . . . a very favorite uncle. They were happy years then. Luc would come sometimes and toss me high in the air and laugh. He would bring sweets, little boxes of bonbons. Always, one for me, one for Mama, and one for Félicité."

"Félicité?" Tory hadn't heard the name before.

"Félicité is the wife of my brother, Armand, his . . . what is the word? His widow. She is of an age that she might be my mother, just as Armand was of an age that he might be my father."

"Oh? And was she like a parent to you, as he was?"

"Only in age," Aimée said guardedly. "It was a marriage arranged between the families when Armand and Félicité were very little children and had not even met. In the very old families that is still sometimes done. My brother married her when I was still a baby."

Tory risked a direct question. "Didn't you like her?"

Aimée hesitated only one instant before saying very positively, "No, I did not. Armand, I think he should not have followed the family's wishes. I hate Félicité!"

"Why?"

"She is very . . . proper. Always she is going to mass. Always she is very right; always she is telling people how they are very wrong. I was not sad, mademoiselle, when Félicité left."

"Why did she move away?"

"Félicité, she was angry when Armand died."

"Angry?"

"Because of the money, mademoiselle. After the marriage of many years she expects to be very, very rich. But how? It was my father who was rich, not Armand. Félicité was in a fury with the Saint-Clouds. Her family is rich and powerful, too, and they also were very angry. They even took Luc to court. Is that not bad, to think so much of money when a husband dies? Especially when Félicité is not even a little bit poor and has no children to think of? She said she did not wish to see a Saint-Cloud again in all her life. She moved back to Rennes."

As soon as possible Tory returned to the topic of Luc. She gleaned a little more information, some of it new, some of it only confirmation of things she already knew or guessed. In his life Luc had traveled a lot, and he had always spent a fair amount of time at sea. As he had told Tory, he had returned to live at the Château d'Ys only after the family tragedy that had left him, as the sole surviving male, head of the

Saint-Cloud clan and heir to all its fortunes. As far as Tory could gather—and she could phrase her questions only indirectly—he had never brought a female to stay at the Château d'Ys, except Tory herself. Nothing she learned confirmed Luc's involvement with Laura, but nothing denied it, either.

Finally, when she had lingered on the topic of Luc as long as she dared, she went on to the equally tricky subject of Aimée's cloistered upbringing. She didn't wish to cast aspersions on Aimée's mother, so she approached the subject obliquely. "You must miss having young people around, Aimée. Did you never have playmates when you were little?"

"Oh, yes. The sons and daughters of people who came to visit. Friends like Jacques, yes? Oh, it was good then! But now they come no more. And I . . ." Something unhappy crossed Aimée's face, and she began to poke at the sand. "Myself, for some years I do not leave this place."

Tory again risked a direct question. "Why not?"

"Because Mama will not permit it." Restlessly Aimée's eyes turned to the sea. Her arms gripped her knees tightly, as if she were trying to hang on to herself. "Sometimes, when I see a boat passing in the distance, I think I will have to swim out and escape that way."

"That sounds a little desperate. Are things so bad?"

"Bad?" Aimée moaned. "Have you not seen how it is at the Château d'Ys? There should be strong men to help, but instead there are only two servants who are not female. Of the two, one is near seventy and the other is already some years past that age. Since I started to change from a little girl to the shape of a woman, it has been so."

Tory murmured an ambiguous "Oh?"

Aimée shot her a look. "Can you not think what Mama is afraid of?"

"I imagine she doesn't want you to meet any young men. I guessed as much, because of Jacques."

"You guessed? But I think, mademoiselle, you still do not understand Mama, or me." Aimée's voice was very embittered for one so young.

"You're still young, Aimée," Tory said gently. "I imagine your mother doesn't want you to fall in love and get married, at least not yet. She probably feels you're all she has left. I can sympathize, because I understand—"

"No, you do not!" Aimée cast an agonized look in Tory's direction and jumped to her feet, her young body tense with feverish adolescent anguish. Her words tumbled out.

"You do not understand Mama at all! She does want me to marry! Since I am thirteen, she talks of nothing else! She counts the days to when I turn eighteen, when the time will come that I am old enough for a man to ask!"

"But I don't see—"

"Can you not understand *who* she intends me to marry? Who is the one man I am allowed to see?" Aimée paused dramatically, leaving the question to tremble in the air. "A man who will not even kiss me or hold my hand, because he is too old and I am too young! A man who treats me like a little child!"

"Luc?" Tory guessed in a whisper.

"Yes, Luc! *Mon oncle!*"

"And he . . ." Tory's voice was very jerky as she asked, "Is he . . . willing?"

"Of course he is! Of course he must be! It is his duty! It is not from love that he will marry me, but for the sake of the Saint-Cloud name. For the sake of the children we make together!"

"I didn't . . . know," whispered Tory.

"And Mama will not rest until I do as she asks. Why do you think she so often tells the story of Dahut? She is not telling it to you. She is telling it to me!"

Explosively, to express what she thought about marrying the man she thought of as an uncle, a man more than twice her age and nearly twenty years her senior, Aimée raced toward the sea wearing her tank top and shorts and dived in. Tory just sat, numb with realization.

Luc and Aimée. A match arranged many years before, and awaiting only the time when Aimée turned eighteen. That was reason enough for any man to keep a marriage secret.

Luc and Aimée.

Luc and Laura . . .

Tory thought she was going to be ill.

Chapter Eight

Tory lived in a purgatory for the next few days. On Monday morning, as she set out for Carnac with Luc, she was still tied in anguishing internal knots. Earlier in the acquaintance, when she had thought her reactions due only to sexual tension, she had been able to cope with Luc on some level, usually that of anger and antagonism. But now she was barely capable of exchanging two rational words. Aimée's revelations had convinced her that Luc must have been married to Laura, but the knowledge had come too late. During that long night of doubt, when Tory had decided he might not be the man in Laura's life, she had allowed herself to admit that she was in love, and once that realization had been reached there was no going back. She *was* in love. If Luc had been Bluebeard himself, married to a whole succession of wives and all of them Tory's own sisters, it wouldn't have changed that feeling. He flowed in her heart, as necessary as its beat, as essential as its blood, as vital as its muscle. To excise the pain of loving, she would have to excise her heart.

She had other reasons to writhe. She was sorry she had ever delivered the note from Jacques Benoit, and even sorrier she had promised to return Aimée's answer. It was one thing to promote an innocent young romance, but quite another to interfere when Luc was involved. She had tried to return the note to Aimée, telling her she would prefer not to deliver it after all. Aimée's face had taken on some of the harder character of her mother's. "You promised, mademoiselle," she had reminded Tory, her chin stubborn and her young voice tight.

So at the end of the previous week Tory had delivered the note—but at the same time she had told Jacques Benoit the messenger service was to be discontinued. "I want no more to do with it," she had said. "I'm sure Madame Saint-Cloud has her reasons. Why don't you wait for a little while? Aimée will be eighteen in less than a year—an adult. Then she won't be so subject to her mother's wishes. Besides, if you're patient, Madame Saint-Cloud may change her mind."

Madame Saint-Cloud most certainly would change her mind, reflected Tory unhappily, when she discovered Luc was already married. Oh, God, how had she managed to get herself emotionally entangled in such a mess?

It was a long drive to Carnac, well more than two hours along the southern motor routes of the Brittany peninsula. They had covered no more than five minutes of it, enough to take them a short distance past the gates of the Château d'Ys, when Luc pulled the car off the side of the road, switched off the ignition, and jerked on the handbrake. He turned to face Tory, his eyes hard as flint.

"Now do you mind telling me what this is all about? Yesterday and the day before both, you pleaded headaches and exhaustion when I suggested getting to work on our project. Considering the story I gave Tante Marie about urgency, that sort of excuse doesn't wash too well."

Unconsciously Tory cringed a little further away from him, her eyes wide and her heart beating harder.

Luc raked his long fingers through his hair, a gesture of frustration. "What *is* the matter with you? What happened to the female who lashed me with her tongue and attacked me with her fists? Today you're like a scared rabbit!"

"Because you're married to Laura," Tory burst out. "You're really married."

He frowned at her, puzzled. "And what's new about that contention? You've been attacking me with it for days. Usually, I might add, with a little more spunk and spirit. What's changed?"

Tory swallowed hard and looked away, her eyes anguished. "I found out the reason you kept the marriage secret. Why you didn't tell the Saint-Clouds at the time."

"Please don't keep me in the dark," Luc said sarcastically. "I should hate to be the last to know."

"Aimée," said Tory.

"Aimée? What's she got to do with it?"

"Your arrangement to marry her."

Luc took his time about answering, a faint frown

creasing his brow before he did. "The arrangement at the moment is nonexistent," he said dryly. "Aimée hasn't agreed. And although her mother would like me to proceed, I haven't actually asked Aimée in so many words. I've promised to do so, yes—but I refuse to do it before she comes of age."

Tory's eyes turned back to him, ravaged by emotion. "But you can't deny you've been prepared to marry her, and for some years!"

Luc's face was darkly quiet, his eyes steady. "No," he said evenly, "I don't deny that."

"It's a terrible way to bring up a young girl! Hiding her away just so, so you can—"

His voice was dangerously still as he said, "So I can what?"

"She's only an inexperienced girl . . . a *virgin* . . ."

It wasn't until those agonized and unthought words tumbled out that Tory recognized the truth of the terrible feelings that had been wracking her over the weekend. Must the ghosts of her own past always affect her reactions to Luc?

"If you want to get angry at someone about that, get angry at my aunt." Luc's voice was very controlled. "I'm not Aimée's parent and I'm not her guardian. I've argued until I'm blue in the face, but the fact of the matter is, I have no say whatsoever in her upbringing. Why do you think I insist on holding off until Aimée's eighteen? Because then she'll be an adult and her mother won't have control. I intend to make quite sure the child sees something of the world—*and* other men—before she makes up her mind."

Tory subsided and calmed a little, conscious that she was making a fool of herself, allowing too much of her shakiness to show. Luc was watching her closely and he had a capacity for reading her feelings, had had from the start. When she spoke again her voice was still strained, but more controlled. "I know you're not marrying Aimée out of love, because you told me you loved no woman as you love the sea. It's a family arrangement, isn't it? Just as Armand's marriage was a family arrangement."

"I don't deny that either." It took him only a moment to understand her circuitous line of reasoning. His eyes glittered angrily in the moment of realization. "I suppose you've jumped to the conclusion that this agreement goes back to the years when Aimée was hardly more than a toddler? And that's why I kept some other marriage secret? That's arrant nonsense. If you're going to play amateur detective, hadn't you better ask me the truth of the situation?"

Tory's lips felt wooden, her facial muscles rigid with the effort of concealing her feelings. She was torn apart inside, no longer thinking of Laura but only of herself. "What is . . . the truth of the situation?"

"Tante Marie wants me to marry Aimée. I feel an obligation to do so, in order to return what I owe to the Saint-Cloud family. My uncle's will was oddly phrased—he provided support for the women, but left the bulk of his estate to his closest surviving male heir. He wrote that will sixteen years ago when Armand married, and he never meant the estate to go to me. He meant it to go to his son or his son's sons. Armand's dead, and his marriage produced no children. And so the estate came to me—a distant cousin, and not even a legal Saint-Cloud at that. Yes, my father was a member of the clan, but he didn't marry my mother. I'm a bastard Saint-Cloud, and I shouldn't be robbing the hand that fed me. Don't you see the position I'm in?"

Luc waited until Tory nodded, misery making it hard for her to speak. "I have no right to the Saint-Cloud fortune, and I can't even return it, because my uncle wrote in safeguards so that the estate couldn't possibly be handed over to Tante Marie or Aimée. Don't ask me why! Perhaps he felt women weren't capable of running the Saint-Cloud enterprises. I'm returning what I can, in the only way I can, by agreeing to marry Aimée, if she'll have me. Eventually, if she does, the Saint-Cloud estates will return where they belong—to her children and her children's children. When I marry her—and not before!—I'll take the Saint-Cloud name, as my aunt wishes me to do. If Aimée marries someone else, it should be that man who changes his name legally to Saint-Cloud. Does that answer all your wild accusations? Yes, there is an arrangement, but it dates only from some months after my uncle's death. In other words, *after* my amnesia. Eight years ago the arrangement simply did—not—exist!"

Tory felt like a tightrope walker badly shaken by a near miss, halfway along a very long wire. She put her head into her hands and started to cry quietly, not a full relief of tension because there were still too many dangers, too many chances to slip from the narrow line of safety before any haven was reached. She would have preferred to hold back the slow tears, but she couldn't help herself. After the past few days she was not in good emotional shape.

"Tory . . ."

Luc's low groan was hardly more than a whisper. As he uttered it he reached for her. He pulled her gently against his chest and held her there. He didn't ask why she was crying and he didn't tell her to stop. His language was the language of true comfort, for he didn't talk at all. His arms enfolded her. His hand moved over her hair, stroking it slowly and with no passion. There was nothing erotic in the embrace, only the consoling personal contact, a fortress against trouble, a bulwark against pain. In a time of sore need, he offered strength and understanding to help Tory through, and he demanded no explanations in return.

And yet she knew he knew. He hadn't been told all the reasons for her inner tumult, but he knew the tumult was there. He was calming her, soothing her, telling her it was all right to feel the way she did. His message seeped through her pores, just as her messages must have seeped through his. Luc knew what was wrong.

And there, against the warm wall of him, enclosed by his arms, with his mouth at her temples and his hand gradually becoming still against her hair, peace stole slowly into Tory's soul. The tears stopped. She knew she was safe. The tightrope had been traveled, and she had reached her haven already. She knew she loved him and always would, but she also knew she had strength to resist the tidal pull of sexual attraction as long as there remained the slightest chance of Luc being married to Laura.

And she knew, with no words spoken, that even if she were weak, Luc would be strong.

As simple understanding slowly grew, she began to know the man he was, and not the man she had imagined in her mind. He hadn't changed. He was the man who had allowed her to drum him with her angry fists; the man who had been patient and sometimes driven to impatience; the man who had been at times sympathetic and at times humanly angry; the man she loved. He was a man with faults and foibles and virtues, too, a man it was not so terrible to feel this way about. He hadn't changed, but she had. She knew him now.

In time, when she was ready, she extricated herself from his undemanding embrace and returned to her own place in the car. Her tears had been absorbed into the fabric of his shirt, and there was no need to wipe away the little glistening moisture that might remain. "I'll survive," she said, her mouth trembling into a smile.

Luc searched her face for a long moment, his mouth grave and his eyes very sober. "Yes, I believe you will," he muttered.

He started the car and edged it back onto the gravel, his concentration returning to the road and the rock-strewn, enduring land. On Tory's side, stretching far into the distance, lay the broad horizon of the sea, unruffled in the sunshine of a calm, pure day. She watched it, feeling humble and oddly content. There had been no overt statement of desire in Luc's arms or in his dark eyes. And yet, for the first time in many, many years, she knew herself to be truly desired, not just because she was a woman, but because she was herself.

They talked a little during the long drive to Carnac, not as enemies but as valued and respected friends. Tory knew she would never again need the armor of antagonism, that defense of former days. She trusted Luc and she trusted herself, and she knew nothing would happen to cause her to be unable to live with herself. Exactly why that faith and absolute certainty had come to her she was not sure; but come it had, during those moments of unarousing closeness. The intense internal upheavals of a hopeless love had fired Tory in some sort of emotional crucible, and although the pain had been great, she sensed that in some way she had emerged a stronger person.

There were long silences, too, comfortable ones. During them Tory's eyes rested on the passing, peaceful countryside of Brittany. She thought about all the same things she had been thinking about for days, but with a difference. She was calm, and she accepted.

In an odd way she felt as if she had completed the process of becoming an adult since meeting Luc. Her marriage had damaged her image of herself at a crucial time, when she had been emerging into womanhood. It had arrested some part of her development, robbed her of essential confidence in her own desirability. It had destroyed her trust in men. It had left her reason warring with her emotions and instincts, so that although men had sometimes wanted her, she had always felt unwanted. She had become incapable of believing that any man would have any real interest in her. Luc, with his grave gray eyes and his undemanding hands, had told her without words and without caresses that what she had believed simply was not true. He desired her, and the desire had no physical goal, and Tory was at rest with herself.

She understood Luc now. No matter what they might discover in Carnac or in the days to come, there was no place for her in his life. If it turned out that he wasn't Laura's husband, there was still Aimée. Luc was an honorable man, and provided Aimée consented, he would honor his promises. Tory couldn't say why she knew this to be true, but she knew it was so.

And Aimée . . . Aimée might give in to her mother's pressure at any time, or she might resist for years. If allowed freedom at any point, she might very well become involved in a romance with Jacques Benoit or some other young man. Tory sensed that Luc would simply stand by, and watch, and wait. He would bide his time for years if necessary. Unless Aimée actually married someone else, he would never be a free man.

And even if he were free, there was still the sea, his first love, his abiding love, his great love.

Tory thought about these things, and understood them, and accepted.

The little inn where Laura had stayed eight years before looked as though it had seen no changes for a century. Constructed of granite and slate, the enduring building materials of Brittany, it nestled amidst long grasses overlooking a quiet blue cove—a "family beach," as the guidebooks fondly called such economy *pensions*. It was within bicycling distance of the Carnac megaliths, on the picturesque west shore of the Quiberon Peninsula, a location less expensive than the touristy town of Carnac. With its coves and grottoes, the shoreline was jagged and impressive, but despite the name of Côte Sauvage, not as bleak as the promontory guarded by the Château d'Ys. Perhaps the word "savage" applied to the strong tidal currents. At every turn signs said *Baignades Interdites*. "No swimming," someone had translated during Tory's previous visit to this place.

The keepers of the inn, a man and wife of comfortable years, had owned the place for three decades. It catered for the most part to French families. As fewer

English tourists patronized the place, the owners spoke only a little of the language, and that quite brokenly. But Tory had managed to communicate during her short former visit, when she had stayed overnight and had been allowed to examine the hotel register.

They both remembered Tory from her former visit and greeted her warmly. At the time, Tory had provided them with a missing person story, an easy excuse that didn't call for too much explanation. The couple had been very helpful. Both observant by nature, they had recalled Laura's face from her photograph. Without being told, they had placed her as one of a group of bicyclists and remembered that she had stayed on when the rest of her party had left. If Laura had become involved with any man during her stay, it must have been discreet, for the proprietors were unaware of it, although they appeared to have excellent memories for other small details. They had also located the name Devereux in old registers, but in that regard they had been less helpful, claiming they had little memory for names. They had not remembered that Laura and Luc Devereux had signed out on the same day, a fact confirmed by the register.

Tory explained that she was still looking for information about her sister. In hopes that French might produce clues missed in English conversation, she said, she had brought with her a friend who had agreed to help in the search. She didn't introduce Luc by name.

The proprietress offered Tory a cup of tea, and she accepted. Trusting Luc now, she left him to talk to the man of the establishment. As the conversation would be conducted in French, she wasn't going to understand it in any case. She went with the woman to a large, homey, old-fashioned kitchen that smelled of newly baked bread. The woman had also been making butter, and on the scrubbed wooden table there was a huge bowl of it, creamy and fresh from the churn. Nothing, Tory had discovered weeks ago, tasted quite like the butter of Brittany. The wonderful wafting of smells piqued her appetite, the first time in many days that food had tempted her at all.

It took Luc quite a time to finish with his questions. By then, because it was already past noon, Tory had negotiated the purchase of a simple picnic lunch and even helped to put it together—fruit, cold chicken, slabs of local cheese, and a bottle of *vin ordinaire* having been added to the warm, fragrant bread and new butter.

After emerging from the kitchen, Tory told Luc about the picnic and suggested they take it to the site of Carnac, which she was curious to see. She didn't wish to question him about other matters in front of the innkeepers, so before broaching those she waited until they had emerged into the sunshine. "What did you find out?" she asked, halting in her tracks now that they were alone.

"Nothing much. I'd prefer to do some thinking about it before we talk." Luc's evasive reply caused Tory to stop stock-still and look at him more closely. There was a grim white line around his mouth, and that throb of a tiny muscle in his temple, near his scar. By now she was aware that those things signaled stress.

"Did you recognize your signature?" she asked, realizing in that moment the reason for some degree of her inner calmness throughout the car ride. During the flow of tears that morning a subconscious part of Tory had decided that Luc would not have been capable of hurting a woman as Laura must have been hurt.

"I told you, I'm not ready to discuss it."

"Luc, I want to know now." Tory's voice was perfectly steady and so were her nerves. The calmness was still there, a sense of fatality that allowed her to accept even what she might not like to hear. Whatever Luc had found out—and she was certain he had found out something—it had not been good. And what wasn't good for Luc wasn't good for her, for it must mean he now had reason to believe he'd been involved with Laura.

He held her with dark, unfathomable eyes. "Trust me," he said in an even voice.

Tory did trust him, but she still needed to know. In the enigmatic set of his face, she saw that he didn't intend to tell her anything. Tory placed her hand on the inn door. "If you won't tell me exactly what you found out in there, I'll ask for myself. I have to know, Luc, for once and for all."

His hesitation was so slight it might have been no hesitation at all. "There's no need to continue the search. I'll accept responsibility for your sister."

"Is that all the answer you're going to give me?"

"That's answer enough for now."

Without another word Tory turned and went back into the inn. Luc neither followed nor tried to stop her, and so he was not at her side when she approached the alcove fronted by a plain built-in desk of darkly smoked wood, with a small office occupying the space behind. The innkeeper was bent on his knees behind the desk, restoring the old records to their pigeonholes. He rose, smiling pleasantly, as Tory approached.

"Thank you so much for helping," she said. "It's lucky my friend recognized the signature."

"Pardon? But, mademoiselle, he does not. Or, if he does, he does not say this to me."

"Please, do you mind going through what my friend said to you? He told me quickly, but I'd like to hear it all from you before we leave. I want to make sure he didn't forget to ask any important questions."

"Questions? Most questions, I have no answer. But he ask about Belle-Île-en-Mer, and that is when I remember."

"Belle-Île?"

"Oui, mademoiselle, it is . . . island, *n'est-ce pas?* Very close."

And a week before, Luc had asked Tory if it meant something to her. What did it mean to Luc?

Tory was in a state of suspension, hanging on the innkeeper's answers. "And that's when you remembered the important part?"

"Most certainly, mademoiselle. Me, I have trouble to remember a name, but I do not forget the face, and when your friend speaks of the new . . ." Forgetting the word, he stroked his chin to indicate his meaning.

"Beard," Tory guessed.

"No, not beard, but—the hair of a week, yes? When he speaks of that I start to think a little. But still I do not know if I remember. In many years there are other men who do not shave on holiday. But in my head it is not only faces that remain. I do not forget what . . . happen, the things people say when they talk. When your friend speaks of Belle-Île, I know him at once, this man Devereux."

Tory's internal calmness stood her in good stead. "Then you did recognize my friend after all," she concluded.

"Your friend?" The innkeeper looked surprised. "*Mais non, mademoiselle.* Do I mix the English, when I speak? I have never seen your friend before, in all of my life. Of that I am most sure. It is the man Devereux I remember, the man who came to here from Belle-Île. And that is not your friend!"

Chapter Nine

Tory kept her thoughts to herself until she and Luc had reached the site of Carnac and carried their picnic to a place well removed from the wanderings of sightseers. And even then she simply sat for some minutes, matching Luc's silence with her own, soaking up the warmth of the sun and the serenity of the quiet day. There was no tension to be released, because she had released it all some hours before. Her feelings were simple, and they could be described in one word. Peace.

The timelessness of very great age pervaded the place, and although no words were spoken, Tory had a sense of communion with Luc. She had not visited Carnac before, but she had read about it and needed to ask no questions. Scrubby grasses covered the flat heath between the great menhirs, the rows of mysterious long stones erected by a lost Celtic civilization.

The tall megaliths had been raised on end so many centuries before that the very reason for their existence was lost to antiquity, left to the guesses of scholars. On some of them, conquering Romans had chiseled drawings and inscriptions, and the stones had been old even then. Some bore marks of the Middle Ages, when men of religion, seeing the stones still venerated by superstitious Bretons, had crowned them with crosses and carved them with Christian symbols.

And yet, although there had been changes, one sensed that nothing much had changed. Centuries had come and gone, Romans had come and gone, the Middle Ages had come and gone, but in these megalithic monuments remained the strength and continuity of the mystic, simple Celts, earliest forebears of the Breton people.

Because Tory and Luc had not come for sightseeing, they had avoided one of the more popular sights, the immense Tumulus of Saint-Michel with its burial chambers and tunnels. Instead they were near Mênec, where over a thousand of the tallest prehistoric stones were aligned in regular columns that stretched more than a mile toward the horizon, an awesome vista. They leaned their backs against one of the time-eaten granite slabs and allowed the sun to warm their faces. Tory was happy. It was a quiet, bittersweet happiness, because it contained no selfish hopes for her own future. If she had had to express the reason for her happiness, she would have said simply that she was glad it wasn't Luc who had destroyed Laura.

"You weren't going to tell me a thing," she said at last.

"I told you as much as you need to know."

"There's no reason you have to assume responsibility for Laura."

Luc reached for the picnic, which had been packed in paper bags so that no hamper would have to be returned to the inn. "All the same, I plan to do exactly that. Shall I pour you some wine?"

Tory accepted some in one of the plastic cups that had been provided. "Do you have some idea who the man might have been?"

"How do you know it wasn't me? A beard changes a man's appearance, and so does a scar."

"The innkeeper would know that. He has a good memory for faces and he was positive he didn't know yours. The man Laura met didn't have a beard, just a stubble from not shaving, and that wouldn't hide features."

"And for those silly little reasons you've decided it's not me?" he scoffed.

"How odd you are. For the first time I'm absolutely convinced it wasn't you, and you're trying to put doubts in my mind."

"How perverse you are. For the first time I'm prepared to accept that your sister is my responsibility, and you're trying to deny that she is."

Tory merely smiled at him contentedly. Seduced by the languor of the day and the serenity that had seeped into her soul, she didn't wish to argue with Luc about anything at all. She reached for the bag containing their food. For a time they occupied their mouths without talk, wiping buttery fingers on the grass, returning the chicken bones to the emptied paper bag, washing great chunks of the fresh bread down with draughts of robust wine.

"How did you know to ask about Belle-Île?"

Luc shrugged. "Just because it's quite near. As your sister left here on a yacht, I thought she might have visited the place."

"But the man wasn't going there, he'd come from there. Do you know someone from Belle-Île?"

"Offhand I can't think of a soul."

"Do you think they may have been married on Belle-Île?"

"Who knows? There are other places one can sail to easily enough from the Quiberon Peninsula. A man of my inclination might have chosen to go to England, to Portugal . . ."

"Luc," Tory pleaded, "don't try to mislead me. I know you weren't married to Laura. Are you trying to protect some other man?"

"Please don't jump to conclusions. When I reach some myself, I'll let you know. For the moment the only thing you need to know is that your sister will be taken care of. So will the boy. More than that, I just can't discuss."

"But—"

Luc turned until he was facing her directly. In his steadfast eyes there was a promise, but there was also a grim warning. Tory was not to talk about it anymore.

"If you have any faith in me at all," he said quietly, "you'll leave the matter in my hands from now on. As far as you're concerned, Tory, it's over, it's done. I want you to stop thinking about it altogether. You've accomplished what you came to Brittany to accomplish. Do you still trust me so little that you have to pin me down with hard evidence? I started trusting you long ago, that first night in Quimper, or I wouldn't have even started this whole investigation. Isn't it time you returned the trust?"

Tory held her breath for a second. "I already do," she said, exhaling. There was relief in leaving it all to Luc. It was the same secure feeling she had had earlier in the morning, the sense of reaching safe harbor after troubled waters. She thought he must know or guess who had been married to Laura, but perhaps he wished to accuse no one without hard proof.

"Then let's not talk about your sister anymore. Agreed?"

"Agreed."

Luc eased himself into a prone position, stretching full length on the grass and leaving the backrest of the granite slab to Tory. Earlier he had shed his suit jacket and she had shed her sweater. Grass pricked at her stockinged legs and the granite was hard against her spine, but she was comfortable and content just watching Luc.

She was utterly aware of him, of the virile power, of the long muscular legs and the easy grace of his lean hard thighs, but with her new frame of mind the sensations he evoked were no longer troubling ones. Knowing he wasn't married to Laura, had never been married to Laura, she could gaze at him without constraint. She saw him and loved what she saw—loved the man himself and not just the physical presence of the man. But she wanted him physically, too, and no longer hated herself for wanting.

"I'd like to hear about you." Luc was looking at her, too, a quiet look that had nothing to do with desire. Tory couldn't read the expression on his mouth, but it filled her with warmth. Today she felt her whole world had been set to rights, and that look in Luc's face had something to do with the feeling. "I want to know about your marriage. Why don't you ever talk about it?"

For once, the mention didn't cause a tightening of Tory's chest. "A lot of reasons. For one, I don't like to speak ill of the dead."

"He died? Is that how the marriage ended?"

"No. He died a year later."

"Tell me about it," Luc directed quietly.

For a moment Tory felt as if her lips wouldn't move. And then, almost of their own volition, they began to. She closed her eyes, feeling the sun warm and gentle on her lids, a balm to old hurts. She had struggled so long to keep the past to herself, but she no longer wanted to struggle. "It can hardly be called a marriage. It lasted only ten days."

She had told the whole truth of the story to no one, not even her parents, but she found herself telling it now. She felt she had known Luc for a very long time. In a strange way she had been bonded to him for years by the bonds of hatred, and now there were newer and even stronger bonds, the bonds of love and trust. Circumstances had created a depth to the relationship that years of acquaintance might not have done. Perhaps, too, the weeks of truth-seeking had left Tory with a need to remove some of the veils from her own past, and not just Laura's.

"I was very young when I married Griff Rammell. I had just turned nineteen . . ."

And a very young nineteen at that. During adolescence she had been awkward with the opposite sex. Reliving that time, Tory opened her eyes and began the story at the beginning, because without the beginning the end made no sense.

"When we were growing up, Laura and I, our friends had a nickname for us. Beauty and the Brain. Need I tell you which nickname was mine? Yes, I had lots of friends, but Laura was the really pretty one. I wasn't quite sure of myself around boys, partly because they never looked at me when Laura was around. I think I was a little shy."

She told Luc a little more about those feelings, which hadn't made her too insecure at the time. Tory had had some strengths that Laura, lovely will-o'-the-wisp Laura, hadn't had. Tory had been the dependable twin, the one who tidied more than her share of the bedroom and tended to take more than her share of the blame for youthful infractions. Laura had often escaped punishment by taking refuge in tears, and because she'd had psychiatric problems all through her growing years, their parents hadn't been overly harsh. Laura had always had difficulties adjusting to the realities of life, a tendency to fall apart when things didn't go well. Without labeling Laura's problem, the psychiatrist had spoken vaguely of the symptoms of manic depression. A broken possession, a failed exam, a lost boyfriend—these things had crushed her easily all through youth, and she didn't rebound at once. Yet when all went well with Laura, she was effervescent, giddily happy, unfailingly popular.

Tory had been less flighty, more retiring around the opposite sex, more given to quietness and introspection. She seldom shone at a party, but she always shone in her studies. That had given her confidence and status of a sort, but not with boys.

"In high school Laura and I both knew Griff Rammell, and although he was quite a few years older, Laura went out with him a few times. I . . . I had a hopeless crush on him. I didn't outgrow it, as I might have done if I'd been more outgoing. Now I can't understand why I thought he was so wonderful—I must have been wearing blinkers. Griff was tall, very charming, very good looking, very sure of himself. He was considered the town catch. His family was very rich and also socially prominent. They owned a department store, a large one. What Griff wanted, he usually got, and it seems that what he wanted most of all was to initiate young girls, the prettier the better. To Griff, I wasn't worth bothering with . . . just another pair of calf eyes. I saw his charm at work on Laura and was sick because it wasn't at work on me. Griff knew I was mooning over him, but other than that I might have been part of the furniture.

"Then Laura went to Europe and I went to college. By that time Griff was long out of school and well into learning the family business. He had started at the bottom—for about one day—and already he had a big title, sales promotion manager or some such thing. When I came home for the Christmas holidays, I took a job as temporary sales help at his family's store, during the seasonal rush. Griff began another kind of rush, probably out of boredom. By then he'd sampled most of the local talent, and he was getting a little too old to be seen around town with the younger teenagers. He wanted some new amusement, and he decided I was worth his while after all. He thought it would be easy."

"But it wasn't." Luc's quiet prompting came after Tory had spent a silent moment with her bitter memories.

She sighed. "No, it wasn't. Perhaps he would have succeeded if he'd started the pursuit sooner, but by the time I went to college I was mature enough to recognize some of the truth about Griff—that he always discarded girl friends as soon as he'd had his way. God knows, I'd watched him in operation often enough, lovesick idiot that I was. What he couldn't have, he always wanted, and what he had, he didn't want anymore. I should have been warier, but he was so damn attractive, so dangerous. . . .

"It's funny about men like Griff. He couldn't believe he couldn't talk me into bed. I think I was . . . an insult to his image of himself. He couldn't understand me, especially when I'd been wearing my heart on my sleeve since the ridiculous age of sixteen or thereabouts. And at nineteen it was still out there for all the world to see. Even though I understood that Griff's interest was purely in the chase, the way I felt about him just . . . spilled out of my eyes. I couldn't help myself. I was desperately in love, adolescent love maybe, but it seemed real enough at the time. And I wasn't very good at hiding my feelings."

"You still aren't," Luc said, his voice a little gruff. Perhaps he was thinking about the way Tory had attacked him physically on the first day of their acquaintance.

"When Griff didn't succeed in sweeping me off my feet after a few days, he proposed. No doubt he thought a proposal would be enough to bring about instant surrender. But I . . . I knew he'd tried the same thing on other girls. He'd been engaged before, but never for more than a few days. The engagements always ended when Griff succeeded. For the price of a ring, he had nearly always managed to buy himself what he couldn't get any other way. So he bought me a ring. It didn't work quite as he hoped. You see, I was wearing blinkers, but I wasn't completely blind. I didn't want to be dropped."

"And so he married you."

"Yes, although in retrospect I wish I'd just given in," Tory said wearily. There was a note of bitterness in her voice. "I was naive enough to think that marriage might change a man, and I guess I was flattered that he actually intended to take the big step. I thought maybe I *was* different from all the others, as he kept telling me. We eloped on New Year's Eve, at his insistence. It was a whirlwind thing. He didn't even tell his parents at the time, although I told mine at the last minute, for I wanted them to know I wouldn't be returning to college. They were startled, but they didn't try to talk me out of it. They just . . . hugged me and wished me luck and cried a little."

There was a great stillness in Luc's outstretched body. He had raised himself on one elbow to listen to Tory's story, absorbed but not intruding on the progression of her thoughts, except when her words seemed to falter.

"Griff's family owned a small ski lodge several miles from Aspen, on a remote private road. It was well stocked with food and seldom in use—except, I found out later, when Griff used it as a lovenest. He took me there for our honeymoon, the long New Year's weekend."

"And?"

"We were snowed in for longer than that. It was ten days before that little back road was finally cleared, so that's exactly how long the marriage lasted. Ten days. When we got back to town, Griff dropped me off at my parents' home and said he'd be in touch later in the day. It didn't seem extraordinary at the time, because I knew he had to hurry to work—he'd missed a whole week because of the snowstorm. Also, I thought he would want to pave the way by telling his parents about what he had done. I spent the morning pacing my bedroom floor, wondering what to do, wondering if it might begin to work out if I tried very hard."

Tory had dropped a clue in her words, and Luc homed in on it immediately. "*Begin* to work out? That sounds as though the honeymoon hadn't gone too well."

Tory studied Luc's hands, for the first time avoiding his eyes. It wasn't easy to tell this part. "It didn't," she admitted reluctantly. "The first night, he told me I was a rotten . . . partner." Griff's hurtful comment had been considerably more explicit than that, but to repeat it verbatim would have involved a crude vocabulary Tory didn't use. "After that I couldn't enjoy the rest of the honeymoon too much."

She could see Luc's fingers flexing murderously and could imagine what he was thinking. She thought it herself. Griff Rammell had been overly arrogant about his sexual prowess, in the way of a man used to too much gratification. Marriage to someone not in his own social strata had been very high on the list of things he hadn't wanted. He had deeply resented Tory's failure to succumb without that distasteful step, and he had vented some of his resentment by accusing her of a different failure altogether.

Tory knew Griff hadn't lied. She *had* failed, and although reason told her it wasn't entirely her fault, she had been deeply mortified and hurt. On first taking her, Griff had been interested in his own satisfaction, not hers. Although she lacked experience, he had initiated her crudely and with no care whatsoever. There had been no helping through the hurt, no tenderness, no attempt to use the techniques of arousal he had employed during the whirlwind courtship.

And during the ten days of lovemaking that had followed, he had been no more considerate. During that long snowbound spell spent indoors, there had been more times than Tory cared to remember. Griff had claimed that her failure to please left him with unsatisfied needs, and that was very clearly the case. At first Tory had responded to some degree, even though she had been filled with a great sickness about her own ineptitude. But she had married him, hadn't she? And she had felt she ought to try. Each time Griff had rewarded her with small cruelties, sometimes during the act of love. She was unskilled; she was awkward; she was not passionate enough; she was too shy about displaying her body; she was too hesitant to do the erotic things that would stimulate a man. Her breasts were too small and her hips too slim and he wished to God she would get that wounded doe look out of her eyes. To sum up, she was boring in bed, and the only reason he wanted her there so often was that she was even more boring when she was out of it. If there'd been another female available, he wouldn't have bothered with Tory, especially as she had started to freeze whenever he touched her. If she didn't want him to touch her, why in hell had she driven him into marriage in the first place?

By the end of the ten days Tory had been in misery, sure that she had no attractions of any kind. Despite the forced freezing with which she had started to greet his advances, she had still reacted unwillingly to Griff's physical attributes. She had hated him, and feared her responses to him, and been sickened with herself for feeling anything at all when he touched her.

She could not tell all this to Luc.

"The honeymoon was a dismal failure," she said, in a very considerable understatement. She cast her eyes to the cloudless sky. In thinking of Griff, the sense of peace had deserted her, and it showed in the restlessness on her face, in the evasiveness of her eyes. She added in an aching voice, "It's true, I wasn't very good in bed."

Luc came to a sitting position, his body tense with contained anger. "I don't believe that. The first time—"

"And every other time."

"If there were other times, then he must have enjoyed something about making love to you!" The tightness of Luc's voice betrayed powerful emotion, as if he had read between the lines and knew many things she hadn't told him.

"I don't think so. He told me over and over that I was a rotten failure."

"Over and over!" Luc exploded. "My God, how often did the brute satisfy himself at your expense, without taking the trouble to arouse you? Doesn't it occur to you the *man* can be at fault? From everything I've heard so far, I'd guess that Griff Rammell was selfish and spoiled. He was punishing you because he had wanted you badly enough to marry you. And perhaps for having a little fastidiousness! If you weren't responding properly, then what the man did to you is little better than rape."

"It wasn't rape," Tory said dully. "I consented. But he made me feel . . . rejected. Undesirable."

"Undesirable . . ." Luc's harsh little laugh was devoid of humor. "How can you think that? For one thing, it's obvious that that . . . excuse for a man desired a very great deal more than he deserved to get." He added between his teeth, *"Mon Dieu! Quel bâtard."*

Tory's eyes returned to Luc's, calming a little as they did. "I know that," she said, "but I couldn't help how I felt."

Rationally Tory knew she wasn't unattractive. She knew she wasn't cold. She knew she would have responded with the passion Griff wanted if his verbal cruelties and callous self-centeredness in lovemaking had not been so destructive to desire. She knew much of the blame for her wretched introduction to sex could be laid at Griff's door. But knowing something rationally didn't always allow one to change one's emotional makeup, and since her marriage, Tory had never been sure of herself with men.

"Go on," Luc said in a grim voice after a minute. "You spoke about being home with your parents, wondering what would happen next. That was the same day your sister, Laura, arrived home in bad shape?"

"Yes, but not until later in the day. First . . ." Tory laid her head against the old stone. For a few moments the muscles of her throat worked. Even now, so many years later, that scene still seemed so clear, so close, so painful.

"What happened?"

Tory swallowed hard. She found Luc's eyes again, and something she saw there, a kind of anger, made the rest of the story easier to tell. Her emotions were usually transparent, but for the moment her voice was flat and completely toneless. "Griff had said he would be in touch. About noon the doorbell rang. It was Griff, but he had others with him. His father and a lawyer. They said they had come to talk about an annulment."

Luc sucked in his breath. *"Annulment . . . ?"*

Tory nodded. "We all went into the front parlor, my parents, too, because they had come home for lunch. First Griff's father looked around the room, a sort of . . . supercilious look. He made some comments about how a little money could go a long way toward fixing things up. Then we all sat down to talk."

"He offered to pay if you went along?"

"Not in so many words, because my parents and the lawyer were present. I didn't misunderstand, though. He was prepared to buy his precious son's way out of a bad match. First the lawyer turned to Griff and said he understood the marriage hadn't been consummated. Griff said that was so."

"And then?"

"My father is quite a hot-tempered man. He got very angry. He broke in and pointed out that after ten days of two young people being closeted together, that was impossible to believe, especially when the man was someone like Griff."

"And what did you say?"

"Nothing at that point. My father was . . . shouting, beside himself with anger. At the first opportunity Griff said . . . he said I'd been trying to trap him into marriage, just for his money and his social position. He said he'd gotten the license just for a gag. He said he'd been drunk on New Year's Eve, and when he sobered up he'd found himself married, with me driving both of us through a snowstorm to the lodge. There was a little truth to it. He had had a couple of drinks, and I had done the driving. But he had never been drunk, not even close to it."

"What else did he say?"

"He said at that point, because of the snowstorm, there was no possibility of turning back, although he would have liked to. He said that being a normal red-blooded male snowed into a cozy lodge with a female, he might even have made the best of a very bad deal, except for one small detail. He said he couldn't be bothered to touch me, because I was the most frigid female he had ever had the misfortune to kiss. He said he'd as soon have made love to a board. He repeated the same things later, in the proper legal surroundings, in order to get the annulment."

"My God!" Luc exploded. "Didn't you disagree with a thing he said?"

"Why would I?" Tory said tiredly. "It was an easy way out. That day at my parents' house, I told all of them it was absolutely true, except for one part. I said I hadn't married Griff for money, and I didn't want any. You see, I didn't want to be paid for providing the services of a whore. Everything else, I swore to in proper legal fashion. It got around, of course, but I didn't care if the whole town knew I was frigid."

"You can't actually *believe*—"

"No, I don't actually believe that, although it's true I hadn't enjoyed anything much with Griff. By then I would have sworn to anything. I didn't want him for a husband, and annulment was simpler than divorce. As far as I'm concerned it was just a ten-day affair, and not a very pleasant one at that. The only satisfaction I got out of the whole thing was flushing his great big diamond ring down a toilet. I feel sorry for the woman he did eventually marry! Two months after going through the motions of forswearing all others, he crashed his private plane while flying to some other private family retreat for a private weekend. His wife wasn't on the plane, but another female was. A young girl of fifteen. You see, he hadn't changed. He still liked virgins—and he was starting to like them younger all the time."

"No wonder you were so upset this morning," Luc muttered hoarsely.

He said no more than that, but Tory knew he now understood some of the wretchedness she had felt after learning about the arrangement with Aimée. Luc and a young virgin: the parallel had been a parody of her own past. So much of their relationship had seemed to be a parody of her past, a terrible mockery perpetrated by the cruel hand of fate. . . .

Thinking about it now, Tory recognized that she must have transferred to the unknown Luc Devereux much of the anger that for years she had not been able to express. Pride had not allowed her to express it to Griff, and circumstances had prevented her from expressing it to anyone else. Wanting the annulment, she hadn't been able to reveal the truth of those terrible ten days, even to good friends. She had felt unable to talk freely with her parents. Nor had she been able to confide in the one person she would have told, the person who had always been the confidante for her most private secrets and thoughts, the person with whom she had once shared the special communion of twins.

"I was never able to talk to Laura about it," Tory whispered. "That was the worst part of all."

"Because of her illness, I suppose. Yes, I see—"

"Because of that, yes. But even if she'd been well, I don't think I could have talked to her. That day in the living room, when my father lost his temper so badly, he blurted out something I hadn't known. He shouted that . . . he and my mother had caught Laura and Griff together, a long time before. I hadn't known. Laura hadn't told me. *They* hadn't told me when I went off to marry Griff, probably because they were thinking it might be nice if I married a rich man. I wanted to die. I was so angry with them. And I was so angry with Laura, so very angry . . ."

Tory briefly covered her face with her hands, shuddering with the dreadful emotions and hurts she had been holding inside all these years. How could you direct anger at someone in Laura's condition? How could you feel something like hatred for your own twin? And all that anger had simply had nowhere to go.

Calming, she started to talk again. "I used to think Laura told me everything. It hadn't occurred to me she might have kept some secrets to herself. I'd never, never have married Griff if I'd known. It was awful to be so angry at her. Awful."

"I think I begin to understand more of the reason for those fists," Luc said gruffly at last, his eyes rising to Tory's. In them there was an acute feeling, almost a pain. "All that must have hurt like hell. You've been holding too much inside, for too long."

"I supposed I endowed you with all Griff's faults," Tory acknowledged. "And then it was so dreadful to be attracted to you. I felt . . . sick with myself. Sick to think of you with Laura. Sick to think of you with Aimée."

"I'm not a Griff Rammell. Very few men are, thank God."

"I know that now."

"Isn't it time you let go of the past?"

"I think I just did," Tory said with a wry smile. For a long time they sat in silence. Then she said, "I let go of Griff Rammell long ago. At some point I even stopped blaming Laura. How could I really blame her? She had leaned on me in a lot of ways, but she probably didn't like me to know all her weaknesses. If my parents already knew about Griff, that was one scrape I couldn't help her out of."

Tory added after another moment, "It was myself I couldn't let go of, myself I blamed. I should never have found Griff attractive in the first place, whether he had been to bed with Laura or not. And you . . . you brought all sorts of things to a head. Thinking you had been intimate with my sister, I couldn't . . . bear the way I was feeling about you. It was like history repeating itself."

Luc bent his head, the little muscle in his temple making a slow staccato beat in rhythm with a pulse in Tory's wrist. For a long time only the notes of a distant birdsong and the stirrings of a warm breeze broke the quiet of Carnac. With the full story told, peace was washing through Tory once more, a very great peace because although Luc was not even looking at her, she knew he was wishing it had been he, not Griff, who had been the man to teach her.

After a long time he spoke, his voice low and clogged with difficult emotion. "Has there been no man since?"

"No."

"Tory . . ."

They looked at each other and there was no need for talk, for touching, for arch expressions, for agreements that had to be voiced.

Luc rose to his feet and helped her to hers, and they both gathered all evidence of their stay. Luc slung his jacket over his shoulder and didn't take Tory's hand. Together, in the golden afternoon, they walked slowly past the tall rows of long stones, a passage through history that put past history behind.

They exchanged no words, but Tory knew he was taking her back to the inn.

Chapter Ten

The couple who kept the inn were not young, but they were familiar with the changing mores of the times. As it wasn't yet the tourist season, there were empty rooms, and empty rooms meant empty pockets. No questions were asked, not even when both signed the register with their own names, not even when Luc said the room would be required for an hour or two only. If the L. Devereux raised a brow, it was well concealed behind the friendly confusion caused by their unexpected return.

The man of the inn led Luc and Tory up some old creaking stairs and into a room with a low timbered ceiling. It vaguely reminded Tory of Luc's rooms, although it was somewhat more rustic. There were rag rugs and polished wood and lovingly embroidered petit point covers on the furniture. The bed was an old-fashioned featherbed, and the couch was an antique captain's daybed in one corner. Sun streamed through open windows at whose edges fresh yellow curtains stirred, blown by a salt-tanged Atlantic air. Inadvertently Tory thought of a poignant line from Shakespeare, and in her mood of trembling anticipation and inner content could not imagine why such a sad line would have occurred to her at all. *Tears shall drown the wind . . .*

Except to arrange for the room, Luc was silent until after the innkeeper had departed. He shut the door quietly and leaned against it, not closing the space between them.

"I'm not really a free man," he said soberly. It was the first thing he had said to Tory since leaving Carnac.

Tory had walked to the window to close the sheer curtains. They lifted and billowed in the breeze and still admitted sun, filtering it to a subtler aura, an old gold afternoon light that shifted and stirred and bathed the airy room in softness and serenity.

At Luc's words she turned. "I know that," she said, for she accepted already that the relationship had no future.

"I've been waiting a long time for Aimée to grow up. Even Tante Marie is realist enough to accept that my promises don't begin until she does."

"Luc, don't. Please don't explain." Tory didn't want to think about Aimée. This was her hour, hers and Luc's, one golden hour stolen from his future. She expected nothing from him except the promise implicit in his bringing her here, the promise that he would help heal the wounds inflicted by a hurtful marriage. She wanted to close out the outside world, past, present, and future. She wanted to live only for this golden moment, pretending that for a little time Luc belonged to her, and to her alone.

She kicked off her shoes and started to unbutton her blouse, but Luc came across the room and stayed her with a raised hand.

"Wait, I have more to say." Luc took some time to formulate his words, as if picking and choosing his way through a minefield. "I've had some difficult decisions to make in the past, and even more difficult ones ahead. No matter what comes about, I want you to know I wouldn't allow this to happen between us if it were . . . wrong."

"I know that, too," Tory said simply, lifting her eyes. They were luminous with the feelings she couldn't conceal. She had not told Luc she loved him, but that look told everything, confessed everything, accepted everything. The physical wants were still there, and he had seen those long ago, along with the little fears. But now, with what her eyes revealed, a man might see right through to her very soul. She loved Luc, and she trusted him enough to let him see that love.

"One other thing. Don't . . ." For a moment his words didn't come. Tory could see his throat working, his scarred forehead throbbing. "For God's sake," he grated, his voice harsh with effort, "don't expect me to fall in love with you."

She didn't trust herself to answer that in words. She hadn't expected him to, but she had hoped he might pretend. She shook her head, her throat hurting. Her eyes must have betrayed her, for in the next instant his arms were around her, holding her close.

"Oh, Tory, Tory. Victoria . . ."

There were other words, gentle words in French, little endearments whispered as he showered her cheeks and her temples and her eyelids with tiny, tender kisses. Tory raised her face to feel them and wound her arms around his waist. With his mouth and his hands soothing her, she managed to voice the words she had wanted to say a few moments before. "Luc . . . could you pretend you do love me? Please, just for this afternoon. I won't ask it again."

He groaned and buried his face in her hair. For a time he simply held her, not even stroking her shoulders. And then he said in a hoarse voice, "If that's what you want to hear, I'll say it before the afternoon's through. But not until I've taught you what it is to be loved. A man shouldn't . . . use words like that lightly. I'll tell you when you're ready to believe me, and not before."

The promise was enough. Tory moved her mouth to offer it, and in the joining of lips found it was not so very hard to pretend he loved her, too. Past, present, and future were forgotten, and her golden hour began.

It was a stirring kiss, more than a mere meeting and melting of mouths. In the past Tory's sexual responses to Luc had deeply disturbed her, but she had come to terms with herself in many ways. There was no guilt, now, in the soaring sensations that filled her. Her desires no longer battled with her scruples, and her passions no longer warred with preconceptions out of a hurtful past. She lost herself in Luc's kiss.

The embrace began gently and became all she wanted and more. His desire blazed and she felt it, not only in the hardness of his body, but in the growing urgency of his mouth and hands. How could a woman think herself undesired when a man kissed her as if he hungered and thirsted for her, and for no other woman in the world?

The kiss broke, Luc breathing unsteadily as he stopped to fold back the covers of the bed. During the embrace he had unbuttoned Tory's blouse, and she started to remove it quickly, wanting to be ready for him.

"No," he said, straightening from the bed and stopping her with his hand. His eyes smoldered darkly but there was patience in them, telling her that although he desired her very much, he intended to be careful with her needs. "That task is mine, darling. I want to undress you slowly. Wait for me."

He pillowed her against the snowy sheets, the warmth of his steaming gaze telling her she would not lie alone for long. Tory lay quietly on the downy bed, cushioned by its sensuous softness, watching him with love and desire moving in her heart and melting her expressive eyes.

Luc sat on the bed's edge to remove his shoes and then stood to divest himself unhurriedly of his shirt. It came free, revealing the smooth, powerful muscular structure of a torso bronzed by long days at sea. A dusting of hair darkened his chest and arrowed downward, disappearing at the flat of his beltline. His desire and his potent need were evident, but as he came down on the bed beside Tory, he had not removed his trousers. She asked no questions. She wanted, but she was content to wait, to let Luc move at his own pace—not the pace of a man who seeks to satisfy his own desires, but the pace of a man who seeks to satisfy a woman.

"Don't move at all, darling, and don't say anything." Luc took her face in his hands and looked gravely into her eyes as he issued the husky command. His voice was soft but stern, warning that he intended to orchestrate the lovemaking at his own speed and in his own way. "Lie still and be silent, and have trust. Don't do anything to arouse me, for I don't need any more arousal than you've already caused. I want you to leave everything to me. Everything . . ."

As he stroked the clothes from her limbs, he murmured the things a woman wants to hear, soft warm words about the shape of her breasts and the curve of her thighs. Tory believed the things he said, not just because she wanted to believe, but because she had such faith in Luc. He gentled her body with his hands and he praised her flesh with his dark smoldering eyes, and when she lay naked before him in the beautiful golden light of the room, her body felt golden and beautiful, too. Luc had told her it was, and she believed.

His hands discovered her first—moving slowly and lightly the length of her, the hardness of his sun-browned fingers belied by the extreme gentleness with which he handled her. His palms grazed her breasts and her thighs but lingered nowhere, asked nothing. He made no move to part her legs. They quivered to feel the featherlight passage of his fingertips, but he had said not to move, and so she lay without moving, trembling with need, feeling supremely wanted in the warm light of his dark and smoking gaze.

He was in no haste to take her. He bent his head close into the curve of her throat and told her things about the silkiness and scent of her skin. Tory believed and felt beautiful. The texture of his furred chest shifted and stirred against her bare breasts as he muttered how desperately he wanted her. Against her naked thigh the hard, contained readiness of his body told her his words were true. He wanted, but he would wait.

And then his lips moved lower. With his warm breath stirring against her dusky tautened nipples and his fingers describing light traceries in the valley and over the pale round rise, he told her how much he wanted her, and she believed.

And then he was silent for a time, for his lips and his tongue were engaged in a different language of love. He bathed her breasts, circling each nipple with his unhurried tongue, then dragging his lightly parted lips temptingly over the erect tips. He taunted with his tongue and he teased with his teeth, and as each breast in turn submitted to the sweet torment of his procrastination, the other surrendered to the feathering of his long, lean, strong fingers.

It was growing hard for her to lie still. Her body felt wonderful, honeyed by desire, quivering with readiness beneath his expert and ardent caresses.

At last, after a torturous space of time, his mouth fastened over a nipple. The strong sucking caused a shock wave of intense pleasure to shudder along the length of her limbs. No longer able to attend to his stern command for stillness and silence, she began to moan and stir.

As she did so, one bronzed hand traveled downward to brush lightly over the triangle of her thighs, a strange reward for her disobedience. Instead of taming, the touch enflamed. She gasped and arched high against his hand, seeking a greater closeness, and although he made no move to nudge her legs apart, they parted of their own accord.

And still he did not take her. His fingers stroked and tarried at her thighs until she was frantic with need. She groaned and writhed. His mouth moved, leaving erotic liquid trails across her skin, so that her skin felt like moist velvet in the wake of his progress. Behind the confines of cloth she could feel the surging power of his manhood, the mightiness of his desire, a containment that had become as maddening to her as it must have been to him.

And still he waited. She wanted him to be a part of her, and she wanted it at once. She had long since been driven to the brink of ecstasy by the intimate ingressions of his strong, skilled hands and the progress of his moist, impassioned kisses. He needed, and she needed, too, and although his ministrations were wild and wonderful, they had become almost agonizing to her, unspeakable and exquisite tortures to her flesh.

Stretched on a rack of delicious agony and desire, she could bear the sensuous pleasures no more. She clutched his hair hurtfully in the extremity of her need, nails digging, fingers winding and twisting into the dark vital strands. "Luc, make love to me," she pleaded, gasping. "Don't do this. Have mercy. Don't make me wait."

"I am making love to you," he murmured huskily, his words muffled against her skin. "How could I ask you to wait for me, when I love you as I do? I never wanted you to wait."

Her world exploded into pure gold. Love and need were inextricably fused in that long and marvelous distillation of desire, and as she floated back to earth the golden moment didn't end.

Luc had moved his length alongside her on the bed. He was holding her very tightly, his impassioned kisses now raining over her face, his hands now folding her nakedness achingly close against his half-clad body. His virile frame was tense with unslaked needs, the hard shuddering of it telling her how very difficult the long minutes must have been for him.

"I love you, darling," he whispered thickly, not once but again and again. And because he had thought of her needs first, Tory believed.

When he at last joined his nakedness to hers, finding his passion's goal and deeply fulfilling hers, her senses once again soared and sang. In the twining of arms and limbs, in the fusing of mouths, she believed. She loved and was loved. In that golden hour Luc belonged to her, only to her, and to no other woman in the world.

Chapter Eleven

Tears shall drown the wind . . .

The quotation came back to Tory toward the end of the long, silent drive to the Château d'Ys. Her sense of deep content had been a fragile thing, and its fragility had been shattered. With the quiet southern shores of Brittany giving way to the wild westerly reaches of Finistère, the day was no longer golden. As it darkened to a close the pure peace of the afternoon had been broken by a gathering of leaden storm clouds rolling ominously in from the northwest. The wind was not yet high, but already cattle huddled and lowed in the shelter of windbreaks, warning of the coming Atlantic gales. As the car wound along coast roads and past restless seascapes gray as the granite cliffs that rimmed them, Luc's dark and introspective mood mirrored her own and nature's.

Her mind had been dragged back to reality, to the unanswered questions about Laura, to the unhappy reflections about Aimée. The sense of guilt had returned. Even though Luc's promises to marry were a thing of the future, not of the present, Tory couldn't help but feel that she had in some way caused him to be unfaithful—not to a wife, but to a future wife. Yet how could he be truly faithful to a half-grown girl when he had the needs of a full-grown man? Luc had said that even his aunt accepted certain realities, but in her present troubled and reflective mood, the thought gave Tory little comfort. In her heart she was aware that there ought to be no repetition of the afternoon. Physical ecstasy might be recaptured, but never again that sense of rightness, of golden contentment, of loving and being loved in return.

She knew she must stay in Brittany no longer. For reasons she still didn't understand, she had accomplished what she had come to do, and to stay was to risk an unhappiness so great it would be insupportable. She knew, also, that for Laura's sake she must accept Luc's offer of financial help, for the time being at least. Once settled in a job, she would repay him as best she could. And by then, if Luc continued to investigate as he had promised, Laura's real husband might be found. Luc had said to ask no questions, and so Tory hadn't, but even without questions she could make guesses. Luc, she thought, must have some strong suspicion of the man's identity. He would tell nothing until he was sure. And perhaps, if he saw reason to protect some other person, he would never tell anything at all. But Tory knew it was as he had said: she must now leave it in his hands.

As they neared the Château d'Ys she told Luc that she intended to return to the States as soon as a flight could be arranged. He merely nodded his agreement and said, "It's best if you don't stay. I imagine I can get you on a flight tomorrow, if you have no objection to taking advantage of a little Saint-Cloud influence."

"No," Tory said, with her eyes on the road and her hands very still on her lap. Although she wouldn't have stayed under the circumstances, a part of her had wanted him to try and talk her into staying.

It was shortly before the dinner hour when they drew into the garage. Under the black and lowering sky, it was so dark that the falling night might have already come. In the long slitted windows of the château, lights shone dully behind drawn curtains. The wind had not yet risen. There was a stillness in the air, but it was a heavy, waiting stillness, the calm before the storm. Wordlessly Luc took Tory's arm and helped her to pick her way across the darkened cobblestone forecourt.

She stood back to watch him as he freed her arm in order to open the door. A sudden gust spattered her with the first drops of rain, foretaste of the storm to come, but Tory hardly noticed. Love and longing were a deep ache in her heart. She had taken her stolen hour and even deceived herself into believing for a time that Luc loved her, too, but she could not deceive herself now. She looked at the dark, shadowy length of him and felt nameless yearnings for things that could never be.

The door was flung wide before Luc had had time to open it, before Tory had thought to search in her purse for the horn-rimmed reading glasses. At the door was Madame Saint-Cloud herself. She clutched at Luc's arm and drew him into the gloomy entrance hall, her hands shaking with urgency. Anxiety scored her face and there was a piteous plea in her eyes.

"Luc! C'est Aimée . . ."

Tory closed the front door because no one else thought to do so. The flood of French made little sense to her, but it was easy to understand that something dire had happened. Luc's concern was instant, his frame tensing as he listened attentively to what his aunt had to say. The governess and several of the old servants were hovering nearby, wringing their hands and looking almost as shaken as Madame Saint-Cloud herself.

Moments later Luc started barking commands. The ancient Émile hobbled off toward the back rooms of the château, presumably on some errand. Three female servants scuttled to a nearby cloakroom and emerged with armloads of heavy-weather gear of the type used for sailing. There were boots, too, and one large flashlight. An outfit was handed to Luc and a jacket to Miss Pritchard, and the rest of the garments were placed on the stone floor near the front door.

The governess jerked her arms into the jacket, picked up the flashlight, and rushed out into the gathering gale. The wind had begun to lift, bringing a blast of sudden rain through the opened door. The storm had broken.

Luc doffed his suit jacket and donned the heavy-weather gear, boots and trousers as well as jacket. He waited in the hall, impatient, his lean body as tense as a coiled spring. With his hand on the doorknob, he watched the direction in which Émile had vanished. Madame Saint-Cloud was standing with her fingers pressed to her lips, as if to stop their tremble.

In the alarm Tory had simply watched, unimportant details like reading glasses the last thing on her mind. Now she could no longer contain her concern. In the pause she asked Luc urgently, "What's happened to Aimée?"

"She's missing," Luc said curtly. "She's nowhere in the château, for the servants have just finished scouring it high and low. Her governess will search the orchard while I search the rest of the property."

"Can I help?"

"Yes—stay with my aunt. Or better still, go and get something to eat in the kitchen, for there'll be no proper dinner tonight. Then you might go to your room and change into old clothes. If I don't locate Aimée within the next short while, you may have to join a more careful search of the area just around the château, along with some of the servants. On a night like this they won't be going outside unless it's absolutely necessary."

"Luc, she might have gone . . . down the cliff, to the cove."

"At this time of night, with a storm breaking? That's madness."

Yes, it was madness. Tory had no clue why she had even suggested it, beyond the remembrance that Aimée sometimes went there when she wanted to be alone. All the same, once the idea hit her, it stuck.

"I have an idea she's there."

"Impossible," Luc said. "She's been missing for an hour at the very most, since she went to bathe and dress for dinner. The storm's been threatening for at least that long. And even if she had gone there, she'd have started up the cliff the moment it began to get dark. She's not a fool."

"Yes, but . . ."

"I'll try the cove if I can't find Aimée anywhere else," Luc assured Tory patiently. "It's far more likely she just stepped outside to have a look at the storm clouds. She might be lying somewhere close at hand, with a sprained ankle or a concussion."

Émile returned with two additional flashlights, both powerful. Luc took one and left, banging the door behind him as he strode into the night, where rain now drove down furiously.

Pale and overwhelmed with a sense of impending calamity, Tory stared at the closed door, feeling as if fate were exacting some just due for the illicit happiness of the afternoon. Aimée was missing and she felt oddly responsible, as if the stolen hour with Luc had been to blame. Or perhaps her sense of guilt stemmed from the exchange of notes between Jacques Benoit and the young girl. Suddenly Tory remembered more of the conversation she had had with Aimée and realized with a ghastly sinking sensation why she had thought of the cove. *Sometimes I think I will have to swim out, and escape that way. . . .*

Was it possible that Aimée's note had directed Jacques to meet her by boat, on a prearranged day at a prearranged hour?

Instantly Tory knew that someone would have to search that cove. She didn't want it to be Luc. To think of him undertaking that dangerous descent in the black of night, with the wind beginning to rise and the rain driving blindingly in his eyes . . .

Tory turned to Madame Saint-Cloud. "I'm going to help," she said, making her conscious decision in that moment. She gave herself no time to think about things like bravery and cowardice, nor did she reflect on her familiarity with the terrain and her capabilities for the climb. It was a simple choice and she made it.

Luc wouldn't have to do something that had already been done.

Madame Saint-Cloud nodded assent absently, but with concern for her daughter lining her face, she looked as though she had hardly heard.

Tory grabbed some heavy-weather gear and ran to the nearby cloakroom to remove her skirt. Within moments she was out the door, bundled in waterproof pants and jacket, with a heavy flashlight in her hand to pierce the downpour. A driving wall of water greeted the powerful beam. She could see barely enough to pick her way. In seconds her hair was soaked, her face streaming, her feet squishing inside boots a size too large. The wind was not yet too high, but still it was a battle to walk against it. She made her way along the orchard wall, groping it for direction and using it for shelter as she went. She remembered the rocky trail Aimée had used to reach the cliff, and she remembered that a large boulder had marked the point where the descent began. And beyond that . . .

She stopped thinking altogether and concentrated on each single step she took. In places the deluge had slicked the sparse grasses, but the roughness of time-pocked granite aided the grip of her rubber soles. She tried to aim her flashlight at the hard rock.

With the orchard wall put behind, each step had become more of a struggle. She bent into the wind. Its strength seemed to be increasing by the moment. The rain lashed at her eyes, and even with the lantern the path was almost impossible to discern. She had no very certain idea of the exact distance to the cliff, and after a time it seemed that each step must bring her to the boulder. If she missed it, there might instead be a precipitous drop, but the fierce concentration required for battling the elements prevented Tory from thinking such terrifying thoughts.

At last the boulder loomed out of the rainstorm, only a foot ahead. Tory reached for it and clung, leaning her face against its soaked abrasive surface for a few moments while she gasped for air, needing a renewal of strength to fight the heightening wind on the downward climb. Hair and rain streamed into her mouth, and her overlarge boots were heavy with water. If she had been thinking at all, she would have turned back. But she wasn't thinking, only acting and reacting, and that out of some instinct far deeper than fear itself.

And then she began the tortuous and tortured descent into the black maw of the dreadful night. She shifted the lantern to her left hand, for the right was needed to cling to handholds on the jagged and formidable cliff. In places her feet slipped, for even the grip of rubber would not hold where the angle of rock became too steep. She inched her way down, step by perilous step, leaving each handhold only when she had managed to discern the next. Rain knifed at her face and wind tore at her arm, as if the sole purpose of its growing fury was to dislodge her grip on the rocks and the flashlight. At times the beacon of her lamp seemed the only real thing, other than herself, in the dark nightmare. Many times, she pointed it far down the cliffside, but below she could see nothing, nothing but a black hellhole concealed by the dense wall of rain.

She wasn't yet afraid. With each step a lesson in simple survival, there was no time to feel fear.

It seemed she had been descending for an eternity and must be near the bottom. Out of sheer necessity she moved with great caution, using the beam of her lantern as a guide. Precarious step followed precarious step as she worked her way downward, the forces of night and wind and rain powerful adversaries to her progress.

Tory was sure she must be very nearly at beach level, and still there was no sign of Aimée. She almost turned back. Surely Luc was right. If Aimée had ever been down here, she would most certainly have started up before now.

Unless she was hurt? Or hadn't been able to see? Tory shouted and felt the words thrown back in her throat. But how could anyone have heard above that screaming wind?

She was clinging to a large projection of rock, searching with the flashlight for a safer footing, when suddenly her breath was dashed from her lungs by a new enemy, the Atlantic. A wall of salt spray hit her from below. The force and unexpectedness of it flung Tory against the cliff face. Flashlight forgotten, her left arm clutched wildly for the solidity of rock. In a moment of black terror her light was extinguished.

Whether the flashlight had been washed away from her hand or had simply dashed itself to pieces in the impact, Tory didn't know. Its light no longer existed. The night and the dark maelstrom had swallowed her, and so had fear. Pure fear, primitive fear, nameless fear, all the fear she had forgotten to feel until now.

Engulfed by it, she clung to the rock projection with both arms, too terrified to move. She could see nothing, not even the stone she clung to. She could feel nothing but the lashing of rain from above, the furious dashing of spray from below, the tearing force of the gale. She could hear nothing but the crash and thunder of the sea, the wild whine of the wind.

The night had a name and its name was Fear.

And then the high wind became higher still, a wild, tearing, whining, raging, ripping fury of a wind, no longer a wind but a shrieking, vindictive tempest. . . .

And with the great wind came the great waves. Whipped into a frenzy by the gale, unseen in the blackness of night, one after another crashed over Tory, engulfing her entirely, receding only long enough to give the wind its turn, then crashing and thundering and frothing over her frail flesh once again. It seemed as if all the elemental forces of nature had been unleashed and were concentrating their furies against her and her alone. Against such mighty forces she could no longer move. She could hardly even breathe.

Tears shall drown the wind . . .

For the next eternity of moments only a few rational thoughts pierced Tory's mind, and those that did multiplied her terror instead of alleviating it. Luc might have found Aimée elsewhere. After the scare of the girl's disappearance, Luc had said there would be no proper dinner hour. No one would miss Tory at the table. Madame Saint-Cloud might have forgotten that she had gone out into the night, if indeed she had noticed at all. The servants might or might not have seen her exit, but even if they had, in the confusion of the evening they would be thinking of Aimée, not of Tory. Everyone might be safely back in the Château d'Ys by now, believing her in her own room. And no one would know she was here, alone in a wet black hell where all nature was trying to commit mayhem.

Or was she alone? Were those screams she had heard above the screaming of the gale? Terrible screams, terror-struck screams, screams torn from the lungs of someone who suffered a fear too awful for words?

The screams penetrated Tory's terror a little. She began to expect the impact of each wave, schooled herself to breathe only when no mouthful of salt would be swallowed. Between each assault she listened and heard no more above the wild keening of the gale. But there had been screams; she knew there had been screams. And they must have been Aimée's screams, for there was no one else to scream.

Luc would come for Aimée. Luc would come. Luc would come. Luc would come. Luc would come.

The refrain calmed Tory and she took a fresh hold on the rock projection, pressing one sodden cheek closely against it. She wrapped her arms around its bulk and locked her hands together tightly on the other side, so that neither wind nor wave could pry her from its safety. She pretended the rock was Luc's chest, the chest that had offered her comfort and strength and security hardly more than a dozen hours before, at the beginning of this day that had lasted such a lifetime. A gigantic wave of water crashed over her, trying to suck her into the sea. But Luc would come, he would have to come for Aimée. . . .

Tory didn't know the screams had been her own.

Chapter Twelve

Less than twenty minutes after Tory had set out on her disastrous voyage into the night and the storm, Luc gained the door of the Château d'Ys with a sodden and very subdued Aimée in the shelter of his arm. As his weatherproof garments had been transferred to his young cousin several minutes before, he was thoroughly soaked, his hair plastered to his head, his shirt plastered to his shoulders, his trousers plastered to his hard thighs.

With eyes narrowed against the rain's onslaught, he noted that no electric lights shone from the château's windows. The power lines, as always, had been knocked out by the storm. Luc already knew it was so, but all the same, his mouth thinned to see it. He guessed the telephone line would be out, too, another inevitable happening.

In the blackness of the foul night, beneath the

rivulets of water that coursed down his face, his expression was not prepossessing. During the trip back to the château, his relief in finding Aimée had been replaced by a grim and fatalistic determination. A few hours ago he had been faced by a terrible decision to be made between two impossible alternatives, and he had not known which decision to make. Aimée's attempt to run away had made the decision for him.

As he ushered Aimée through the front door, the water from their bodies ran in long rivulets onto the stone floor, darkening it under the flicker of the branched iron wall sconces, where a dozen fat candles burned to dispel the gloom of an otherwise lightless hall. At their entry the gust almost caused the flames to gutter. The wind was beginning to rise.

Her daughter's wetness didn't deter Madame Saint-Cloud, who rushed forward and clasped Aimée close against her heaving chest. Tears of relief ran down her face, their salt moisture lost in the tangle of Aimée's wet hair.

"Aimée! Aimée, *ma chère* . . ."

In the first moments no explanations were asked for. Some of the ancient servants had donned weather wear preparatory to joining the search if needed, and their expressions showed vast relief as they started to remove the garments. Miss Pritchard, the governess, had returned several minutes before and already removed hers. Where the jacket hadn't given protection, her hair and the bottom of her skirt were still soaking wet.

After Madame Saint-Cloud had released her initial joy and relief, she assured herself that her daughter's ashen face didn't portend any actual physical damage, beyond a few surface scratches and a very bad scare.

Then, at last, she asked the natural questions about what had happened. Aimée's eyes turned to Luc in an anguished plea for help.

"It's a very grave matter, Tante Marie. I'll explain in a few minutes." As Luc spoke he gripped his aunt's arm to prevent her departure. He turned to the governess. "Take Aimée to her room and see that she's bundled into bed at once," he ordered. He issued other crisp directions, and other servants scurried off to attend to them—some to light candles on the second-floor landing and in Aimée's room, one to prepare a tray, one to fetch a hot water bottle. Émile was sent to search the liquor cabinet for brandy, with instructions to send a glass to Aimée and bring the rest of the bottle to the living room. The other male servant went to find a dry sweater for Luc.

With all servants occupied in their various urgent errands, Luc put down his flashlight and lifted one of the candles from its wall sconce. By its light he led his aunt into the great salon giving out onto the Atlantic, the same room where Tory had first heard the story of the lost city of Ys. Tonight, with a howling sea gale rattling the panes of the French doors, there was no thought of walking onto a parapet beseiged by storm. Luc knew too well what a gale like that could do. He settled his aunt in a chair and walked around the room, using the candle in his hand to light others.

His expression was grave when he finally faced his aunt, remaining on his feet because of the seriousness of what he had to say. Expecting servants bearing brandy and his dry sweater to arrive at any moment, he spoke in English. "Aimée was trying to run away," he said.

Madame Saint-Cloud tensed a little, but her answer

to Luc was level. "She would not try to run, if she had children to hold her to this place. She is old enough to bear a child. Not long after I became seventeen, I was married, and Armand was soon on the way. If you would take the girl for your wife at once, instead of waiting . . ."

"I'm never going to marry Aimée," Luc stated harshly.

His aunt's body turned rigid. Had Émile not arrived at that exact moment with two snifters of brandy, the storm of invective in the room might have equaled that raging outside. Luc downed his brandy in a swallow, the burning liquid proof against the day's difficult decision as much as against the weather. He indicated his need for a refill.

Émile left the brandy tray on a small table and lit a few more candles. Before he left the room, dry clothing also appeared—socks, trousers, and a sweater, as well as a heavy towel for Luc's hair. He stripped himself of the soaked shirt, gratefully pulling on a black cablestitch sweater. The socks, too, he pulled on. From his hip pocket he extracted his leather wallet and dried it on the towel. He set it on the tray with the brandy. The dry trousers he ignored, not from modesty but because he wanted to rid himself of the servant who stood by, waiting to receive the dripping clothes.

At last Luc and his aunt were alone.

She had drawn herself up with fearsome proudness, a bearing that had at times intimidated lesser men than Luc. "Have you forgotten your promises?" she lashed at him, trembling with fury. "Have you forgotten your duty? You are a Saint-Cloud, Luc. Where would you be . . . *what* would you be if your uncle had not taken you into this house and raised you as his own? What have I ever asked of you, Luc, but this one thing? With what your uncle left you, is it so much to ask in return? And you agreed."

"Tante Marie, listen to me and listen carefully. Aimée could have died tonight. She had been waiting for a storm and the power failure that always comes, so she could climb the fence. She watched to see the light at the gates go off, and then she tried to go over. That's where I found her—trapped on the top of the fence, her hair and her clothing caught on the barbs. Beneath that heavy-weather gear I gave her to wear, her clothing was shredded from trying to get herself free. If the power had flickered on, even for a moment . . ."

He stopped and let the full enormity of Aimée's actions sink through to his aunt.

Madame Saint-Cloud's face was pale in the unsure flicker of small flames that lit the large, dim room. She swayed on her chair and took a hard grip on its arms, then fortified herself with brandy. She didn't answer Luc at once.

"You can't shelter the child anymore, Tante Marie. This is the twentieth century, not the seventeenth! Aimée needs to meet young people of her own age. She doesn't want an arranged marriage, and she certainly doesn't want to become a brood mare out of duty to future Saint-Clouds. She longs for some freedom. Tonight should tell you how desperate she is."

"She is desperate only because you will not give her what she needs. A husband!" Once recovered from the impact of Luc's revelation, Madame Saint-Cloud was unshaken in her determination. Like the wind outside, her voice was rising. "Is it so much to do, Luc? There have been women in your past, yes, but never one woman. Will you stay single all your life? Aimée is young, she is beautiful, she will make a good wife. Yes, the child has romantic notions. If you would talk to her of love, she would not think to look for it elsewhere. Would she yearn for unskilled boys, if you used a man's kisses to teach her that her duty is not a painful one? Instead you keep your distance and treat her as a child. How can you refuse to marry her, when—"

"I already have a wife and child," Luc cut in forcefully.

The words had the impact of a slap in the face. Wanting his aunt's full and undivided attention, Luc had made the statement intentionally strong. When he saw that she had turned stiff and silent, frozen with shock into listening, he began to talk slowly, first explaining the true reasons for Tory's arrival in France. For once Madame Saint-Cloud did not interrupt with lectures about duty.

When Luc had covered most of the facts, he quietly took the brandy snifter from his aunt's nerveless fingers. He refilled it for her and handed it back, along with a damp photograph extracted from his wallet. He carried a candle close to the likeness and held it so his aunt could see.

Madame Saint-Cloud sat with her head bent over the snapshot of Nicholas, her hands visibly trembling.

Luc said evenly, "You talk to me of duty, Tante Marie. If I have a duty to the Saint-Clouds, I also have a duty to that child."

"Yes," whispered his aunt, her voice ghostly.

"No, the wife's not truly mine. No, the child's not truly mine. I knew that almost from the first. How could I have met and married some girl in Brittany when I was in the States at the time? At first I listened because this supposed wife was American. And then, even after I realized she was no wife of mine, I listened because I saw the picture of the boy. At first I had no idea who the father was. Was it just a startling chance resemblance? But why would someone use my name? It must be someone who knew me or knew of me. Had the boy's father been another Saint-Cloud indiscretion, just as I had been? Over the years there must have been other bastards fathered in other ports by other Saint-Clouds. Had my mother borne another Devereux, another child to my father? Wild guesses, yes. I knew I had to find the answers. Until today I wasn't sure. Now I know."

"Whose . . . child is he?" The whisper was hardly heard above the storm.

"Armand's."

"But no, that is impossible . . ."

"Impossible? No, Tante Marie. Armand's marriage was barren, true, but that could have been Félicité's fault."

"But Armand had a wife! He could not have married again."

Luc placed the candle on a table and sat down on a chair facing his aunt, his face very serious. "But he did, Tante Marie. Armand committed bigamy. Shall I tell you how I believe it happened? You remember Armand always used to go to Belle-Île in August, at least until after I returned from the States. In the years before our yachts began to enter larger events, they used to take part in the international races from Belle-Île every year—sometimes to Plymouth, but always to Santander. Eight years ago the Saint-Clouds were entered, but because of some problem with the keel my uncle decided at the last minute not to sail either of those races. I know that because I've phoned to check. With the large yacht out of commission, the regular crew dispersed. Armand left Belle-Île and checked into an inn near Carnac, using my name. I imagine he had used it before, not once but many times. In Brittany it's hard for a Saint-Cloud to be discreet in his affairs. Perhaps he had come across some identification of mine—I was missing my passport one year, if you remember, and had to get a new one. Considering the striking similarities in our appearance, it's not inconceivable that Armand could get away with using it. In the inn he met a girl. Soon after, he leased a smaller yacht, with a different crew. I haven't yet been able to track down the men he hired, but I think they would confirm part of what I'm telling you. He had arranged to take a sailing holiday, and so he sailed—with this young American girl, Laura, as his companion."

"But he would not have married her!"

"I'm sure the evidence will show he did—if we care to follow through and collect the evidence. The whole thing is far too sensitive for me to hire investigators in Brittany, but I've already confirmed one or two facts by retaining a firm of private detectives in Spain. Armand always loved sailing to Santander, and it occurred to me that he might have decided to go there at some point, even though he had missed the race." Luc paused and asked his aunt, "Wasn't there a year when Armand took an extra-long holiday? Because of the pressure of business, as I remember. He was gone for more than two months."

"Yes," came the low and reluctant admission.

Luc leaned forward and laced his fingers together tensely, giving his next revelation dramatic impact. "A man using my name married a woman named Laura Allworth in a civil ceremony in Spain that year, not in August but at the beginning of October. Because the girl lied about the date of marriage, she had also been purposely vague about the locale where it had taken place. Who knows why Armand did such a thing? I think he loved the girl. Perhaps the stress of business had impaired his judgment. Perhaps when she found she was pregnant she became hysterical and talked of an abortion. It's possible. Given the child's date of birth, it's evident that the affair must have started almost as soon as the two met. The girl, Laura, didn't have the mental strength or moral fiber of her sister."

"Armand, a bigamist . . . I cannot believe . . ."

"Remember, Tante Marie, that Armand had asked Félicité for a divorce more than once. He had been very young, God knows, when he married her, and he had never been in love. She wasn't a warm woman, and he desperately wanted the children she didn't give him. That was one arranged marriage, Tante Marie, that simply didn't work."

"But still! Armand would not . . ."

"But he did. Whatever his reasons, he married this American. Today provided proof enough for me. I didn't dare show a photograph of Armand, but the innkeeper remembered his cleft chin. I recognized his handwriting, too. The fact that the man had just come from Belle-Île, where I know Armand had been, provided the final corroboration. There's no doubt in my mind, Tante Marie."

"*Mon Dieu,*" whispered his aunt.

"Armand returned to Brittany immediately after the marriage. He took an apartment in Brest for his new wife, close to the shipyards, again in my name. When he dined out, he used the utmost discretion, for of course he had to avoid being seen in public with the girl. Because he returned to Félicité and the Château d'Ys most nights, he told his new wife that his occupation kept him at sea most of the time. He probably talked vaguely of fishing fleets, or perhaps implied that he was a ship's officer of some kind, being careful not to mention which ship. It worked for a few months—until the girl discovered what was going on."

Luc paused long enough to take a cigarette from a box on a coffee table and light it from one of the candles. With most of the story told, he spoke more slowly now, giving his aunt time to get used to the idea.

"I know the exact date she ran away from Armand. The day before, in a Brest newspaper, there was a large photograph of Armand with Félicité on his arm, taken at a concert. It was an excellent likeness. Who could miss that cleft chin of his? The girl, Laura, certainly didn't. Perhaps she confronted Armand. Perhaps she simply phoned the Saint-Cloud shipyards and asked for him, and heard his voice, which was easy enough to recognize. Perhaps the picture itself was enough, especially as she had probably begun to wonder why he introduced her to no friends or family. She may have become suspicious because they always dined in such seclusion, when she wanted to try some of Brest's other restaurants. How would she feel when she discovered her husband was a bigamist, using a false name? I know, from what I've heard, that the girl was emotionally immature and psychologically unstable. She had just turned nineteen and she was five months pregnant, in a strange country with no one to turn to, and probably still in love. Her mind cracked. No wonder she could never bear to hear the name Luc Devereux!"

Madame Saint-Cloud's face was ravaged. "But what are we to do? Mother of God . . ."

Luc rose and walked away a few feet. His back was turned to his aunt, and his shoulders were tense. "The boy must be acknowledged as a Saint-Cloud. When he's older, he should be brought here. The estates are rightfully his—not mine. I'll have to admit paternity, Tante Marie, for I see no other choice. Otherwise how can we establish that the boy is a Saint-Cloud? If we say he's Armand's bastard, Félicité won't rest until she knows every last sordid detail. She'll be angry and spiteful. She and her family are rich and powerful, and they bear a strong grudge against the Saint-Clouds. They're furious about losing the court case. Remember how they tried to drag my name through the mud? How they tried to prove that will invalid, my uncle incompetent? How they said Armand had made promises we know he couldn't have made? My God! Can you imagine how furious they would be if a bastard son of his became heir to all the estates? Given the boy's age, they can easily count backward to the time of conception. They'll scour that chapter of Armand's life, and they won't hesitate to expose it out of sheer venom. The facts aren't that hard to find. The bigamy is bound to become common knowledge. Félicité's family would make sure of it! Can you imagine the scandal? Can you imagine how Aimée would feel, to find her brother was a bigamist?"

"It cannot be allowed," acknowledged his aunt in a cracked voice.

There was a little bitterness to Luc's voice as he said, "At least, Tante Marie, you have the Saint-Cloud heir you wanted. A true heir! The son of your own son. If I say he's mine, no one can prove otherwise. Laura . . ." There was a hesitation before he went on. "My wife is fit to testify to nothing."

"And what of her sister, this Victoria?" Madame Saint-Cloud's voice was anxious. "How much does she know?"

"She knows some other man used my name. She didn't recognize the handwriting in the inn register, naturally. Nor did it mean anything to her that the man had recently come from Belle-Île. She knows nothing about yacht racing."

"Then you must tell her at once it was you, so she does not start to suspect Armand!"

Luc's hoarse answer took a long time in coming. "I'll have to tell her the truth," he said.

"Luc! You cannot! I forbid it!"

"She has to know."

"She must not know! What if she breathed some words of this thing? It cannot be allowed. You owe me that much, Luc, to protect the name of my son! The name of Saint-Cloud . . ."

Luc turned to face his aunt, his eyes stony, his mouth deeply etched with harsh lines. "I can do only so much for you, Tante Marie. Don't push me too far! Don't you think I know you raised me out of duty? I agree that I owe you duty in return. To satisfy you, I was prepared to marry Aimée. But I owe even more to my uncle! He loved me as you never have. He wanted to adopt me, when you didn't. Yes, I was young, but I remember overhearing the two of you argue about me. You said you wouldn't have a bastard brat using the Saint-Cloud name."

"You heard," whispered his aunt. She looked almost as shaken as she had on learning the news of her son's bigamy.

"Not much, but enough. After that do you think I really want to take the name as an adult? For my uncle's sake, I was prepared to do it. Not for yours, when you refused me the use of the name as a boy! Also, it's for my uncle's sake—not yours, not even Armand's—that I'm prepared to accept responsibility for a wife I didn't marry, and for a son I didn't father. To give a name to his grandson, the child that should be his heir, I'll pretend to all the rest of the world. But I refuse to pretend to the woman I love that I'm married to her sister!"

Madame Saint-Cloud's face had crumpled along the lines of old pain, her cheeks turning withered as she stared wordlessly at Luc, her eyes tragic and bearing a silent plea. The pride that normally sustained her had deserted her, and she looked far older than her years. Her throat worked and her hands clutched each other tightly, as if she wanted to talk. It was almost the posture of a supplicant.

Luc didn't much care what his aunt had to say. He hadn't made his decision for her sake. He put his emptied brandy glass on the tray and told her tersely, "Tory Allworth has to be told the truth, because I refuse to lie to her. She can be trusted completely. She has already accepted the fact that there can be nothing between us. I agree with you about one thing, though, Tante Marie—I should speak to her without delay. Where did she go, to her room?"

"I do not . . ." Madame Saint-Cloud's voice trembled, but she no longer tried to divert Luc from his purpose. "I do not think . . ."

"Never mind," Luc cut in impatiently. "I'll find her."

Taking a candle, he started to stride from the room. The decision he had made soured his very soul. After the events of the afternoon he hated to tell Tory, but now that his course of action had been decided upon, he knew he must tell her quickly. He knew she had fallen in love with him. If she harbored even the slimmest of hopes for the future, he had to lay them forever to rest.

"Luc!" There was a sudden wildness in his aunt's voice that stopped him in his tracks. He turned and saw that she had risen to her feet. Not for the first time that evening, her face was drained of color. "Luc . . . I forgot. She went outside, to help you look for Aimée."

"What?"

"I forgot to tell you," Madame Saint-Cloud repeated helplessly. "I forgot."

Luc's face turned ashen. "The cove," he said hoarsely. "She talked about the cove. But she must have come back . . . perhaps before I came in with Aimée?"

"No," whispered his aunt. "I did not leave the door for a single moment then."

For a frozen instant they both stared at each other, and knew. No one had returned to the château since Luc had brought Aimée into safety. The salon gave directly onto the entrance hall. If the front door had opened, its banging would have been heard and the draft would have disturbed the candle flames.

Madame Saint-Cloud's eyes turned to the rattling French door at the far end of the room, where the pelting rain and the high whine of the Atlantic gale had mounted and continued unabated. She knew, just as Luc knew, what a storm like this could do. Fastnet had killed her husband and her son, and Fastnet had been just such a storm. For the past hour the wind and the waves had been rising. By now, towering combers of fifty or sixty feet in height would be battering against the mighty cliffs that guarded the Château d'Ys.

"God forgive me," muttered his aunt, fingering the cross at her neck.

Luc took time for a few more words, lethal in their ferocity. "He may," he grated, "but if she's dead, I won't!"

One second later he was at the front door, taking no time to struggle into heavy-weather gear. He pulled on boots, picked up a flashlight, and snarled an order for one of the elderly servants to drive out and fetch some able-bodied men.

"And a doctor, too!" he shouted as he hurtled into the teeth of the terrible night.

Chapter Thirteen

In all the world there was only the rock and the sea. The howling wind was drowned by the sea's thunder; the driving rain was lost in the sea's fury. The sea was mighty in its rage. The sea was terrible in its vengeance. The sea was savage in its hatred. It wanted to dash her to pieces on the rock; it wanted to tear the very rock from its foundations. And then it would suck her down, down, down. . . .

She mustn't let go. Luc would come. She mustn't let go. Luc would come. She mustn't let go. Luc would come.

She was secure if she kept her arms locked tightly around the rock that was Luc's chest. But some force was prying her fingers loose; some force was dragging her arms from safety; some force was pulling her cheek from the place where it had found haven. She gasped a mouthful of salt water as another great comber swelled and thundered in and dashed against the rock and swallowed her entirely, sucking her from safety. For a moment she was awash in a great, raging, violent sea. And then she reached wildly and found another rock and clung. And clung. And clung.

A golden light warmed her lids. A breath of air stirred her hair. Her arms were still locked around the rock, but the rock was warm and dry and safe, and so was she. Slowly the rock lifted and fell, a gentle movement in rhythm with the warm stirring at her ear, in rhythm with her own even breathing, in rhythm with her own quiet heart. . . .

She opened her eyes and saw that the rock was Luc. He slept, and in his embrace she had slept, too, and the light that lay on her lids was the golden light of morning. She lay still and gave thanks for morning, thanks for life, thanks for Luc.

She remembered the rescue. It was Luc's chest she had reached for, Luc's strong arms that had wrestled her to safety, Luc's gentle hands that had undressed her and dried her and laid her in a bed. His own bed.

A woman's voice had objected when Luc carried her to his own quarters. Luc had silenced the woman with a few savage words. "Do you think I give a damn about that? Let people think what they like! This is my house, not yours! In any case, who knows the story yet but you? Now out of my way!"

It must have been Madame Saint-Cloud, Tory realized. The words had been in English and she had understood them. She vaguely remembered other faces, concerned faces dimly lit by candles, concerned voices, too. But her eyes had clung to Luc's face, just as her arms had clung to his shoulders. Her fingers had been so tightly laced around him that someone else had had to pry them loose.

She had been sick to her stomach from swallowing too much salt water. Luc had held her head and washed her face. Others had been present, and she hadn't cared. She hadn't cared that there had been people in the room when Luc stripped her. One had been a doctor, perhaps? She remembered being checked. And one had been Madame Saint-Cloud, hovering and concerned, her face looking very old. There had been brandy and towels and warm blankets supplied by female servants. Remembering the confused candlelit scene now, Tory realized that Aimée must have been found, or everyone would have been occupied elsewhere, not paying such devout and concerned attention to her.

Last night, after the doctor had at last made some favorable pronouncement, Luc had ordered everyone from the room, cursing them roundly when they took too long to go. He had closed the door and locked it and removed his own wet clothes. He had toweled himself dry. And then he had slid naked into bed beside her, gathering her into his arms to warm her with his own body heat. And the things he had whispered into her hair. . . .

Tory stirred, slowly and gently so he wouldn't wake, and moved her mouth to rest alongside his cheek. It was beautiful to be loved. And Luc loved her, he truly loved her. Yesterday's golden hour hadn't been mere pretense.

Although her movement had been almost imperceptible, Luc came awake. His arms tightened their hold. "I love you, darling," he murmured huskily. "I love you so. . . ."

His mouth moved, too, sliding gently over her face,

touching her lashes and her cheeks and coming to rest against the edge of her lips. "I love you, too, Luc," Tory whispered simply, feeling the rightness of the way his warm breath mingled with her own.

They lay in silence for a long time, folded against each other, neither talking nor moving. There was a oneness in the twining of their naked bodies, a oneness in the flow of feeling between them. It was not desire and not even the beginnings of desire. It was love, and they both knew it was love, and after last night neither had to say it anymore.

At last Tory asked, "Is Aimée all right?"

"Yes."

Tory hadn't wanted to break the mood. She didn't want to ask Luc why he had dared to bring her to his own room, flaunting convention and risking his aunt's deep displeasure. She didn't want to ask about his promises to Aimée, and why he had decided to put them aside, as she was sure he must have done if he had brought her here. She didn't want to ask about anything. She wanted only to accept the gifts of life and love, and she wanted to accept them with no questions at all.

But reality, once it had intruded, was persistent. Luc shifted in the bed. Still cradling her close with one arm, he turned his eyes to the ceiling. The pensive, brooding expression that had taken possession of his face told her that reality was troubling him, too, and that his thoughts were not easy ones. Optimistic in the aftermath of the broken, desperate love words he had muttered in the night, Tory wondered if he was considering the implications of abjuring his promise to the Saint-Clouds. How could he think of marrying Aimée now?

A soft knock sounded at the door that led directly into the hall, and Luc extricated himself from her arms. Moments later, clad in a brown velour bathrobe, he was receiving a breakfast tray from some servant invisible to Tory from the vantage point where she lay. Luc spoke to the servant briefly before he closed the door.

Tory sat up, unconcerned about the nakedness of her breasts. She stretched, feeling multiple aches and pains but not minding them at all. Her hair was tangled and tousled and caked with salt and she didn't care. She was alive. She was glad. She was loved for herself and she knew it. Her face glowed with the knowledge that in Luc's eyes she was beautiful; and despite the ravages wreaked by her battle with nature, the inner glow did indeed create a true beauty.

"Tell me about Aimée," she said as Luc brought the tray to the bed and set it on a small table.

"I just heard that she had an excellent night and is quite back to normal. All the rest, I'll tell you in a moment," Luc temporized. He moved across the room to a tall, old-fashioned mahogany highboy. He found a clean shirt, one of his own, and spent the next minute helping Tory into it. He buttoned the front gravely, not allowing her to help. In truth, her fingers were scraped and still sore, although not seriously damaged. Broken fingernails, of which there were several, couldn't be considered serious.

"I'll have to get hold of some of my own clothes," she said, looking helplessly at the dangling shirtcuffs that covered her hands.

Luc rolled the sleeves to a manageable length. "Not yet," he said firmly. "You're staying right where you are, all day. And I'm staying here to watch over you."

"In bed, all day? I don't feel sick, just a little sore."

"You'll stay in my rooms, at least. I may allow you to go as far as the studio later on. But only if you behave yourself and allow me to pamper you a little." He bent and kissed her on the nose. "I've just finished telling Émile that all meals are to be brought up, and that I'm not available to anyone, under any circumstances."

Tory smiled up at him, the tremulous smile of a woman very much in love. "He doesn't look half as formidable as Annette," she said.

"Unfortunately he's not," Luc agreed wryly. He puffed several pillows behind her back, poured coffee, and sat down on the edge of the bed facing her. Only then did he answer her earlier question.

"I found Aimée on the property line, about ten minutes after I set out. I brought her in a little more than an hour before I found you."

Tory's eyes were puzzled. "She wasn't in the cove?"

"No."

"Then there was no one else down there," Tory murmured, thinking of the terrorized screams she had heard. Had they been imagination, or just the raging of that terrible maelstrom in her ears? Would she have had the strength and courage to hang on if she hadn't heard those screams and thought Luc was coming? And had that lifetime of terror been only a little more than an hour?

She repeated in an awed whisper, "There was no one down in that cove but me. Oh, God . . ."

"You weren't down in that cove, either, thank God," Luc said with heartfelt gratitude. "You were only about thirty feet below the top of the cliff."

"Thirty feet!" She stared at him disbelievingly.

"But I thought I went down so far. And I felt those great salt waves crashing over me, pouring over me . . ."

"You felt the spray dashing upward on the cliffs. If you'd felt the waves, you wouldn't be here to talk about it. As it is, you escaped with no more than a couple of small bruises and a few minor scrapes. One very beautiful one right here." Gently he touched the curve of her cheekbone, the part that had been pressed so achingly close against rock. She winced.

"I'm glad I knew exactly where to look for you," Luc said unsteadily.

Tory shuddered and bent her head to the hot coffee he had handed her. "Tell me everything that happened last night," she said in a low voice. "First tell me about Aimée."

Slowly Luc started to do so, taking no food for himself, only watching Tory as she ate. For the moment he told only of the short search for Aimée, the gravity of her predicament. He kept all else to himself. Time enough for the difficult things, when the breakfast was put aside.

For her part, Tory confessed about the notes she had carried between Jacques Benoit and Aimée. She told of her remorse for acting as messenger, after hearing of the arrangement between Luc and Aimée; her worries that Aimée might have vanished because of a prearranged meeting with Jacques; her sense of guilt at Aimée's disappearance. The only thing she didn't tell him was exactly why she had decided to make the search on her own.

At last Tory pushed the food aside and smiled at Luc, the kind of smile that warmed her entire face. If there was a little uncertainty in her eyes, it was because she had hoped Luc might tell her he didn't intend to marry his young cousin after all. In the past few minutes she had given him enough openings.

"Perhaps your aunt will stop trying to confine Aimée now," she remarked.

Luc would have preferred to leave some matters to another day, but after the things he had whispered to Tory in the night, he knew he mustn't. It would be cruel to extinguish the love and hope shining in her eyes, but it would be even crueler to let her go on believing that the catharsis of last night's storm might have left him a free man.

"I imagine she will give Aimée more freedom," Luc said guardedly. His face was very sober, his eyes worried. "Tory, I have a few things I must tell you right away, about your sister's marriage. . . ."

He told her everything, the true facts and the facts that would have to be told to the world. Tory was quiet and asked few questions. Why had it never occurred to her that Luc might have lived in the States long past his college years, learning his craft by working with master yacht builders? That he might not have been in Brittany at all at the time? That the man involved might have been Armand? That Laura's extreme shock had been caused by something as serious as bigamy? Tory realized she had too easily dismissed Armand in her thinking because he had been married, and because according to things she had heard, he hadn't been truly a man of the sea. And yet he had died at sea, hadn't he? Some of the salt Saint-Cloud blood must have run in his veins, too.

After a time she stopped watching Luc's face because she couldn't bear the bleakness in his eyes. They mirrored too much of what was in her own soul.

How was it possible to feel like this when one had life and limb and a man's love to be thankful for?

"If it's any comfort to you, I imagine Armand must have loved your sister very much," Luc said quietly at one point. "He wasn't happy with Félicité. I happen to know he had broached the subject of divorce a number of times, but she had refused. She was a very straightlaced woman from a very dogmatic family—a cold woman, I think. When she bore grudges, she could be vengeful. I'll admit, Armand wasn't a saint, but perhaps he had reason. All the same, he must have been under great stress to go to the lengths of committing bigamy. Why did he do it? We'll never know, but I think he may have been afraid he would lose your sister, or your sister would lose her child. Perhaps she was upset by the pregnancy and talked about having an abortion. Armand desperately wanted a child, a son. For whatever reason, he took the risks. I imagine he suffered a good deal when your sister ran away. But under the circumstances, how could he go after her?"

Tory took what solace she could in hearing those things. Perhaps Laura had been loved. Perhaps, for a time, she had not been unhappy. But Laura's love story was an old one, a sad one. It was a tragedy of the past, and this was the present. For herself, Tory felt hopeless. No matter how much she wanted to let go of the past, it didn't want to let go of her. It ruled her life, it ruled Luc's, perhaps it ruled everyone's.

Why had she believed, even for one moment, that it was possible to escape the tyranny of the past?

"If Félicité and her family weren't so angry with the Saint-Clouds about other things, it might be possible to acknowledge this boy Nicholas as Armand's natural son, and leave all question of marriage out of it. But under the circumstances . . ." Luc paused and finished wearily, "They'd be only too happy to tarnish the Saint-Cloud name. The boy has to be acknowledged as either Armand's son or mine. I've decided it has to be as mine."

Tory studied her fingers and said in a flat voice, "Because you want to protect the Saint-Clouds."

"I have to protect the Saint-Clouds! But it's protection for your nephew, Nicholas, too. Would you want him to grow up knowing his father was a bigamist?"

Tory shook her head. "No," she said.

"Yesterday I told you I had to make a decision. The decision was between doing this, or fulfilling the old promise to marry Aimée. The purpose of that promise was only to produce a Saint-Cloud heir, and this boy is that heir. Don't you see that I *must* do something to pay off old debts, in one way or another? After last night you can't believe I'm happy to put myself in a position where I can't . . . marry according to my choice."

Tory merely nodded, for her throat was too knotted to answer. She knew the things he had told her in the night.

Luc seized both of her hands and waited until his silence forced her to look up and meet his eyes. They were deep, somber, and filled with regret. "You must know I trust you a great deal to tell you about Armand. With what you now know, you could easily take the Saint-Clouds to court. By the terms of my uncle's will, your nephew, Nicholas, is the real heir to . . . a very great deal. Ships, shipyards, fishing fleets, canneries, even this château. Everything but the boatworks, which my uncle left to me."

Tory nodded, wordless. She knew she could tell no

one the truth of these things, not even her parents. Like herself, they had spent many years hating Laura's husband for what he had done. If they learned of the bigamy and of the fortune that could be had by exposing it, might they decide to exact some raw justice? Tory wasn't sure. Her parents weren't vengeful by nature, but her father was hot-tempered and he was human. Given the weapon, he might decide to use it, probably not in order to hurt the Saint-Clouds, but in order to acquire a sizeable fortune for Nicholas. It was a thing that couldn't be risked.

"I could deny I ever married your sister, which is true enough, or I could try to divorce her, though it would be risky since I am not the man who really married her. But then, would your parents prevent all access to the child?"

"They might," Tory said, understanding the horns of his dilemma. In view of Laura's incompetence, her parents were Nicky's guardians. If they could be told no part of the truth, they would have very little sympathy for Luc and the Saint-Clouds.

"Will they forbid access anyway?" Luc asked.

"They'll want to," Tory said slowly. "But I imagine they'll come around. They wouldn't wish to deny Nicholas any advantages coming to him as your son. As for their attitude to you . . . I suppose the amnesia can be used to excuse a lot of things.

Some of Luc's tension eased. "The boy needn't live in France. Let him grow up where he's happiest. Perhaps there should be some short visits, though." Luc added in a raw voice, "You could . . . accompany him."

Tory was dying inside, at that moment almost wishing the storm had had its way. "No, Luc," she said with difficulty. "I couldn't. I couldn't bear it."

Luc mastered his voice, his tones becoming harsh as he mended the brief break in self-control. "Then perhaps he shouldn't visit at all until he's a little older. Of course, from now on his life will be made a great deal easier in a financial sense—and the lives of your parents, too, naturally. He can go to the best schools and have the best of everything. In time, when he's of age and ready for the responsibility, I'll sign the bulk of the Saint-Cloud estates over to him. In the meantime I'll keep them. The arrangement is simply one of good faith. You'll have to trust me to do what's right."

"Yes," Tory whispered.

"At the moment I can't see another solution."

Silence lay between them for a little while, a silence filled with regret, but acceptance of what had to be. After a few moments Tory said, "Do you think you can get me on a plane tomorrow?"

Luc said raggedly, "If that's what you want."

"Yes. Yes, it is." Tory's eyelids flagged with a sudden terrible fatigue, an exhaustion of the spirit and the will as well as of the body. At this moment she felt as if she had spent an entire month clinging to the cliff, instead of a single hour. "Now do you mind if I rest for a while longer, Luc? I'm aching all over and I'm very, very tired."

Toward the end of day Tory awakened to find Luc watching her from a chair pulled close beside the bed. Her brain felt drugged from too much sleep, heavy with the dark Gothic dreams that had been haunting the labyrinths of her mind, weighted down by the hopelessness of a dilemma for which she could see no easy answer except the answer Luc had proposed.

But the day-long rest had done her body good. Beyond a certain numbness, which might have been a numbness of the heart, her complaints were few. Even her sore hands felt considerably better. With the resilience of youth, Tory's flesh was fast mending.

Luc's hand came to rest over one of hers. Now it was he who looked exhausted, his face deeply marked with signs of strain. "How are you feeling?"

"I'm fine now." Tory extricated her fingers from beneath his.

"Tory, don't," Luc groaned in a hoarse voice. His hand recaptured hers, his thumb this time probing the palm gently. He gave her a tormented look she understood. It spoke worlds. There was deep pain in those dark eyes, but also grim determination, and more. Luc's expression said that a man could not be expected to deprive himself of everything, for all time.

Tory didn't fight the clasp of his fingers. "It's only going to get harder, Luc. Don't you see we have to stop it now, while we can? I must go back to my own room."

"Not tonight." The low savagery of his tone was directed not at Tory, but at fate. "Surely not tonight. I don't give a damn what my aunt thinks, nor anyone else in the house either. Stay with me tonight, darling. Don't you think we owe ourselves that much?"

Tory's mouth moved and made a decision not dictated by her mind. "Yes," she whispered.

Luc's long, darkening look told her he understood the promise implicit in her acceptance. He raised her hand to his mouth and kissed it with lingering tenderness, a promise that he would treat her bruised body with great gentleness in the stolen hours to come.

He rose to his feet. "Our dinner should be arriving quite soon. Émile has already set a table for two in the other room. Shall I run you a hot tub?"

"That would be lovely."

When she heard the water running, Tory slipped out of bed and followed Luc into the attached bathroom. He was on his knees at the side of the tub, testing the warmth of water to adjust it.

"Somebody took my wet clothes last night," she said. "I have nothing to put on. I can't possibly eat dinner in one of your shirts."

Luc came back on his haunches. "You can as far as I'm concerned," he murmured, capturing one of her long naked legs. His hand slid disturbingly beneath the flap of the shirttails while his parted mouth moved gently over the soft skin of her thigh.

The trail of his kisses laid siege to Tory's senses. She swayed. Under the extreme gentleness of his hands and lips, the little aches of her bodily injuries were forgotten. Luc's warm mouth was a balm, a benediction, a seal of deep love and longing.

If he hadn't risen to his feet, choosing to leave the lovemaking till later, the bath might have gone forgotten. Still pampering her, he unbuttoned the shirt she wore and slid it from her shoulders. "I'll fetch some clothes from your room if you wish. What shall I bring? Or will you trust me to choose? I warn you I'll choose to please myself, as I did the first night we met."

With love spilling from her eyes, Tory lifted her fingers to trace the line of his scar. "Tonight is your night, Luc. I want it to be perfect for you. I'd wear anything . . . or nothing . . ."

"Stop tempting me before bedtime," he murmured huskily. With an effort he drew himself away and went to the door. He paused there, one hand raised and braced against the doorframe, and watched while she stepped into the tub.

"I'll look in on Aimée quickly at the same time," he said. "I didn't like to leave the room earlier, in case you wakened and needed me."

He left. For a short time she soaked in the tub, feeling the aches of the flesh ebb, and wishing the aches of the heart could be as easily assuaged. But tonight she must put thoughts of tomorrow's heartache aside. Luc had given her one perfect afternoon, and she wanted to give him one perfect night. No, it was not too much to ask of fate.

She had washed her hair and wrapped it in a towel when she heard a knocking at the door—not at Luc's bedroom door, but at the door of the room he used as studio and sitting room both.

Luc's warm brown bathrobe was lying in view on a chair in the bedroom. Tory put it on, walked through into the studio, and answered the door, expecting one of the servants with dinner.

It was Madame Saint-Cloud. Her face still wore that old, trembling, troubled look it had worn the previous night. The pride of her bearing had suffered from the events of the past twenty-four hours. In that space of time she seemed to have aged a decade. Her eyes were ringed with dark circles; the network of her facial lines seemed to have spread and deepened; her whole body appeared to have shrunken and sagged. Tory thought she knew why. It would not be easy, on one and the same night, for a mother to face the trial of a daughter's disappearance and possible brush with death, and the tribulation of a son's bigamy. The old Saint-Cloud skeletons might haunt Luc's life, but they also haunted the life of his aunt.

"Luc is . . . not in?" Even her voice seemed hesitant, wavering, almost apologetic.

After spending the night in Luc's bedroom, Tory

might have expected to feel awkward in his aunt's presence. For some reason she didn't. She felt too sorry for the other woman. "He'll be back soon. Won't you come in?"

"It is best if I return when Luc is here." Madame Saint-Cloud remained in the hall, reluctant to step through the door. "You are . . . well today?" Her eyes searched Tory's face. "I asked for news of you and was told you do not suffer too much."

"I have very few aftereffects, only a bruise or two. Thank you for being so concerned. I remember you were around last night, too."

"How could I not be concerned, when it is on my head that you are so nearly lost to the sea?"

"On your head? Oh, no, Madame Saint-Cloud. I was foolish to go out into the storm."

"Yes, but I think you did not know how foolish you were. Me, I knew that the gales were coming, and I know what the gales can do. At that time I was thinking only of Aimée, or I would have stopped you from going through the door. And then, for so long, to forget that you had gone . . ."

The apology was sincere. At one point during the previous evening, Tory had guessed that her exit might be forgotten, but at no time had Luc blamed his aunt for the tardiness of the rescue. "But you didn't forget forever," she said with a gentle half-smile.

Madame Saint-Cloud bent her head. "I would not have thought of you at all," she admitted in a low voice, "if Luc had not wished to see you. When he went into the storm . . . I confess, I still did not think so very much of you. It is of Luc that I thought. It is for Luc that I was afraid. He was so much a madman, so wild . . . I wished him not to go at all. In that time when he was gone, I died some deaths, too, to think what might happen."

Tory touched Madame Saint-Cloud's arm and said, "Please, won't you come in? Luc really will be right back. He only went to get some clothes for me and look in on Aimée. He'd expect you to come in and sit down."

At last the invitation was accepted. As the two women walked into the room, Tory reflected wryly that considering the improprieties of her situation, she might expect to feel self-conscious. But after last night what difference did it make that she was in Luc's bathrobe with a towel around her hair?

A table for two had been set near the fireplace. With the household not yet back to normal, it occurred to Tory that there would probably be no proper dinner hour again tonight. Deeply touched by Madame Saint-Cloud's penitence and concern, she was fleetingly tempted to invite the older woman to join the fireside meal. But then Tory thought of what Luc's reaction might be and kept her peace. She doubted that any of last night's happenings had mended the slightly strained relationship between the two. Tonight of all nights, Luc would hardly give thanks for his aunt's presence.

Madame Saint-Cloud settled herself in the same wing chair Tory had used on an earlier occasion in this room. Tory lowered herself to a settee and asked, "How is Aimée?"

"She is well, very well. There is no damage to her, only scratches." The other woman's lined eyes were a little remorseful as she added, "Today she was to Quimper."

"Oh?"

"Yes. With her governess, she went shopping. The . . . blue jeans that were bought, they did not fit too well. Aimée, she wished to choose her own."

Tory's smile was genuinely warm. "I'm glad," she said. She wanted to ask if Aimée had also managed to see her friend Jacques, but thought better of it. For now, it was enough to know that Aimée's unnatural seclusion was to end.

Tory made efforts at polite chatter, but Madame Saint-Cloud was too distracted for small talk. Anxious for Luc's return, she was watching the door, fingers plucking at the stuff of her dark blue silk dress or at the simple gold cross she always wore suspended from a chain. A tense woman at the best of times, she was doubly tense tonight.

At last, Tory's attempts at conversation dwindled. She had things on her own mind, and private contemplation was less awkward than trying to sustain a one-sided monologue.

Wanting no pall of gloom over the coming evening, she was trying to mold her thoughts into optimistic patterns. Again the remembered quotation pricked her mind. *Tears shall drown the wind* . . . but wasn't it an ill wind that blew no good? Out of happenings that were unhappy for herself, some positive things had come. More freedom for Aimée. An heir to continue the centuries-old bloodline of the Saint-Clouds. Someday a vast inheritance for Nicholas. Support for Laura, too, and an end to the terrible financial burdens that had plagued Tory and her parents for some years. No, life was not all tragedy. And for herself and Luc, there was still tonight, a night in which they would compress a whole lifetime of love. She wouldn't think of tomorrow.

Luc's entrance put an end to the silence that had

fallen. He had come in through the bedroom, evidently having deposited Tory's clothes on the way. His face tightened when he saw his aunt, the tensing of muscles around his mouth and jaw suggesting no particular pleasure in her presence. "Well, Tante Marie," he acknowledged testily. Tory could have sworn he added something vehement in a mutter too low to be heard.

"Luc, it is important that I speak to you at once. Do not be—"

"If you've come to tell me to hold my tongue, Tante Marie," he said harshly, "it's already too late. Tory knows the whole story. Now I think you'd better go. Haven't I done enough for you as it is?"

His aunt bowed her head as if under a great burden, then raised her eyes beseechingly. "Do not be angry, Luc. I think you will not be so angry when you hear what it is I wish to speak of."

Tory rose to her feet, ready to escape.

"No, you don't," Luc objected, curling firm fingers around her wrist and forcing her to remain standing by his side. "Anything Tante Marie wishes to say, she can say in front of you."

When Madame Saint-Cloud looked uncertainly from one to the other, perceptibly hesitating, Luc added, "This is the woman I love, Tante Marie. If she leaves the room, I leave too. Well? What is it you want?"

His aunt was still reluctant. "There is a part that she can hear later," she agreed slowly. "But first there is a decision to be made, Luc. And I do not think you will wish to make it in front of . . . anyone."

Luc sat down on the settee, pulling Tory after him, his grip still firm on her wrist. "And what is this great . . . decision?" he asked with an edge of sarcasm. "I thought I'd already had my moment of decision, and decided to your satisfaction."

"Luc," pleaded his aunt. "Let her go to the other room. It is possible you may wish to make a choice that . . . " Her voice trailed off.

"Go on, Tante Marie," he said in a steely voice, after a short uncomfortable silence. "There's no choice that I can't make in front of Tory."

"No?" Madame Saint-Cloud took a deep breath to fortify herself. "Perhaps there is one. Perhaps when I talk, you will be wishing that you had allowed her to leave." She looked at Luc more steadily, some of the old strength of character firming her face. "It is a choice between the Saint-Cloud fortune, and . . . and her."

Luc's mouth thinned grimly. "If it were that easy, Tante Marie, there'd be no choice at all. I never wanted the Saint-Cloud fortune. As soon as possible, I intend to sign it over to the proper heir. I can hardly give it to a mere boy, but when he's a grown man he'll get it. In the meantime, as far as I'm concerned, I'm only holding it in trust."

Madame Saint-Cloud looked neither surprised nor relieved. A little pain flitted across her face and she said, "In that case it is easy."

"Easy?" Luc laughed harshly. "I wish it were."

His aunt steadied herself by taking hold of the cross at her neck. "There is a way, Luc," she said in a trembling voice. "A very easy way, if you are willing to part with . . . very, very much. The suggestion I make, it will answer for everything. The American wife, the child . . . and they do not have to be yours."

Luc leaned forward toward his aunt, instantly alert. His grip on Tory's wrist might have been painful, but she herself was in too suspended a state to notice. She was riveted with tension, her breath bated to hear what Madame Saint-Cloud had to suggest.

"Don't play with words, Tante Marie," Luc said urgently. "If you have a solution, out with it."

"We will say that the boy is the son of my husband."

For a moment Tory and Luc simply stared. Then Luc whispered, "*Mon Dieu.* You joke, Tante Marie."

"No, I do not joke. From the things you tell me, I think very little is known of the boy's father, except that he was a Breton, a wealthy man, and a man much away at sea. Is that not so, mademoiselle?"

"Yes," Tory said. "But still, I can't imagine . . ."

"Will your parents wish to question too much, if this boy Nicholas becomes at once heir to a very great deal? I do not think so. When my husband died, he was not yet sixty. He could have fathered the boy. Who will deny it, if I say it is so? And for the matter of taking a wife that was not legal . . ." Her voice lowered and quivered a little. "Perhaps, mademoiselle, your parents will keep such questions to themselves, for the sake of their grandson. They know there was a marriage, but who in this country knows? They may believe very bad things of the Saint-Clouds, but I think they will say nothing to the ears of the world, unless they wish to be cruel to a child. A man who is dead cannot be punished by law for old sins, and to talk of bigamy, when there is nothing to gain, would be only to punish the boy. Is that not so?"

Madame Saint-Cloud seemed to be waiting for Tory's opinion about her parents' reaction. She thought for a moment and realized the other woman was right. No advantage could be gained by exposing bigamy, when all advantages had already been gained. With Nicholas declared heir, her parents would have no reason to take the Saint-Clouds to court. She nodded, concurring. "Under those circumstances, they'd certainly hold their peace."

Luc's fingers had moved and were now clasped around Tory's. Neither could quite believe that the tides of fortune were changing, but there was hope in that handhold, a joining of hearts as well as hands, a promise for the future.

"Then it is agreed," said Madame Saint-Cloud. Her voice was tremulous. "You see? You will be free, Luc."

Luc said in a very still voice, "Why are you doing this, Tante Marie? It can't be easy for you."

His aunt's fingers were twisting around the chain of the cross. "Because . . . because I owe it. Have I not always said that duty is important?" She tried to smile, not too successfully, for her eyes were pained. "For me, it is time to discharge an old duty."

"Surely not a duty to me," Luc said disbelievingly.

"Yes, to you. There is a thing I should have done for you many years ago."

"I don't understand."

"I will tell you if you permit Mademoiselle Allworth to leave the room," Madame Saint-Cloud said in the lowest of voices.

Luc was looking at his aunt with puzzlement, his eyes narrowed as if he were seeing things he had never seen before. His manner was considerably gentler as he said, "Tante Marie, whatever you tell me, I may very well decide to pass it on to Tory anyway. She's going to be my wife."

It was the first time such a thing had been mentioned, because it was the first time circumstances had permitted such a thing to be considered. Tory squeezed Luc's hand, a private acceptance of the public proposal. There was a great joy swelling in her heart, and only the very real anguish on Madame Saint-Cloud's face prevented her from expressing it.

"What you murmur of in privacy, no one can prevent," Luc's aunt whispered in a strangled voice. "But there are some things that can be told with only two people present. There is an old sin I wish to live with no longer. I beg you, Luc, let her go. I do not speak of duty now. I speak of pain."

Luc released Tory's fingers. She understood the message. Wordlessly she stood up and slipped out of the room.

Chapter Fourteen

Luc waited in silence. In his life he had not seen his aunt like this, except very fleetingly the night before. She sat before him, mouth troubled, head bowed, fingers trembling, no longer a tower of strength but an unsure old woman with something on her conscience. She started slowly.

"You have many times heard me tell Aimée the story of the lost city of Ys. How many times? More times than I myself remember. But I think, it is not to Aimée that I was telling the tale, but to myself. . . ."

Luc listened without interrupting, his face grave. From the pack in his pocket, he took a cigarette and lit it. The smoke curled slowly upward, almost the only movement in the room.

"I tell the tale not because the princess Dahut slept with sin, but because she caused a great city to die. By her actions, she allowed the waters to flood in and destroy her family, and all the people of Ys. How could I allow the house of Saint-Cloud to die, when I so nearly destroyed it myself?"

"You? But—"

"I will start first at the end of the story, Luc, and in a little time you will understand. Aimée is not a Saint-Cloud. She is not your uncle's daughter." She held up a hand, telling him not to talk. "I was growing near to forty years of age when she was born, and I had lived without love for many, many years. Perhaps you will remember that your uncle was seldom here. Yes, when his duties allowed he would come to the Château d'Ys—and then he would vanish, sometimes the same day, to take you or Armand for a week or two of sailing on the big yacht, or on one of the little ones. Me, I was left alone. Perhaps the blame was not all his, but . . ." Her voice almost broke. "I will come to that in time."

Madame Saint-Cloud spent a moment with her own unhappy thoughts. "Aimée's father . . . it is not important who her father was. He was a man I have not seen since, an officer of the navy who had come with papers to be signed." Her voice turned a little bitter. "Did I do it out of need for love? No. I did it out of need for revenge. And revenge, it has the bad taste of a mouthful of water from the sea. If a person thirsts and drinks, it gives a sickness inside, a sickness that makes a person wish to die.

"I think, Luc, you will now begin to understand the matter of your uncle's will. He wished no Saint-Cloud fortune to go to Aimée, and so he wrote many things in his will to make certain it could never be so. Did he forget to make a new will when Armand failed to have sons? Did he forget that it is possible that Armand might die too? Did he forget that next to Armand, you are the closest male in blood? No. None of these things are forgotten. Your uncle, Luc, he knew all these things. And now I go back to the beginning of the story . . ."

Her eyes came up, haunted, to meet Luc's. "The beginning is the time when my husband came into this house with a little baby in his arms. I already knew of the baby, and I knew his name was Luc. I had agreed the baby could be brought into this house, because your uncle wished to raise him as his own son. I had heard of the bad place where the baby was born, in a city still bombed-out from a war not long in the past. I wished to help, because I loved my husband and was proud of the Saint-Clouds. Oh, I was young then, hardly more than a bride, and I was in love. And life was good! Will you believe when I say I was truly happy on the day the little baby came? That I loved him when I saw him? He was only months younger than my own Armand. They would grow together, they would be friends, they would be brothers. Three years later the baby's mother died, and in this house adoption was talked of. Will you believe I was happy? It was by accident, just before that adoption went through, that I saw some papers about that little Luc's birth. And I found that he had been brought into this house not out of charity, but because . . . because he was my husband's own son."

Luc had frozen into total stillness. On his face there was no expression. In his fingers the cigarette burned forgotten, the ash lengthening as the moment extended.

Madame Saint-Cloud's face was tormented. "Do you wonder that I could never truly love you after that, Luc? I tried. But I had a child of my own, a child I had thought born of love. And yet while I had been bearing Armand, another woman had been bearing you! How can I tell of my feelings? I cried. I raged in my heart. I cried again. I sinned in my soul, for I wished to kill my husband. I wished to die. I wished to kill you."

The cigarette began to burn Luc's fingers and he tamped it out, the initial shock of discovery replaced by deep disturbance. And he had expected his aunt to give him love?

She bent her face into her hands, the fingers pressing against her weathered cheeks as if to prevent the start of tears. "After a little time the rage was held inside. I stopped crying, because I knew there were lives to be lived, little children to be cared for, a house to be run. I told myself that you were only a little boy, and the sin was not yours. I had loved you for more than three years. How could I throw you from this house? But the next time my husband came home, I would not let him lie in my bed. I locked my door. He was angry. He said he loved me. He said he was human, that his men had been sweeping mines in the Brest harbor that year. He said that some had died, that he had needed a woman's comfort. I would not listen. In time he began to stay away. It is hard to think of those long nights, those long years . . ."

After a time Madame Saint-Cloud looked calmer. "Will you understand, if I tell you that I loved him always? And yet I could not forgive. Do you think it was to regain the Saint-Cloud fortune that I wished you to marry Aimée? No. It was because you bore Saint-Cloud blood, and she did not. It seemed a way to . . . heal the past, to join what could never be joined in life."

"This child in America does that more than any child of mine and Aimée's could ever have done,"

Luc said. "He's Armand's son, and Armand was born out of love—a love I think you never stopped feeling, Tante Marie, despite everything."

"Yes," she whispered. "Do you see, that to acknowledge this boy as your uncle's—your *father's*—child, it is only a payment for old sins. His sins and my sins! He wished to acknowledge you as his true son. I refused. But that is not the sin I talk of, the sin against you, the sin for which I owe—"

"You don't have to explain, Tante Marie."

There were some moments when both lived with their own thoughts. Luc's were not turbulent. For the first time in many years he felt at peace with his aunt, understanding things he had never understood before. She was not by nature a cold and rejecting woman, and yet since his early childhood she had always been a little cold with him. On the surface she had not rejected him, but underneath there had always been that little reserve, that lack of warmth, that undercurrent of resentment. How could it have been otherwise?

As to the story of his parentage, after the initial shock he found he accepted it with a sense of content. He had deeply loved his uncle—his father—the person who had continued to give him warmth and love throughout his growing years.

Luc saw moisture start to gather in his aunt's eyes. He stood and went across to her chair. For the first time in his life since he had given her the dutiful kisses of a child, he bent and touched his lips to her furrowed cheeks.

"Luc, I wish . . . I wish I did. I wish I could. It is a great sin on my head."

He knew what she meant. "It's all right, Tante Marie," he soothed. "A person can't force love to happen. You did what you could, more than I had any right to expect. You accepted me, didn't you? If there's a sin, I'm guilty, too. I haven't loved you, either."

"I did, once," trembled his aunt.

"So did I, once, when I was so little I can hardly remember," Luc said softly. Then he added, using the same words he had used not long ago to Tory, "Isn't it time you let go of the past?"

In a slow slide of relieved tears, she did.

"I hope you didn't mind that I asked my aunt to eat with us," Luc apologized to Tory some time later as he closed the door behind a departing servant. They were alone at long last, with a warm fire burning and the remains of dinner cleared away.

"Your aunt seemed a lot . . . easier in her mind after she talked to you. Softer and more relaxed."

Luc gathered Tory into his arms without delay and bent his head. "Mmm," he murmured, testing her lips. "You taste like dessert."

Tory smiled secretly to herself. She knew he was evading her curiosity. With the confidence of a woman who feels herself loved, she thought he would tell her everything in time. Hadn't he said he might? And she could wait, for a lifetime if necessary. . . .

She wound her arms around his neck and looked lovingly up into his eyes. "With your aunt around, isn't it lucky you provided me with the jacket this time, instead of just half a dress?" Luc had brought the same clinging caramel confection she had worn on their first night together. "The under part isn't even a real dress. It's an un-dress."

"What a wonderful idea," Luc breathed, fingering the first of the long row of little buttons down her front. Tory melted against him for a slow, lingering kiss. All through the meal she had kept reminding herself that there was no desperate hurry to be alone with Luc. She knew the importance of what Madame Saint-Cloud had agreed to do, and hadn't begrudged her presence at the meal. And yet this was the moment she had hungered for. . . .

"Oh, God, I thought of nothing but this all through dinner," Luc breathed huskily when the embrace had reached a point where it could become no more passionate without being horizontal. Tory's buttons had been undone one by one, and the dress had been pushed from her shoulders. Luc's jacket had long since been shed, too. Tory had been loosening the belt of his trousers and making dramatic inroads at the opening of his unbuttoned shirt. She had been running her fingers over the warm surface of his bared skin, her sense of touch thrilling to the texture of crisp hair, the firmness of flesh, the hardness of muscle. This was her man and she loved every part of him. Could it be true, really true, that nothing stood between them now except a few clothes?

"No more of that," Luc groaned, "until I have you in bed."

"I thought you'd never ask," Tory murmured throatily, withdrawing her adventuring fingers.

They led each other to the bedroom and finished undressing each other. Luc was gentle as he stripped her of her clothes, his ranging hands and his warm mouth urgent yet reverent on her body. He bathed her breasts in burning kisses, whispered wonderful things in her ears, stroked her thighs, tangled his long fingers in her hair, held her face with his hands to receive his deeply possessive kiss. Tory felt loved and lovely. In return she offered herself and her caresses with complete openness. Luc had taught her to love, and she loved without reserve, now and for all time.

He mastered her tenderly, wonderfully, leashing his passion in order to draw out the long moments of full possession. She quivered beneath his power, filled by him, fulfilled by him, imprisoned by his thrusting strength, yet beautifully free. . . .

And at last, joined in one, they rose to rapturous heights—mouths melded, thighs merged, hearts bonded in a union that seemed to seal the promise of the future.

In time the long shuddering was over, the drawn-out moment of rapture passed. Still clasped together, they lay content, not only with fulfillment of the body but with fulfillment of deeper desires.

"Next time you don't have to be so gentle with me," Tory murmured contentedly.

Luc growled tigerishly at her throat, pretending an animalistic attack. His teeth were gentle. "Next time I won't be," he muttered.

"Is that a promise?"

"A solemn one! I couldn't possibly have been so patient if I hadn't been thinking of your bruises. On second thought, the promise holds only if the next time isn't later tonight."

"You couldn't!"

"Couldn't I? Don't underestimate me, Madame Devereux. Several recent events have strained my patience more than a well-bred lady like you would believe possible."

"Haven't you forgotten something? At the moment I'm not madame anything. I'm your mistress."

"Details." Luc stroked her stomach. "I'll look into correcting that tomorrow. We'll go on a long, long honeymoon, a sailing cruise . . ."

"I wouldn't dare write that to my parents!"

"We'll fly over and pacify them first. Does that please you?"

"*You* please me. You flow in my heart, Luc Devereux. You flow in my veins. Oh, Luc, kiss me like that again . . ."

There was a silence broken only by the shifting of skin on skin and the murmurous sound of little, lingering kisses discovering new and untried places—the back of an ear, the bend of an elbow, the hollow below a chin. In time, Tory murmured, "Luc. Did you mean what you said last night?"

"I said a lot of things I meant last night. Things I ought never to have admitted to you, considering that I was about to pretend I was married to your sister. What thing in particular did you have in mind? That I adore you to distraction? That you're the only woman I've ever truly loved? That since you came into my life, I feel like only half a person when you're not around?"

"No."

"What, then? Would you like me to repeat it all in French? *Je t'adore . . .*"

Tory pulled herself to a sitting position in the bed, arms locked around her naked knees, looking at Luc with a warmth that put amber depths in her extraordinary eyes. "No, Luc, it was something else, something you said when you were rescuing me."

"I don't remember using any soft words then."

"You didn't. You had just brought me up the cliff, me in one arm and a flashlight in the other. When you reached the top, you stopped and shook your fist at the sea and shouted something at the top of your lungs. Do you remember?"

"A black curse word, I'm afraid."

"Yes. Do you remember the rest?"

"I don't remember the exact words. Something about never wanting to see the sea again, if you were hurt. At that point I thought you might be. You had gone limp—with relief, I suppose." His eyes darkened and sobered, their message so somber, so sincere, that it warmed the very depths of Tory's heart. "And yes, I meant it, every word. If you hadn't survived intact, I would have hated the sea forever."

Tory's mouth trembled with emotion, and tears of pride and happiness shimmered in her eyes. "Oh, Luc. Those were the finest love words a woman ever heard. Don't you think I remember how you feel about the sea?"

Gently Luc pulled her back beside him on the bed. He raised himself on one elbow and wound his lean brown fingers into her silky hair, hovering over her so he could look down into her eyes, so he could lose himself in the warmth of them, bathe in the glow of them, drown in the deep pools of them.

"How I *used* to feel about the sea," he murmured huskily. "If I had to make a choice between two loves, there would be no choice at all." He bent his head to her throat, and his husky whisper stirred against her skin. "I could choose only you. My one love, my great love, my life's love . . ."

MORE ROMANCE FOR A SPECIAL WAY TO RELAX

$2.25 each

79 ☐ Hastings	87 ☐ Dixon	95 ☐ Doyle	103 ☐ Taylor
80 ☐ Douglass	88 ☐ Saxon	96 ☐ Baxter	104 ☐ Wallace
81 ☐ Thornton	89 ☐ Meriwether	97 ☐ Shaw	105 ☐ Sinclair
82 ☐ McKenna	90 ☐ Justin	98 ☐ Hurley	106 ☐ John
83 ☐ Major	91 ☐ Stanford	99 ☐ Dixon	107 ☐ Ross
84 ☐ Stephens	92 ☐ Hamilton	100 ☐ Roberts	108 ☐ Stephens
85 ☐ Beckman	93 ☐ Lacey	101 ☐ Bergen	
86 ☐ Halston	94 ☐ Barrie	102 ☐ Wallace	

LOOK FOR SUMMER COURSE IN LOVE BY CAROLE HALSTON AVAILABLE IN SEPTEMBER

AND A THISTLE IN THE SPRING BY LINDA SHAW IN OCTOBER.

SILHOUETTE SPECIAL EDITION, Department SE/2
1230 Avenue of the Americas
New York, NY 10020

Please send me the books I have checked above. I am enclosing $______ (please add 50¢ to cover postage and handling. NYS and NYC residents please add appropriate sales tax). Send check or money order—no cash or C.O.D.'s please. Allow six weeks for delivery.

NAME ______________________________

ADDRESS ______________________________

CITY ____________________ STATE/ZIP __________

Silhouette Desire 15-Day Trial Offer

A new romance series that explores contemporary relationships in exciting detail

Six Silhouette Desire romances, free for 15 days! We'll send you six new Silhouette Desire romances to look over for 15 days, absolutely free! If you decide not to keep the books, return them and owe nothing.

Six books a month, free home delivery. If you like Silhouette Desire romances as much as we think you will, keep them and return your payment with the invoice. Then we will send you six new books every month to preview, just as soon as they are published. You pay only for the books you decide to keep, and you never pay postage and handling.

MAIL TODAY

Silhouette Desire, Dept. SDSE 7S
120 Brighton Road, Clifton, NJ 07012

Please send me 6 Silhouette Desire romances to keep for 15 days, absolutely free. I understand I am not obligated to join the Silhouette Desire Book Club unless I decide to keep them.

Name____________________

Address____________________

City____________________

State________________ Zip__________

This offer expires March 31, 1984